# PLASTIC

# PLASTIC

## SCOTT GUILD

PANTHEON BOOKS

NEW YORK

Copyright © 2024 by Scott Guild

All rights reserved. Published in the United States by Pantheon Books, a division of Penguin Random House LLC, New York, and distributed in Canada by Penguin Random House Canada Limited, Toronto.

Pantheon Books and colophon are registered trademarks of Penguin Random House LLC.

Library of Congress Cataloging-in-Publication Data
Name: Guild, Scott, author.
Title: Plastic / Scott Guild.
Description: First edition. | New York : Pantheon Books, 2024.
Identifiers: LCCN 2023014895 (print) | LCCN 2023014896 (ebook) |
ISBN 9780593316764 (hardcover) | ISBN 9780593316771 (ebook)
Subjects: LCGFT: Dystopian fiction. | Science fiction. |
Social problem fiction. | Novels.
Classification: LCC PS3607.U478 P63 2024 (print) |
LCC PS3607.U478 (ebook) | DDC 813/.6—dc23
LC record available at https://lccn.loc.gov/2023014895
LC ebook record available at https://lccn.loc.gov/2023014896

www.pantheonbooks.com

Jacket design and illustration by Tyler Comrie

Printed in the United States of America
First Edition
2 4 6 8 9 7 5 3 1

*For Rachel Cochran and Marc Pfister*

# PLASTIC

*This is the secret: forget the water. Do not see water in the pool below you, only motion. When you hear the blast of the starter gun, when your back foot pushes off the block, when your front foot carries forward your momentum, you are not plunging into a substance any different from yourself, you are not flesh and bone in a foreign element, an element denser than air—you are motion encountering motion, two forms of fluidity. There are no swimmers in the other lanes, no best time that you're chasing, just your skin and muscle alive in movement, just this sky-blue tunnel where you soar.*

*But I haven't felt alive like that in years. When did I last dive into a pool? Or think of myself as a bird? It's like the waters gathered over me after my sister vanished: turned cold, hard, inflexible, a substance that held me like death. Who could see me under so much ice? Who could recognize my face through all the layers?*

# 1

---

# A DOLL'S HOUSE

The episode opens on a plastic woman driving home from work.

The camera follows her from outside the car, filming her through the window, showing her hard, glossy face inside the dim sedan. She is in her twenties, a pale figurine, with sunken eyes and hollow cheeks, nylon hair cut short above her ears. Houses whisper past on the street beside her, the sun setting over their rooftops, their shadows long in the last hour of twilight. Her surface, smooth and specular, reflects the fading light; her fingers, bent at their hinges, grip the upper rim of the wheel. The name tag pinned to her polo shirt reads, *Erin: Ask Me Anything!*

She rolls to a stop at an empty crosswalk, drums two fingertips idly against the wheel. A single drone is swimming through the smog above her suburb, like a fish seen from the bottom of a frozen lake. Then, as she glides through the intersection, Erin's voice begins to narrate on the soundtrack. It is a quiet but expressive voice, just louder than the hum of the tires on the pavement.

*A year ago,* she narrates, *I was a very different person. On a night like this, a Friday, I'd be hurrying home from Tablet Town, dying to hang up my uniform and start the weekend. Patrick was in my life back then, a reason to get through the hours on the sales floor. I thought—no, knew—that nothing could ever take him away from me.*

The street that scrolls beside her car is dusky and deserted, no vehicles in the driveways, no pedestrians on the sidewalks, no curtains open behind the barred windows. The houses slide past her in a continual sequence, like a succession of blurred photographs, each different in their color scheme but not in their basic construction, shades of pastel siding on the same one-story frame. The backyards are also identical, save for an occasional razor wire fence that glistens above the hedges.

The camera leaves the street, cuts to a close-up of the plastic woman. Shadows drift across her molded face.

*Last year, if someone had asked me—that other, naive Erin—I would have told them my life was perfect. And it's true: I was happy, in my own way. Each night I drove home to Patrick, hid from the world in his arms. I stayed in with him every weekend, barely went out except for groceries. Oh, Patrick. I lost him in the end, of course. Like I'd lost my father, my sister. Like I've lost almost everyone else.*

Erin slows the car and steers onto the pitted slope of a driveway. At the top sits a small blue house, its aluminum siding faded, its gable roof missing a few shingles. She stops at the garage, takes out her phone and taps a garage-shaped icon. The wobbly door rattles upward.

*These days I spend my weekends alone, just trying to stay distracted. I sleep in as late as I can. I binge episodes of* Nuclear

Family. *I clean the entire house, room by room. And on Friday nights, when I miss Patrick the most, I cut myself some slack. I go online and order a Hot Date. I don't think too much about it. It just helps.*

Erin stares at the house in the half-light, her plastic eyes glazed with sunset. The camera holds the shot for a few seconds before the scene fades out.

·       ·       ·

The next scene opens on a slender kitchen, a clean but timeworn room. The floor is a scuffed linoleum, the oven range missing two knobs; columns of blue poppies bulge along the lumps in the wallpaper. A modest yard is visible beyond the window bars: a square of grass enclosed in hedges, a lone pine tree looming at its rear. The pine tree casts a slanted shadow, stretched out on the lawn like a stilt walker.

A door opens on the wall of poppies, revealing the figurine as she steps from her garage. The camera follows Erin as she strides across the kitchen, her gait jerky and mechanical, her upper body unbending. She passes into the dining room and down a brief hallway, the wallpaper darker in patches where a row of picture frames once hung. At the end of the hall is a narrow bedroom, its curtains wan with twilight, a bottle of prescription pills open on the bureau. A stuffed seal smiles at her from the shadows of the headboard, its fluffy flippers reaching out in a gesture of embrace.

Erin sits stiffly on the bed, crosses her legs with a murmur of hinges. She slips her phone from her Tablet Town slacks— a neon *T* on either knee—and taps in the passcode. Soon she is scrolling through profiles on Hot Date, picture after picture of plastic men, some stubbled and some clean-shaven, some with innocent smiles, others with coy, seductive smirks. Above them glitters the heading: *Pick Ur Boytoy!*

*Before Patrick died,* she narrates, *I never dreamed I'd pay for a Hot Date. Why would I? We were settled down, the two of us, starting a family. Even after his murder, I only considered it when these Fridays became so painful. It made me nervous at first, the thought of some stranger coming into my house. But in the end I felt so lonely, I took the chance.*

She taps the photo of a twenty-year-old Hot Date: a long-haired man with a mellow grin and 4.9 stars, sitting bare-chested in a canoe with a Labrador curled at his feet. *Confirm?* the app inquires. She confirms. Then she takes off her Tablet Town sneakers—a *T* on either toe—and leans back against the headboard.

TV on, she says to her flatscreen, mounted above the bureau. Open *Nuclear Family.*

The show begins to play, resumed at the opening notes of a musical number. On the screen a teenage figurine paces through his bedroom, a circle of spotlight following him across the sitcom set. He sings a tender ballad to a photo he holds in his hand, a picture of his secret love: a giant waffle boy with rubber arms and legs. As a pedal harp plucks on the soundtrack, he closes his eyes and touches his lips to the waffle's enormous mouth.

Erin lifts her stuffed seal off the headboard. Volume up 3X, she says to the TV.

She pets the plush pinniped, staring at the lovelorn boy on-screen.

·        ·        ·

Two candles burn on the table in the flickering dark of the dining room, immersing the space in a soft, undersea light. A vase of fake tulips gleams on the bureau, under an oil painting of a lighthouse in a storm. A wave explodes off a boulder below the tower, the soaring spray frozen in a fan of vivid brushstrokes.

The camera pans across the table, where a male figurine sits alone in the shadows. He is a slim but athletic plastic man, his smile relaxed as he scrolls his lambent smartphone. He wears a sapphire pinky ring, jeans so tight they look painted, a tank top whose neck reveals the smooth ridge of his upper pectorals. On the bureau a wireless speaker plays a track of plaintive whale calls, their ululations drenched in reverb, synched to a bassy beat. "Baleen Blues," reads the song name on the display screen.

The table is set for two. In the kitchen a drawer clatters shut, a faucet dashes a basin.

Just sec! Erin calls through the doorway.

No prob! the young man answers.

He scrolls his phone further, laughs to himself at a post. Then footsteps approach from the kitchen and Erin strides in through the doorway, holding a serving dish before her like a full baptismal bowl. She now wears a blouse and capri pants, heels that show the boneless tops of her feet. Her eyelashes curl out, crisp with mascara; her sunken cheeks glimmer with a fresh coat of polish. She places the dish on the table and lowers herself to a chair, her knees bending at their hinges, her upper body rigid.

Glad food, he says. Okay if start?

Def. Enjoy.

He picks up the carving fork, plunges it into the dish. With a pleased murmur—*mmm*—he removes the limp comma of a boiled chicken breast.

Forget eat lunch, he adds. Big hungry.

Hope chicken good. Just throw on after work.

Really? It look wow wow.

He scrapes the meat to his plate with a wet slap.

After she serves herself, Erin sets down the dripping fork and shuts her eyes. With the tips of two fingers, she quickly crosses herself to bless her food. The young man pauses in cutting a slice, his head tilted with interest.

You religious? he asks.

She shrugs. Kinda.

Cool. You go church?

Yeah. Now then.

Where go?

CODA, she says. But it not like normal church. No God or weird stuff there.

He gives a startled laugh. You go Church of Divine Acceptance?

You know?

He laughs again, louder. Know? That where I go!

With Pastor Mark?

Never miss Sunday, he says, his voice suddenly serious. Go lot Wednesday, too. It big help me.

Craze. Prob pass you thousand time.

Prob!

The camera cuts to a wide shot, showing both figurines in profile, smiling across the candles at each other. On the speaker a different whale track plays, two chirpy belugas dueting over the beat. He shakes his head and forks the slice of chicken to his mouth; a brief lump bulges his plastic throat.

You my first CODA client, he says. This shiny. How long you go?

Three year. Almost. I go with relative.

Real shiny. Two year me. CODA like . . . no explain even. So amaze.

He taps at his phone and hands it to Erin, his stiff forearm swinging on its hinge. She chuckles at a recent picture of him

with a middle-aged figurine, both men dressed in teal T-shirts—
*CODA 5K Fun Run!*—a crowd of joggers bustling in the street
behind them. The older man, his jowly face sharpened by a goa-
tee, offers a playful, knowing wink to the camera.

You luck, she says. I only see him on stage. When this?

Last year. I volunteer race. Raise money.

She returns his phone. I need volunteer more. Mean to.

Should! Craze fun.

The figurines discuss the church further. Both, they find,
have had a similar experience. Religion had once seemed to
them a collection of myths and fables, an artifact of the past,
irrelevant to contemporary life. Before their time at CODA, neither had guessed that religious teachings could give them practical guidance, or provide a dose of the inner peace that Pastor
Mark termed "mega chill" in his many videos and podcasts on
the subject. Both figurines had fallen in love with the message of
the church: that religion, far from some dead superstition, was
an ancient form of "technology" for pursuing a happy life.

He shows her another picture, this one of himself at a nightclub, squinting as he takes a hit on a zing-stick. The slogan
FAITH=TECHNOLOGY runs in bubbly letters down his tank top.

By way, she says with a laugh, no mind if you zing.

He looks at her slyly. Serious?

Sure. No prob.

Rising in his chair, he slides a petite cylinder from his pocket,
its metal spangled with periwinkle stars. Erin watches his movements closely, sipping from her wineglass.

What kind you smoke? she asks him.

Oh, I buy many. But right now, lot Breezy BigThink. I study
for National Aptitude Test, take in just few month. My all-time
fav prob Airy Awestruck, but Breezy def best think good. Want
try?

She lifts a polite palm. No thank. Get anxious.

Ah, he says with a grin. That when I zing more.

He fits the mouthpiece between his lips, inhales with his eyes closed.

So, why start CODA? she asks him after he exhales.

He takes a shorter drag. That kinda sad, if honest. Prob kill mood.

Sad okay.

You sure?

Def.

Well, he begins uncertainly. My family have bad tragic. Uncle get killed.

Oh. So sorry hear.

It ecoterrorist, of course. We no get body back, just head. Janitor find it. Toilet stall.

The camera zooms in slowly on Erin. She gives a sympathetic sigh.

*I need to be more careful,* she narrates. *Talking like this—it could get me thinking about my sister. If this man knew where he is right now, the house where Fiona Reynolds grew up . . . but I can't let my mind go there. These Hot Dates are supposed to help me forget.*

So awful, she says to her guest.

He rests an elbow on the table, takes a lengthy hit on the zing-stick. And that what they want, he says in a pinched voice as he holds the smoke. Scare shitless. Make think. Your uncle die like that . . . it haunt you much.

He exhales a dense cloud, like breath on a winter night. He continues:

Maybe bad I say, but I no hate all these terror group before. Before my uncle. I think good cause, think they hero maybe. Who else fight for nature, make us take HeatLeap serious? Who else drive home message—that it suicide keep burning Ground-Up-Bone? But then, such big horror. Hate them much now.

The figurine tells her how, the weekend after the funeral, his family had decided to go to church. How they had somehow known they needed a church, a place to take these feelings, even if they had no faith, no belief in God or salvation, no desire to be religious in a traditional sense of the word. A friend had mentioned CODA to his mother at the funeral, and so, at a loss, the family attended a service there the following Sunday, stepping into the beautiful worship arena at the former Smile-Mile Mall. That day they had found their permanent spiritual home. Now, with the National Aptitude Test approaching—his second, final chance to pass the exam—he's so grateful for the focus CODA gives him. If he fails the NAT again, he'll never be allowed to attend college, will get sent to a government training camp instead, then assigned to some random work post far from his family.

And you? he asks her. You go CODA three year?

Erin reaches for the wine bottle, pours herself another glass. Go same reason you. Big big death. My dad.

They monster. They enjoy kill, I think. They enjoy.

Oh, it not terror group. He just get bad sick.

What with?

BPD, Erin says.

The young man hesitates. Brad Pitt Disease?

She nods.

Damn. I hear it . . . well . . . rumor, really. No know much.

She presses a thumb against her glass stem. It rough. Bad way go.

He sick long?

Erin lifts the glass as if to drink, then sets it back on its coaster. She stands abruptly from her seat, her hip bumping the table with a hollow thud. The candles wobble and settle, the shadows swaying around her as if in the hull of a storm-tossed ship.

Need bathroom, she says. Be back minute.

Sorry, no mean—

No prob. Honest. Need bathroom.

The camera follows her as she strides down the hall, passing a glimpse of the bathroom, the patches of missing picture frames on the walls. In her bedroom she quietly shuts the door and sits on the edge of the mattress. She holds her stuffed seal in her lap, attempts to slow her breathing.

Then, without warning, the bedroom is plunged into darkness. Not a trace of light remains: no glow from the bedside lamp, no sheen around the doorframe, no streetlights paling the curtains. From the ceiling shines a sourceless beam, circling the plastic woman in the luminous hoop of a spotlight. Her glossy surface reflects the beam, shimmering as if it blazes from within.

Erin turns her head and looks into the camera. On the soundtrack plays a dreamy guitar, a swell of synthesizer. In a soft soprano she sings:

> *With all the losses that I've grieved*
> *I should have known my limits:*
> *I can't discuss Brad Pitt Disease*
> *When a Hot Date visits.*

> *My father dead, my sister fled,*
> *My Patrick lost forever . . .*
> *I'll need to chase them from my head*
> *To have sex with this stranger.*

> *But is there any hope of that,*
> *As triggered as I am?*

> *I'll give him five stars on the app*
> *And send away this man.*

She glances away from the camera. The synthesizer goes silent; the lamplight returns.

Erin stands from the bed, steps over to her pill bottle on the bureau. *SettleSelf,* reads the label, *Take as need when anxious bad (max 4 pill per day).* She shakes three capsules into her palm, then presses her palm to her mouth. She winces the tiny bulges down her throat.

*     *     *

The young man remains in the dining room, smoking his Breezy BigThink. He takes a delicate pull on the zing-stick, holds in the smoke with a tight, savoring face. He parts his lips and watches the smoke curl above the candles, rising in lazy tendrils toward the ceiling.

Footsteps advance in the darkness beyond the doorway. Erin emerges into the candlelight, her face void of expression. Avoiding his eyes, she sits back down and sips from her glass.

Okay? he asks.

She nods.

He gives her a gentle smile. Then, with a whisper of hinges, he leans across the table and takes her hand. Her face suppresses a shudder at the unexpected touch.

It okay feel bad, he says. No need embarrass. I get—I get total. Life just . . . creaky, no? So tough sometime.

Erin makes no response. On the wall behind her hangs the lighthouse painting, the beacon raying brightly through the rain. He continues:

What I mean, what want say . . . you no deserve it. You no

deserve pain. No grief. You shiny woman, Erin. Only know you short time, but I see. And want you know: I good you tonight. Way way good, he adds with a sultriness in his tone.

Still she does not speak. Though she stares at the Hot Date's face, her eyes have now gone empty, as if she is looking back into herself, not seeing him at all. With a soft scrape of plastic, she slips her hand away from his.

.    .    .

In the final scene of the episode, Erin, alone, prepares herself for bed. She stands in her robe at the bathroom mirror, brushing her polymer teeth, treating her face with a meshy wipe of Glossy Gal Surface Preserver. Her stuffed seal sits on the sink, its beady eyes reflecting her ablutions.

She carries the seal back to her bedroom, a laugh track booming from the open doorway. On the TV plays a different episode of *Nuclear Family:* the boy now seated on a couch in a living room set, watching a campy horror movie with his waffle crush. The waffle laughs as a haunted oven mitt strangles a terrified chef; the boy glances longingly at his friend's toasted squares.

TV off, she says to her flatscreen. The sitcom vanishes from sight.

Erin kneels down beside her bed, rests her elbows on the thin blanket. Then she opens an app on her phone: PrayZone! Powered by CODA. The home screen shows her Prayer Goals tracker: an avatar of Erin on a steep hillside, a dark wood in the valley below her, a celestial sunlight breaking over the shoulders of the hill. With three quick taps, she enters the number of meals she blessed today. Her avatar, dressed in a medieval tunic, takes three resolute steps up the incline.

She taps the Evening Prayer tab, then scrolls to the Difficult Day section. In a hushed voice, she reads aloud:

*Oh Great Unknown, not every day easy. Some day real blummo, make sad. I just need remember: I perfect. I say again: I perfect. I happy if want be happy, only self-hate hold me back. May I seek peace, seek mega chill. May peace be my whole thing.*

She taps *Prayer Complete;* her avatar takes another stride toward the sunlight. The badge on her tunic reads: *342-Day Prayer Streak!*

After setting her morning alarm, Erin reaches a hand underneath the bed. She slides a rubber helmet from the shadows. The helmet is a smooth oval, its top domed like a bullet, its bottom a rounded opening, its inner surface lined with a wraparound screen. On its exterior are two nose holes, a narrow mouth slit. Erin climbs into bed with the helmet, turns off the lamp with a voice command. A cerulean haze filters in through the curtains.

*These days, I always sleep in my Smarthead,* she narrates. *Back when Patrick was alive, I used to sleep in my entire Smartbody, used to stay with him all night in our simulation. But now that he's gone, my Head is all I need.*

Erin lifts the helmet higher, fits her plastic pate inside the opening. She pulls it down below her rigid jawline.

Smarthead on, she says. Open EZ Pal.

At once the bedroom around her fades from sight. In its place appears a sunny simulation: a bright backyard on a summer morning, a smogless sky above the rooftops, a host of birds melodious in the background. To the right is a small blue house, no security bars on the windows; to the left a single pine tree stirring in the placid breeze. Erin also appears in this virtual setting, seated cross-legged in the grass, her hands in the lap of her indigo dress, her fingers curled together at their hinges.

The yard is an exact replica of Erin's, save for one addition: a granite headstone on the lawn, darkened in the slant of the pine tree's shadow. A single word is carved in the granite: PATRICK.

*For a long time after his murder,* she says, *I couldn't bear to visit this grave. I stayed away from my Smartroom; I tried and tried to forget the night it happened. But then, little by little, I longed to be near him again—as much as I could be. So, every night for the past few months, I've come back to the house I made for us, the house where we were once so very happy. I wear my favorite dress. I fall asleep beside him.*

A bird circles into view, a cobalt-backed swallow. It glides down through the air and lights on the arched top of the headstone. The bird faces the wall of hedges, presenting Erin its long-tailed profile. Then it turns its head and looks directly at her.

## 2

## ATTACK AT TABLET TOWN

The episode opens on an aerial shot of a highway, a bird's-eye view from just below the clouds. The camera shows its winding path, carving across the landscape like a dark asphalt river, headed toward the gleaming coastline on the horizon. On its course to the sea, the road curves through a vast Pacific Northwest suburb, passing the strip malls and office parks made tiny from this height, the streets of houses no larger than game tokens. Hundreds of miniature cars crowd the lanes of the highway this morning, backed up for miles beneath the smoggy sky.

The traffic crawls through a series of military checkpoints, each with a long row of gated stalls. There soldiers inspect the countless cars, running the plates, searching the trunks, patting down the drivers. Sometimes the gate rises and the vehicle drives away; sometimes the gate stays down and more plastic soldiers arrive at the car.

The camera cuts to Erin at the wheel of her sedan, her smooth face glinting in the smog-light. She is dressed again in her Tablet Town uniform, her branded sneaker working the pedals as the traffic starts and stops. Ahead of her, at a checkpoint, two college-aged women wait under guard while soldiers dismantle their hatchback. A few soldiers unscrew the seats from their bases; another fires a scanner gun under the hood. The women stand barefoot in paper robes, their heads bowed, their wrists cuffed behind them.

*To me they look like innocents,* Erin narrates. *Two harmless girls from the suburbs, out for some shopping. But to think like that, to judge by appearance? That's an easy way to get killed.*

She looks away from the trembling women. In the sky above them floats a chaos of commercials, dozens of holographic ads projected from the roadside: DINNER DRONE, ZAPPY ZING-STICK, SUE-EM-NOW.LAWBIZ, NO FEEL NOTHIN'! BULLET-PROOF VEST. The smiles of their mascots stretch deep into the distance.

Erin takes her phone from her pocket, sets it flat on the dashboard.

Morning, Carla, she says.

Morning, Erin! the phone chirps back.

Make laugh, Carla.

Make laugh. You hear about restaurant on moon?

No, Carla.

Great chicken there. But no atmosphere.

Erin chuckles. Carla, call Owen.

Calling Owen, says the voice. A picture appears on her phone of a man in his late fifties, bearded and smiling wryly, his nylon hair thinning at the temples. His forehead is chipped in places, his left ear partially melted; a crooked groove runs down the surface of each cheek. He wears a Tablet Town polo shirt, the collar flipped up ironically.

Owen answers on the third ring. You late, hon, says his warm, bantery voice.

Stuck at checkpoint. They arrest these girl.

Ugh. Well, no rush.

Customer yet? she asks.

Mhmm. He here when open.

Ted?

New one. Worse Ted.

No way, she says. Not possible.

Want see him in Smartroom?

Sure. Show.

Erin taps to accept his live feed. On her screen appears a padded room, its ceiling lined with a network of metal runners. At the center stands a man in a Smartbody: the Head an oval helmet, the Arms and Legs round like tubing, the Torso a thick turtleneck of rubber. A harness with elastic cords connects the suit to pulleys on the ceiling. The man humps the air with steady thrusts, his hips lurching forward with a continual moan of his hinges.

*Take you rodeo,* the figurine gasps, gripping the air as he thrusts. *I take you . . . I take you rodeo.*

Erin laughs. How long he go now?

Twenty minute? I lose track. Dude got stamina.

The figurine drops his arms, falls abruptly backward; the harness cords tighten as he lies supine in the air. *Get top me, get top me!* he pants inside the helmet.

Erin chuckles again and closes the live feed.

He bad, she says. But not worse Ted.

Maybe right. Remember session Ted no sex, just strangle bot whole time?

Wish I forget.

But this guy *loud,* Owen says. I headache today.

You go out last night?

He groans. Yeah, I back on BearDen. Last CODA service, Pastor Mark convinced me: *Go find love! Live best life!* But this guy last night, Paul? He rambled rambled entire date—total self-involve. I needed five beer just stand it.

He your age?

Yup. Fifty-six, work nonprofit. But *me me me* whole time.

Well, no give up. Right guy out there.

You one talk. When your last date?

That dif, Erin says. I still in mourning.

Owen sighs. Oh sweetie. You worry me sometime.

It just so perfect with Patrick, you know? And what happen . . . it all my fault.

Owen hesitates, as if unsure how to respond. Then he says: Wait, wait, our friend near finish now. There he go, final hump. *Damn.* Why twitch butt so much?

Leave suit in Hose Room. I clean when get there.

Nah, I do it.

You the best, Erin says.

That what they tell me. See soon.

He ends the call. The traffic crawls forward, stops, crawls again. At the checkpoint, two soldiers lead the handcuffed women to the back of a dust-colored van. Erin takes her pill bottle from her purse, swallows a capsule dry.

Above her windshield, a commercial plays for Glossy Gal Party Polish: a chic figurine in a cocktail dress, her head thrown back in laughter, her martini glass held up to make the giant *t* in the slogan, DON'T BE DULL!

•       •       •

The next scene opens in the busy Tablet Town parking lot. The camera follows Erin as she strides down a back aisle, her stiff arms swinging beside her, a breeze stirring the fine threads of her hair. Across the lot, the enormous chain store rises from the pavement, its tinted windows three stories high, a holographic banner above the awning: ASK US SMARTBODY PAYMENT PLAN! Under this stands an armed guard, his face blank with boredom, gazing out from his strip of shade.

A middle-aged couple comes trudging down her aisle, the woman pushing their cart with a wearied expression, the man, on his phone, barking, Okay, okay! I *get!* in an exasperated tone. Farther ahead, on the front sidewalk, a man in a ragged cowboy hat strolls up to the entrance, a zing-stick tucked between his tugging lips. He blows out a cloud of smoke as the doors slide open before him, revealing the figurines at the security check in the lobby. A woman in a paisley bow tie lifts her arms in the body scanner, her chipped chin missing a sizable chunk. A one-armed man removes his rubber prosthetic, unhooking it from his shoulder, setting it carefully on the conveyor belt.

The man in the cowboy hat crosses the doorway, joins the line at the scanner. Then, as the doors begin to close, a harsh brightness surges from the back of the store. From the depths of the TV Department flashes a livid yellow light, flooding the building with a sudden radiance, just a millisecond ahead of the explosion's rushing roar. The tall windows shatter outward in a liquid spray of glass, erupting behind the security guard, the back of his shirt shredded apart as he hurtles down to the sidewalk. Car alarms wail awake; headlights flash manically; a blown-off leg twirls through the air and tears its slacks as it skids across the asphalt. The middle-aged couple abandons their cart and sprints toward their sedan with strobing limbs.

The camera swings away from the couple, showing Erin standing farther back in the aisle. Stunned but unhurt, she stares at the humbled storefront. The Tablet Town sign is cracked at the vowels, the doors ripped off their runners. Smoke wavers in the window frames, through which she can glimpse the ruins of the lobby: the figurines strewn on the tile, the shattered body scanner, the pyramidal rains of the sprinkler system. She grips her purse strap tightly, her knuckle hinges creaking.

The security guard, covered in glass shards, groggily raises his head. He pushes himself up on his elbows, and then, as he starts to stand, a gunshot thumps through his temple with a sharp, resonant *thwap.* In a flash the top of his head is gone, torn off in a clean break, the hairy disc of his upper cranium whizzing through the air, tumbling among the glass as he drops back to the sidewalk. Only a jagged ring of plastic now remains above his ears, exposing the empty basin of his skull.

At this sight, Erin snaps from her trance and runs for cover. More gunfire ruptures the air, rapid bursts from a group of shooters who stand in the beds of pickup trucks parked throughout the lot. Their faces are hidden in ski masks, their rifles recoiling against their shoulders. Their lips show no emotion at the mouth holes of their masks.

The camera zooms in on Erin as she drops behind a minivan, clutching her legs to her chest, making her body as small as possible. In the next row over, a sedan under fire rattles like a jackhammer splitting cement. She pulls out her phone and thumbs a text to Owen: *U ok? U hurt?*

Her phone flashes in response: *Terror attack no service. Please use Smart Survivor app.*

Great, she mutters.

Then, startled, she almost drops the phone. Across the aisle, she sees a lumpy octopus rising from a truck bed. The octopus is a parade float, a heap of half-inflated vinyl, swelling above the bed walls like the vocal sac of a frog. On its face is a grim smile, slanted eyebrows. *You burn Ground-Up-Bone. Now we burn YOU,* reads a speech bubble painted beside its lips.

The octopus swells to its full size and then levitates from the truck bed, drifting up on its cord to hover just above the streetlamps. In other rows, a second and third octopus soar up toward the smog, as if swimming below a turbid layer of ice. One wears a vengeful grimace (*You Poison My Home, Fucker*); the other gives an ironic eye roll (*Clean Energy? Ya Think?*). They rotate in the breeze, casting their gaze on the hell of destruction below.

*Octopuses,* Erin narrates. *Shit. These are the mascots for Sea Change, one of the most brutal ecoterror groups in our region. They're known for brief but grisly killing sprees, gone before the cops arrive. Few of them have ever been caught.*

She looks back down, taps open Smart Survivor. The home screen shows a cartoon woman standing in a burning city, her hands on her hips in a fearless pose, a pepper-spray can poking from her fanny pack. *Hi—ERIN JAMES—I Sally Survivor!* reads her text box. *Much sorry you in TERROR ATTACK. How I help?*

Erin taps *Contact Family.* In this section is a single name, Owen Foley. His Survival Status reads: *User near blast zone. Phone offline. Condition uncertain.*

Her eyes tear up at once; she quickly wipes them clear. As she reaches for her pills, a new window appears on the app: Sally Survivor, now dressed in an angel costume, holds out her hands in a gesture of entreaty.

*Good Samaritan Alert!* she says. *Help User in Crisis? (Accept) (Deny)*

For a long moment, Erin stares at the two options. Finally she taps *Accept.*

A radiant halo appears above Sally's head. *You the best, ERIN JAMES—so qunky! Here the info:*

### USER IN CRISIS

*Name: Jacob Sillan*
*Age: 20*
*Gender: Male*
*Height: 5' 9"*
*Body Issue: Legal blind*
*Note: Caregiver—MOTHER—in direct blast zone. Prob*
    *dead. User parking lot.*
*Message User Now? (Yes) (No)*

As she reads the profile, a hand grenade goes soaring through the air above her, clearing her row, bouncing behind a nearby station wagon. A man in hiding shouts for help a second before the car convulses, its tires spewing air, its windows spattering the pavement.

Erin swallows two capsules, then hastily thumbs out a message:

*Need help? I Erin. Work store.*

There is no response.

*I stuck behind minivan,* she adds. *But happy help if can.*

Still no response. She is mumbling a CODA prayer when the phone vibrates:

*You sound worry. This not fun you??*

*Where you now?* she types. *In car?*

A shorter pause. *Yes.*

*By self?*

*Yes.*

*Should get floor back seat,* she says. *Out sight.*

*But how they kill me then???*

*JACOB END CHAT,* the app reports.

She reopens the text box. *Serious, should get floor. Quick.*

*Course on floor,* he responds. *Not idiot.* He ends the chat again.

Soon the gunfire sputters to silence, the car alarms stop yowling. An anxious quiet chills the parking lot, a collective held breath. In the distance a helicopter growls into earshot, growing from a far-off rumble to a thunderous chopping. Next she hears a group of emergency vehicles speeding into the lot, their sirens shrieking, their doors slamming, a sudden din of footfalls. EMTs rush past her row, a SWAT team in a blur of body armor. The stillness shatters into a chaos of noises: voices crying for help, stretchers clacking over the asphalt, the bleeps and squeals of ambulances, cruisers, fire trucks. Now and then a loudspeaker blares: *Stay at attack site until further notice. Order of Terrorism Bureau. Stay at attack site until further notice. Order of Terrorism Bureau.*

The camera pedestals up as Erin rises from hiding. She looks out at the scarred sedans, the octopus floats swaying in the wind, the figurines sprawled unmoving on the pavement. Police tape cordons off the entire storefront. Beyond the shattered windows, she can see the swarm of EMTs who crouch inside the store, tending to victims with blown-off limbs who scream until sedated, ignoring the other victims who—torn in half, or missing heads, or melted beyond recognition—offer no protest at all. Product boxes lie everywhere, dimpling under the rain of the sprinkler system.

Her phone vibrates. This time Sally Survivor wears a party hat, holds a lit sparkler. *Congrat, ERIN JAMES! Your family member—OWEN FOLEY—survive attack! Tap for more info!*

*Condition stable,* the update reads. *Bad hurt left leg. Ambulance to Todd Gordon Memorial Hospital.*

Erin leans against the minivan, her eyes closed with relief. Then, with a conflicted look, she goes back to the Good Samaritan Alert page. She sends another message to Jacob Sillan.

*Still there?* she types.

A few seconds pass. *No. I dead.*

*All clear now.*

*Know,* he says. *Not deaf.*

*Bureau keep us here for while. Maybe few hour.*

*Yes. KNOW.*

*Let give help,* she types. *You need.*

*Tell you already. I dead.*

*Okay, you dead. Now send location.*

*NO,* he says. Then, after a pause: *Fine. But no want talk.*

Jacob sends her a map link; she strides toward the blinking dot. A few rows over, she passes a car with a bullet-riddled windshield, the glass spider-webbed around the punctures. An old man slumps behind the wheel, his plastic face a pulp of gunshot wounds. In the back of the car, a fair-haired boy tilts forward in his seat belt, the cushion behind him visible through the holes in his hollow chest.

Erin looks away from the child, stares down at the blinking dot. The camera switches to a point of view shot, showing the scene through her eyes, Erin glancing up from the dot as she approaches a beige sedan. Through the glare on the back window she can make out a pale profile, a male figurine with sunglasses and long dark hair. He wears jeans and a half-zipped hoodie, a pair of canvas sneakers; on the carpet below him, folded, lies a collapsible metal cane. Something changes in Erin's features as she gazes through the window, her eyes softening, her mouth tightening, a look both troubled and intrigued. Behind her an ambulance wails.

*Outside car,* she texts him.

He taps his phone and listens. He moves his lips in response. *Which side?* appears in her text box.

*Left,* she types back.

Jacob unlocks the door, pushes it open. He waves her inside with a listless hand.

You okay? she asks, taking the seat beside him.

He shrugs.

She shuts the door gently. Lot damage out there. We luck.

Luck, he repeats in a numb, distant voice. In the front seat the AC vents are blaring. As if continuing an earlier thought, he says:

When I little kid, I hurt her sometime. First grade, second maybe. I tap her arm—tap tap, tap tap—when want attention. No care I hurt her. Think funny.

Well . . . lot kid like that.

Jacob, lost in thought, seems not to hear her. Call her bitch today. Own mother. Bitch.

She prob okay. Prob safe in store.

He gives an abrupt chuckle, more an audible shudder than laughter. His clenched toes creak inside his sneakers.

Just one bomb, she adds. Your mom prob fine. Really.

He shakes his head. I feel her go. It weird weird. But I feel.

Jacob slides over to the window, leans his head against the glass. Outside, another vinyl octopus hovers above the parking lot, this one with a pointy dunce cap, a speech bubble that reads, *Even dummy like me believe in HeatLeap!* A bomb squad in disposal suits surrounds the float at a distance, flying a drone that buzzes around it like a timid insect. Erin takes out her pills, swallows two more capsules.

What pill they? Jacob asks her.

She twists on the top. SettleSelf.

ChillDude me. Get bottle?

Sure.

Glove compartment, he says.

She finds the bottle buried under a stack of loose papers. *ChillDude: Cool Down Right!* proclaims its motto. She hands it to Jacob; he opens the top with a practiced downward pressure.

Think play music now, he says after two capsules of his own. Play speaker if want.

Def. I listen.

Carla, open playlist. Fav Rhythm & Noise Song.

Playing Fav Rhythm & Noise Song, says his phone.

The air around them shimmers with a slowly strummed guitar. Above this comes a rhythmic popping, a series of champagne corks bursting open in time to the music.

The song seems to relax Jacob. He tucks some hair behind his ear, revealing the sleek angle of his jawline. His features are birdlike, both delicate and severe, his sharp nose tempered by the gradual curve of his chin. The camera pans from Jacob to Erin, who stares at his face with a deepening absorption.

*It's wrong of me to watch him like this,* she narrates. *I should be thinking about my coworkers: if they're injured, if they're alive. I should be getting ready to leave here, to rush to Owen as soon as the bureau clears the parking lot. But Jacob, it's uncanny—he reminds me so much of Patrick. His hair, the shape of his nose, his lips. The sincerity of his voice. Not that they look exactly the same. Not quite. But enough that it hurts to look away.*

Outside his window, a different drone buzzes toward the octopus in the dunce cap. This drone is equipped with a foot-long blade, jutting like a bayonet from a hole in the front panel. The blade is a few yards from impact when the octopus starts to quake with vibrations, giving off a low mechanical chirring. The drone veers off at once, climbing high above the float; the bomb squad drops to the pavement, ducking below their shields. Erin lets out a quiet gasp.

Then, with a whoosh of compressed air, the top of the dunce cap flips open. From its funnel surges a spume of confetti, a tall spout of colored paper like water from a blowhole, fanning out at the apex of its spray. The camera follows the confetti as it showers onto the parking lot, raining down on the fire trucks, on the ambulances and cruisers, on the few plastic corpses still uncovered among the cars, catching on their eyelashes, piling in their laps. The other octopuses now vibrate as one and shoot their confetti as well, so that, as Erin looks from the window, the chaos of the attack site resembles a giddy celebration.

Jacob pauses the music as he hears her pill bottle open. Something happen?

They shoot confetti, Erin says in a shaky voice. I think it bomb. But just confetti.

Confetti?

She explains about the floats, the eruption of paper.

He does not reply. Instead he reaches into his hoodie pocket and pulls out a pair of earbuds. He pushes them deep in his ears.

Carla, play music on headphone, he mutters. The guitar and corks resume more faintly, the song reverberating from inside his hollow skull.

In his window, Erin watches the drone circle back to the octopus. The blade glides to a stop just before the creature's face, then darts forward and pierces a hole between the painted eyes. At this the drone lurches downward, dragging the wound open with a violent hissing. The octopus crumples in the sky, its face losing form, its arms withering inward, its dunce cap sputtering scraps of confetti.

Erin looks down at her SettleSelf bottle, sees just one pill remaining on the bottom. She tips the tan capsule into her mouth. Then she sifts through her purse and finds her own pair of earbuds. Sitting lower in the seat, she lifts her phone screen close to her face. Carla, play *Nuclear Family,* she whispers.

Playing *Nuclear Family,* the phone replies.

# NUCLEAR FAMILY

## "The Roller Rats"

The episode opens on a sunny sitcom set, designed to look like a quaint backyard in the suburbs. The set is simple but tasteful: a picket fence surrounds the tidy beds of fake begonias; a fake forsythia blossoms beside the birdbath. In one corner is an old stone bench, and there a plastic teen named Max sits below the set lights, a drawing pad spread open on his knees. He bends forward over the pad, his face weak with longing, sketching a sexy picture of his best friend O.

The laugh track chuckles at his drawing: O stands on the steps of a heart-shaped jacuzzi, his lips curved in a sultry smile, a skimpy towel around his waist, some maple syrup dripping from his squares. He is not a figurine but a massive, living waffle, his body a circle of toasted indents, his rubber eyes and nose each fitted into the squares of his grid. His arms, two bendy shoots of rubber, reach down to the knot of the towel, as if about to whisk it off him, revealing the region below his crispy rim.

The pencil trembling in his hand, Max fails to notice when O himself strolls into the scene, appearing behind the long picket fence. The waffle, dressed in jeans and a T-shirt, ambles along on his rubber legs, his upper rim bobbing above the pickets. On the laugh track come titters of anticipation.

"Hey! Watcha drawing?" O asks as he steps into the yard.

Max has only an instant to slap the drawing pad shut. He crosses his legs and grips the pad over the groin of his khakis. The laugh track roars.

"Uh . . . the Eiffel Tower," he says. "The Eiffel Tower at dawn."

"Whoa. That must be hard."

"You've got no idea," Max mumbles to more laughter.

"Can I look at it?"

"No! I mean, not yet. It still needs lots of work."

"You sure? I'd love to see how it's coming."

Max shifts uncomfortably on the bench. "Maybe tomorrow."

"You artists," O says, rolling his eyes in their squares. "Such perfectionists."

The waffle sits down on the bench, turning his breadth to face the figurine. He is thirteen years old, the same age as Max, his bread fresh and plump, no cracks along his crust, no signs of staleness. He goes on: "So, you getting excited for the contest tomorrow?"

Max shrugs. "I guess. Roller Rats is always fun, but Mom . . . she gets so bummed right after. Her rats haven't won in years."

"It's so unfair. That Trish Demarco, she only wins because she's rich. She doesn't even *train* her rats. She just hires some famous guy from the city to do it."

"Yeah," Max says nostalgically. "Mom used to be a champion. I feel worst for Blorko and Daphne, though. Those little critters work so hard."

"Well, at least they have each other. I've never seen two rodents more in love."

Max stares off into the distance, gazing at the painted backdrop of the sky, the strips of cloud blurred behind the smog. A puppet of a monarch butterfly flits above the hedges, its strings glinting whenever it swoops or soars. At last Max says:

"Have you ever been in love, O?"

The waffle looks pensive for a moment, his forehead squares tightening in thought. He gives Max a shy glance, his rubber eyes suffused with a pained desire. Before O can respond, the plastic boy laughs nervously and stands up from the bench.

"Hey, I'll—I'll be right back," he says. "Just need to bring my drawing pad inside. Can I get you some chicken bites?"

The waffle makes a large O with his fingers. "You knOw it!" he exclaims.

The laugh track bursts into applause, cheering for his catchphrase.


Max strides through the downstairs set of his house, headed to the staircase behind the sectional sofa. The bay window shows a bright suburban afternoon outside: a painted backdrop of two-story houses in a more peaceful era, no window bars or razor wire, just flower beds and lawn gnomes. The butterfly puppet has stolen inside through the open patio door; it flutters near a shelf of Roller Rat trophies.

As he crosses the set, Max hears his mother talking on the phone, her voice drifting from a half-open door by the stairs. Wearily she says:

"Yes, okay, that's true. But you know what? I'm not sure I even *want* couple's therapy. It's been fifteen years, we have a son, and

Gary is *still* in love with his ex-wife. Four, five nights a week—I'm not exaggerating—he's on the phone with that woman for over an hour. He uses their daughter as an excuse . . . but Anita is seventeen, she's a straight-A student, she's in all her school plays: there's not that much to discuss. He should be spending time with his son, spending time with *me,* but instead he's off in his study, gabbing away with that motormouth. Sometimes I just want to pack my bags. Divorce him, get the hell out of here."

Her voice pauses. Max, his eyes gone wide at "divorce," steps closer to the door, not noticing the glass coffee table beside him. His left knee strikes a corner; he bites his knuckle, hops about in silence. The laugh track thunders.

His mother resumes:

"I'm sorry to complain like this. It's just . . . it's tough right now. Anita, his daughter, she's visiting us this month. I do my best with her, I really do, but she doesn't make things easy. She's so *particular* about her eating, and it all falls on me." Another pause. "Yeah . . . the contest is tomorrow. That's been hard, too. After this one I might retire, have the rats hang up their skates. That awful Trish Demarco, how can I compete?"

Max, his brow furrowed, now sits at the bottom of the staircase. As he rubs his aching knee, his voice narrates on the soundtrack:

*I knew Mom and Dad were fighting—but divorce? Is that possible?*

The butterfly puppet flaps across the living room. It lands on Max's shoulder, rests a comforting wing on his neck.

*"Awwww,"* coo the voices on the laugh track.

That evening, Max sits on the sofa with his father and sister, watching the news while they wait for their boiled chicken. His mother, across the set, stands at the island in the open kitchen, scooping the limp cutlets onto plates.

Jess is a slim figurine in her forties, dressed in a linen jumpsuit and a lanyard with a rat whistle, still around her neck from a training session earlier. She carries the plates to the living room, sets them down on the TV trays before her son and husband. Then, with an irritated set to her jaw, she turns and makes another trip to the kitchen. Max watches her leave with an apprehensive gaze.

His sister, Anita, has not received a cutlet. The reason for this is clear: Anita is a robot, a metal cylinder four feet tall, set upright on the sofa's taut leather. On her upper half are two googly eyes, a light bulb nose, a narrow slot of a mouth. A frilly pink bow, tied around her top, gestures at her gender. Other than this the robot is bare: no limbs, no other facial features, no attempts at clothing.

Jess returns to the sofa a moment later, carrying a large funnel and a pitcher of motor oil. She approaches her robot stepchild. Careful of the angle, she lifts the funnel and slides the stem into Anita's mouth slot. The googly eyes follow her every movement.

"Please use caution when pouring my hot petroleum," Anita says in a monotone. Her voice is fast and metallic, without inflection. "Last night another error occurred in my feeding."

Jess squints into the mouth slot, a few strands of hair fallen loose from her updo. "I remember," she mutters.

"Errors have repercussions. Mis-poured oil may cause processor delays."

"Yes, Anita, I know. You tell me every meal."

"And yet errors persist."

Jess grips the funnel tighter. "I'd appreciate you not taking that tone with me."

"I am not capable of taking a tone. I am a robot with a single vocal setting."

"I could do without the back talk, too."

Jess starts to pour the oil, the dark fluid glugging down the funnel. At once the robot's light bulb nose flashes a neon pink.

"What? What is it?" Jess says, pulling the funnel away.

"OIL TEMPERATURE ERROR. OIL IS TOO COLD."

"It just came off the stove. It might have cooled a bit, but—"

"IDEAL TEMPERATURE IS 107 DEGREES FAHREN-HEIT."

"Oh my goodness. It won't kill you if it's a little—"

"OIL MUST BE EJECTED."

"Anita, don't you dare, don't even th—"

A gush of oil splurts from the mouth slot, splattering Jess's jumpsuit. The laugh track exults. "Are you *serious?*" Jess cries, looking down at the spreading stain. "You—you—you spoiled piece of scrap!"

Gary, her husband, inhales sharply. He has been watching the news while he eats, trying to ignore their tense exchange, but at the words "piece of scrap" he pulls his napkin off his paunch. He is a balding figurine about a decade older than Jess, a web of crackles forming on his high forehead. On his polo shirt are the words *Muddy Acres Shmuglin Club,* printed under a logo of a mud-spattered bucket.

"Jess? Bedroom for a minute?" he says in an overly polite voice.

"Sure. Fine," she mumbles. She sets the oil on the table.

They trudge out of sight up the staircase, their unsaid words trembling behind their lips. A door closes upstairs with a brusque firmness. Then their vexed voices resume, too muffled to make out the words.

Anita, her mouth caked in oil, revolves her googly eyes toward

Max. "I must apologize for my behavior, dear half sibling. It was not my intention to cause more altercations."

He gives a tired shrug. "That's okay, sis."

"Perhaps my fame at high school is to blame. As our father may have informed you, I landed the lead in the spring production of *Hairspray.* It has brought my inner diva to the fore."

Max lifts his knife and fork, morosely cuts a slice of chicken.

"Ah yes," the robot goes on, "the theater has changed me indeed. I once was such a shy, retiring flower."

Upstairs his parents' voices surge in anger. Jess yells: "Admit it! You're a metal man! You never wanted a plastic woman!" Gary shouts back: "See? This is what I mean—all this suspicion! And you wonder why I'm always at the club?"

Max shuts his eyes. "Volume up 8X," he says to the TV.

On the news is a segment about the president, shown laughing at a podium beside his wife. The leader is a giant waffle like O, a commander made of toasted bread; his wife a stylish figurine many years his junior. The president dresses in a Western style, a Stetson hat on his upper curve, a bolo tie dangling to his lower rim. On a table beside him, in a steel case, sits a gleaming platinum coin.

"Today, in a triumph for President Wafflin," a news anchor narrates, "the Treasury minted a single coin valued at six trillion dollars. This coin will let Wafflin proceed with his expansions of the military, despite his failures to gain the funding through legislation. His goal is to recover the global standing of our nation, largely through tripling the size of our nuclear arsenal. Many waffles have cheered this development, but the nation as a whole remains divided on the issue."

Max asks, "Why is Wafflin laughing like that? What's funny about nuclear bombs?"

Anita considers the question, the motors whirring in her cylinder. "Waffles are not like us. They are selfish, bad from the batter. They crave the syrup of power above all else."

"Well, not every waffle," Max says sheepishly.

"True. My apologies, half sibling. I forgot that your friend O is a waffle of liberal persuasion."

"O *hates* President Wafflin. He fights with his parents about it all the time. But people still yell at him in the street, honk their horns. They see his bread and assume he's a supporter."

The robot's nose glows a soft coral. "I saw your eyes, dear brother, when O left our home today. The look of love you fixed upon his squares. Your amorous feelings were evident."

*"Anita,"* Max whispers. "Mom and Dad are right upstairs."

"Your secret is safe with me, sweet half sibling. But why feel such fear and shame? Attraction to one's own gender is quite normal. Your sexual persuasion is widely accepted."

"Let's . . . let's just drop it," Max says. He lowers his head, forks his slice of chicken.

Upstairs his father shouts: "This again? Your *Christmas* present? Jess, for the last time: I thought it was *nice* to give you money. Then you could get whatever you wanted."

"And your ex-wife?" Jess yells back. "Her you bought a diamond headband!"

"Oh gimme a break. That stone was nothing—a quarter carat."

"A diamond headband. My friends couldn't believe it."

"It was on *sale!*" Gary cries.


Max lies awake that night in the set of his bedroom. The set has an aquatic theme: the wallpaper covered with penguins in bow ties, the curtains with saxophone-playing jellyfish, the bedspread with dolphins leaping from a tranquil sea. A plush squid sits grinning on a shelf above his desk, its rose-colored suckers dangling off the edge.

The boy stares up at the ceiling, his face wan and worried, a stuffed seal hugged against his chest. He breathes an anxious sigh, then looks into the camera that films from above the bed. He begins to narrate out loud:

I keep thinking about Jim Tucker, this kid I knew from baseball. His parents had this nasty divorce, fought over every dollar, even made poor Jim choose between them. Then, after he chose his mom, she packed their bags and moved them across the country. What if Mom and Dad do the same thing? I could end up living a thousand miles from Dad, a thousand miles from O. I'd be here only in the summers, just like Jim.

Well . . . at least I'm not alone right now. I can always go talk to Jesus. I wonder what He'll have to say.

Max swings down his legs and strides across the set, stopping at a wooden cross above his bureau. A tiny Christ is nailed onto its beams. The Savior hangs there in his crown of thorns, no taller than a water glass, his eyes closed, a mournful mouth inside his painted beard. Max reaches out and pokes his gaunt stomach.

"Jesus," he calls, "Jesus. Wake up! I need your help."

Max jabs him again and the Christ figure stirs, his eyes snapping open. "What? What is it?" he says in a gruff elderly voice, decades older than his appearance. "Can't you see I'm napping?"

The laugh track rumbles.

"You're always napping, Jesus," Max replies.

"For the last time, stop calling me Jesus. I'm not your *real*

Lord and Savior, okay? You're thirteen now, Max. I bet you're still asking for toys from the Santa at the mall."

The laugh track erupts.

"Sorry, Morris," he says. "I keep forgetting."

"Eh, don't sweat it, kid. I get that your spiritual needs aren't being met elsewhere."

"Anyway, I'm really worried about something. Can I tell you?"

Morris shrugs his stretched-out shoulders, his palms straining against the nails. "I'm a captive audience," he says to his biggest laugh yet.

The boy explains about his parents. By the time he finishes, he is wiping tears from his eyes. "I just wish I could help them," he says. "They weren't always this unhappy."

Morris gives him a dubious look. "They weren't?"

"Don't you remember? They'd have those weekend getaways. Dad would take Mom on dates. He'd go to his Shmuglin club once a month, not three times a week."

"That man sure loves to play Shmuglin. Me, I can't see the appeal. Too much mud."

"Mom and Dad—all they need is, like, a little boost. To remember they like each other. Then they'll be fine."

"Uh, kid?" Morris says. "I'm not sure it works that way."

"Why not? They got married, didn't they? They liked each other then."

"Listen, Max. Don't you want your parents to be happy?"

"Sure. Of course. Just as long as they stay together."

Morris sighs. "Why don't you take out my nails for a minute. I think I know how to explain this."

The boy gets his pair of pliers, then prises the nails from Morris's palms and feet. The little Savior leaps down to the bureau, where he suddenly stands in a beam of spotlight, dressed in a boater hat and a seersucker suit. He reaches out a pierced hand;

a glittery dance cane whizzes into his clasp. Strolling the bureau like a vaudeville stage, he sings to a maudlin piano:

> *It's awful sad*
> *When Mom and Dad*
> *Are headed for divorce.*
>
> *They used to kiss*
> *But their next tryst*
> *Will be in family court.*
>
> *And you are just a kid who can't believe*
> *A parent could pack up their bags and leave.*
> *It hurts at first—but one day you'll say, "Hey . . .*
> *There's perks for kids of well-off divorcées!"*

The music turns jaunty on the soundtrack, the piano fast and playful, a ukulele strumming to the ragtime beat. The squid on the shelf comes to life and bounds into the air, hooking an arm on a blade of the ceiling fan, spinning in gleeful circles. Its other arms hold gift-wrapped boxes, which it tosses in all directions. The tiny Christ tap-dances with his cane as he sings the chorus:

> *I know that you like Christmas—*
> *Well how would you like two?*
> *I know that you like presents—*
> *Two birthdays just for you!*
>
> *Two bedrooms full of toys,*
> *Two bank accounts to drain,*
> *Two guilty parents overjoyed*
> *To buy away your pain!*

Morris pulls the boater hat off his head, kicks his pierced feet as he sings the finale:

> *Two guilty parents!*
> *They're well aware*
> *Your childhood is ruined.*
>
> *Two guilty parents!*
> *It's only fair*
> *They buy their boy the moon.*

Max has stared down at the carpet throughout the song. In a desolate voice he says: "So there's no hope? They're getting divorced?"

"These things can be for the best, kid. And you should look at the bright side here. Your parents will spoil you rotten. You can't lose."

"I guess," Max says gloomily. Then, with a gasp, he lifts his face to the Savior. "Wait. That's it—that's *it!* Morris, you're a genius!"

"I am?"

"The Roller Rat contest. Mom, if she wins, she'll be so happy! She'll forget all about leaving Dad."

Morris scratches the back of his neck. "Gee, kid. I kinda doubt that. The guy's obsessed with his robot ex-wife."

"It's worth a try, isn't it?"

"What do you mean, 'a try'? You can't just decide your mom will win."

"I have a plan," Max says.

The Messiah winces. "I was afraid you'd say that."

The laugh track explodes.

The next scene features the most elaborate set of the episode, designed to look like an outdoor fairground at sunset. To the right is a teacup ride, the saucers circling a gigantic kettle; to the left the pulsing column of a Test Your Strength; to the back a food truck selling shanks of FairFowl. At the center is a wooden stage, covered with the ramps and hurdles of a rat-sized obstacle course. ROLLER RAT RALLY! SPONSORED BY GORDON WOUND GLUE, reads a banner strung along the back curtains. A crowd in lawn chairs chats excitedly, waiting for the contest to begin.

Max, sunk down in his seat, casts a guilty glance at his father and sister in the chairs beside him. He clutches a backpack tightly on his knees.

*Am I really doing this?* he narrates. *I guess I have no choice. My family needs me.*

Now, from behind the curtains, tendrils of mist begin to seep onstage. His father sits forward in his chair, his aging face youthful with anticipation.

"This is your mom's opening," he whispers. "Looks like they're having her go first. That can be good. Makes an impression on the judges."

Max clears his throat. "Do you . . . do you know when Trish Demarco goes?"

"Trish," Gary scoffs. "That cheater. Right after your mom, I bet."

Max rises to his feet. "I, um—I need the bathroom."

"Bathroom? Be quick, buddy. Soon as the mist thickens, they're on."

"Hurry, my dear half brother," Anita adds. The robot wears

an *I ♥ Blorko* headband, its pink velour wrapped around her metal. "Today your mother debuts her impressive new effect."

Max grabs his backpack and hurries behind the food truck, hidden from view of the crowd. The loudspeaker cries: *Up first tonight, a former regional champion! You know them, you love them: Total Squeakhearts!*

As a cheer goes up from the lawn chairs, two rats in sequined jumpsuits roll as one through the wall of mist. Daphne and Blorko skate on their hind legs, their movements joined and fluid, their forepaws waving like royalty to the audience. They glide to a stop at the first ramp, and then, with an *ahh!* from the crowd, every jumping hoop in the course blazes abruptly into flames. None of this fazes Blorko, the first to face the flames, who not only clears the hoop when he sails off the ramp, but performs a flying spin as he soars through the ring of fire. He lands smoothly on one roller skate, his other leg stretched long. The audience screams like they've all just won the lottery.

Max, kneeling behind the truck, zips his backpack open. It is empty save for Morris, who sits on the bottom clutching a string of rosary beads. He prays with his eyes shut: ". . . and blessed is the fruit of thy—"

"Morris, *Morris.* It's almost time," Max whispers. He takes a whistle from his pocket and hands it to the Savior, who receives it in both arms like a hulking barbell. Morris struggles it to the ground, its mouthpiece angled up toward him.

"So, uh, the thing is . . ." the little Christ begins. "I'm kinda having second thoughts?"

"We went over this last night. There's no way they'll catch us. No one can hear this whistle but rats."

"It just doesn't seem right, kid, cheating and all. I know you hate Trish Demarco, but—"

"This is to save my *family*. Who cares if we mess with that rich woman's rats?"

"Maybe I'm not Jesus. But I still have a conscience."

"Fine," Max says. "If you do this, I'll save up my allowance. I'll buy you that Nativity set you wanted."

Morris frowns to himself, staring down at the whistle. "It'll stay out all year long? Not just at Christmas?"

"All year long."

"I'll need some shepherds, too," Morris adds. "Joseph, the Wise Men—I love 'em, but they never shut up about King Herod. It's like, *It's been two thousand years, guys. Get over it already.* And Mary, she's distracted: the baby and all. The shepherds, though, *they* know how to hang."

The laugh track howls.

"Sure, okay," Max says, "I'll buy you some shepherds. Now you gotta get ready. Trish is up next."

The Messiah bends down to the mouthpiece. "So when you give the signal, I'll just . . ."

"No, Morris! Not yet!"

But it's too late. Morris has blown into the whistle already, and, a second later, they hear the crowd at the stage shriek in horror. Max looks out from behind the food truck: his mouth falls open at what he sees.

On the stage a hoop of fire lies burning on the ground, knocked off its stand by a rat jump gone awry. Blorko skates not far away, his sequined jumpsuit engulfed in flames, unable to stop his momentum as he hurtles like a speeding pyre across the rink. Two rats with tiny fire extinguishers chase behind him, but the burning rodent is skating away too fast. He brushes against a stage curtain, which also bursts into flames. Other teams of rats leap from backstage and scurry from the inferno.

Max ducks behind the food truck. "Oh boy. Oh boy. Oh boy," he says over and over.

Morris, his head sticking out of the backpack, has witnessed the carnage as well.

"So . . ." he says. "I'm guessing the Nativity set is out now. But can I still have *one* shepherd?"

The laugh track wails with delight.


Late that night, Max sits outside on the slanted roof of his house, dressed in pajamas with a seahorse pattern. He leans back on his elbows, gazing at the trails of smog in the painted sky. Morris is beside him on the rooftop set, doing sit-ups under the chimney, his pierced hands linked behind his neck.

"Morris, what's the meaning of life?" Max says.

The Messiah stops mid-sit-up to ponder the question. Then, resuming, he grunts, "Having . . . plenty . . . of time . . . to nap." The laugh track chuckles along with each word.

Max shakes his head. "That can't be it."

"Sure . . . is . . . for me."

"You're sort of like a cat, you know that? A big old lazy cat."

Morris lurches up in a final sit-up, adjusts his crown of thorns. "I'd love to be a cat," he says to appreciative guffaws. "Hell, I'd kill to be a cat."

Max returns his gaze to the sky. "What a day, huh? Did you see Mom and Dad after the contest? How they kept hugging? How he never left her side?"

"I was zipped up in the backpack, kid. You left me there for hours."

"I haven't seen them like that in years. They were so . . . tender. And then, when we got back home, how Dad talked about that cruise? Just the two of them going?"

"I think that was when you left me in the car," Morris says.

"It blows my mind. I never thought making her *lose* would help their marriage."

Morris stares off into the night. "Poor Blorko, though. That was rough."

"Yeah," Max says somberly. "There was nothing those little EMTs could do."

They lapse into awkward silence. At last the Savior says: "Let's make a pact, right now. No more interfering in dangerous competitions."

"Agreed." Max gives a resigned sigh. "Well, I'd better get to bed. Dad's taking us all to the zoo first thing tomorrow."

"And I need to find a priest for confession."

Bellows of laughter follow, sustained applause.

Max stands up on the slanted roof, turns to the attic window. As he stoops to open the pane, a loose shingle skitters from under his foot. He loses his balance, cries out in alarm, and almost crushes Morris as he stumbles backward and plummets out of the camera shot. A thud is heard as he lands on the lawn below.

"My ankle!" he yells. "I think I broke my ankle!"

Morris steps down to the gutter, gingerly peers over.

"Great," he mutters to himself. "Now who's gonna nail me back on the cross?"

The audience laughs with abandon as the credits begin to roll.

# FLIPPIN' CHICKEN
# FUNERAL HOME

The episode opens on a painting of a rooster in a three-piece suit: a waistcoat buttoned down his breast, a jacket flared back over his saddle, his slender legs sheathed in stick-thin pants. He perches on a headstone in an autumn graveyard, his head inclined in sorrow as the leaves waft down around him. A single tear trickles past his beak.

The camera zooms out from the painting, revealing the spacious lobby of a corporate funeral home. Hundreds of plastic mourners mingle near the row of snack tables, talking in muted voices as they eat their boiled nuggets, the elbows of the older mourners creaking as they lift the meat from their plates. Beyond the lobby stretches a long hallway of viewing rooms, the walls lined with wooden doors, the floor equipped with a moving walkway that carries the mourners back and forth below the chandeliers. Beside each door, in vivid detail, glows a life-size hologram of the deceased.

The camera cuts to Erin, gliding on the walkway in a plain

black dress, her finger hinges curled around the handrail. She passes the cheerful holograms of her customers and coworkers, the victims of the Tablet Town attack. A woman in a baseball cap waves from a row of bleachers, a bearded man at a campfire strums a beat-up acoustic guitar, an old man with a sleepy grin lolls in a rocking chair. The victims shimmer above the carpet, the damask pattern of the wallpaper showing faintly through their faces. Erin wipes her eyes with a rigid hand.

As she rides the walkway, the funeral home suddenly darkens around her. The chandeliers extinguish, the moonlight leaves the lobby windows; a ray of spotlight shines down on the walkway. The holograms remain aglow, casting a pale radiance around their ghostly bodies.

On the soundtrack plays a rhythmic bassline, an ethereal guitar. Erin looks into the camera and sings:

> *My ears still hear the frantic screams,*
> *My eyes still see the figurines*
> *Dead on the ground while octopuses loom.*
>
> *Ten coworkers died at the store*
> *But some attacks kill hundreds more*
> *To protest Ground-Up-Bone, our planet's doom.*

Up and down the hall, the holograms break from their static poses. The woman in the ballcap leaps from the bleachers; the old man springs from his chair on youthful legs. The dead gather beside the walkway, swaying with the beat, their voices rising in a plaintive chorus:

> *Oh terrorists, oh terrorists,*
> *Why must we pay the price?*

*We didn't make*
*The world you hate*
*But still you take our life.*

The holograms partner off and begin to waltz down the hall, spinning through the dark in graceful box steps. They sing background vocals as they waltz, spectral *oohs* and *aahs,* while Erin resumes:

*We know why bombs tear off our limbs:*
*To make us face our nation's sins,*
*Three hundred years of poisoned earth and sea.*

*The planet warmed, the oceans rose,*
*But we kept burning chicken bones—*
*The most pollutive source of energy.*

The holograms spin to a spot at the center of the hall, their bodies colliding without an impact, slipping seamlessly into each other. The many figurines form a single luminous body, the face a blur of layered faces, of countless singing lips:

*Oh terrorists, oh terrorists,*
*What does your war achieve?*
*Our souls will rise*
*In smoggy skies*
*Still black with ash and greed.*

*You fight for Earth, but is it worth*
*The legacy you leave?*
*Just graveyards filled*

*With those you killed*
*And families cursed to grieve.*

As the music fades, the holograms stroll back to their separate doors. The chandeliers switch on above them; their faces freeze into smiles.

Erin steps off the walkway and strides to a hologram in a beach chair. She is a middle-aged woman in a floral bathing suit, an unseen umbrella shading her sunglassed face. A gift bag stuffed with tissue paper is reflected in her glasses; her grateful hands reach out to receive it. Her floating nameplate reads: IRENE SILLAN.

Before she enters the room, Erin taps open her PrayZone app. She finds a prayer in the Consolation section, then whispers:

*Oh Great Unknown, I not sure how help people best. They suffer much, so sad. Though I nervous now, I know deep down I perfect. May I bring them peace. May peace be my whole thing.*

She opens the wooden door, carved with an image of the sad-eyed rooster, his comb blown flat as if in a bracing wind. The room inside is small and lamplit, a few mourners in the rows of folding chairs, others shuffling toward the coffin past a screen with advertisements: LOVE AGAIN! DATE APP, GLOSSY GAL LASTLOOK, TOUGHSTUFF TISSUE. A purl of piano ripples from a speaker in the ceiling, mixed with sounds of cats being brushed, soothing feline purrs.

The camera switches to a point of view shot, panning across the room through Erin's eyes. Near the back, a young man sits alone in a black dress shirt, his legs crossed tightly, his long hair framing his face. In his lap he clutches a square of fabric, ragged at its edges. As the camera zooms in on Jacob, he lifts it to his nose and inhales deeply.

Erin slips into the viewing line. Up front, between the flower bouquets, the profile of a dead figurine can be seen inside the coffin, her polished hands folded on the high waist of her dress. Her face is the same as the hologram outside, but uncanny in its stillness, like a wax replica of Irene. Inside the coffin are a few mementos, propped against the lid: a seashell, a smartphone, an onyx bracelet, a school photo of Jacob.

*I've seen that picture of him,* Erin narrates. *There are hundreds of Jacob posted on his mother's profile. Dozens of videos, too.*

Now at the front of the line, she steps to the coffin and lowers herself to the kneeler. She studies the dead woman's face, the limp bangs curled on her forehead, the fractures in her cheeks glued back together. A jagged line at the base of her neck, powdered with concealer, shows where the mortician has reattached her head. Erin wipes her eyes again and rises to her feet.

The only greeter from the family is a woman in her seventies, a stocky figurine in a sable shift dress. A tote purse slumps on the carpet beside her orthopedic sneakers. Her face is lined with crackles, her eyes vague and tired behind the lenses of her bifocals. She seems to recognize Erin, giving her a weak smile as she approaches from the coffin.

*This is Katherine, Jacob's grandmother. She was the one who picked him up at Tablet Town that morning, when the Terrorism Bureau finally lifted the barricade. We talked for less than a minute, and she was crying the entire time. I'm surprised she remembers my face.*

Good see you here, the old woman says. Forgive me, but tell name again?

Erin. Much sorry your loss.

It nice you come, Erin. Must many these today.

Yes. Too many.

I heard ten employee died?

So far.

Ten, Katherine says bitterly. So sad when read that. How you hold up?

Erin gestures at the door. That hall out there . . . feel like I at Tablet Town, so many coworker. But they all hologram.

It lucky anyone survived. I still much grateful you—so brave you answered Good Samaritan Alert. You hero, Erin.

Nah. It no big deal.

Katherine raises her eyebrows. Kid me? No one else answered.

A mourner in a wheelchair rolls up to them, a man with an eye patch and a shrapnel scar in his neck. Katherine summons a smile for him, then says to Erin: Maybe we talk more in minute? You need go soon?

No, can stay for bit. Take time.

The camera follows Erin as she strides across the room, passing a table with four rooster statues for legs. On the table are stacks of pamphlets: *Pick Right PineBox, No Hassle Headstone, Pill for Much Pain.* She heads to the back of the room, where Jacob remains in his empty row, clutching his square of fabric. His face shows no emotion save for an occasional twitch of his lips.

Hi there, she says, standing above his chair. This Erin. We meet Tablet Town? In car?

Jacob stays silent, letting her greeting hang in the air. For a moment, it seems he might ignore her altogether.

You not dead yet? he says at last, his voice soft, ironic.

Not yet.

Well. Sure they kill you soon.

Prob, she says with a chuckle.

He adjusts his grip on the fabric. Sit if want.

Erin lowers herself to the chair. The camera frames them in

a two-shot, a tense young man and an awkward young woman, their faces filmed in a shallow focus, the milling mourners blurred in the background. She opens her mouth but does not speak, as if lost for words in his presence.

Listen, I . . . I need say sorry, Jacob says. I total jerk that morning. No remember much. But remember I asshole to you.

No need apologize. It awful day.

Still, you answer Good Samaritan Alert. Risk life for me. And I treat like crap.

She smiles. Your grandma say I *hero*. The attack over when I go your car.

He turns toward Erin, her absorbed gaze doubled in his sunglasses. He looks uncertain for a second, then asks: You in store when bomb go off?

No, I late for shift. Get there just in time for attack. Lucky me.

Jacob pauses. Better in parking lot than store, though.

Yeah. True.

I hear lot employee die. Such nightmare. They friend?

Erin considers this. Acquaintance more. But they feel like friend when gone, if that make sense.

Sure. Course.

I have relative work there, Owen. He still in hospital.

He be okay?

Lose right foot. But he live.

Jacob sighs. Yeah, that the main thing.

She looks down at his lap, where his fingers tremble on the square of black chiffon.

That fabric. It belong your mother? she asks.

He nods. Shirt from attack. Still smell explosive.

At the front of the room, the last mourners have passed through the receiving line. Katherine stares at the open coffin, the wax-pale face of her daughter, and then turns and creaks down the aisle toward her grandson. She gives Erin a pleased wave at the sight of Jacob talking.

How holding up, honey? she asks when she reaches him.

He tenses at her voice, the hinges murmuring in his shoulders.

Get something you? she continues. Want some chicken bite?

He doesn't respond. The edge of his lip twitches.

Katherine removes her glasses, cleans them with a fold of her dress. She looks more drained than annoyed at his rebuff. Turning to Erin, she says: Come outside for minute? Could use quick break.

Erin rises slowly from her chair, her eyes on Jacob's face. Good see again. You brave get through this.

His sneer softens, though he still says nothing. As her footsteps patter away, he lifts the frayed fabric back to his nostrils.

.           .           .

The next scene opens in the enormous hall, the air humming with the motor of the moving walkway. Erin and Katherine stand on its fluid surface, drifting past the damask walls, the bright-faced projections of the dead. They pass the hologram of a fair-haired boy in ice skates, the child bent forward, blurred with speed as he crosses an unseen rink. Beside him a table holds a stack of coupons: *30% Off YumTum Drumstick! (Max 1 Use Per Purchase.)*

I so happy Jacob talked you, Katherine says as they near the lobby. First time he talked today.

Really? Erin asks.

I drank too much last night. This how he punish.

The walkway ends and they stride through the lobby, past the rooster portrait, the rustle of elbow hinges. They find a spot outside on the crowded sidewalk, near a circle of nuns who scroll their phones in silence. Behind the nuns the massive building stretches back into a wooded area, where trails of smoke waft upward from the chimneys of the crematorium. The smoke climbs on ghostly legs up the ladders of branches.

Katherine digs in her purse and pulls out a zing-stick, covered in spades like a playing card. Two month, she says to Erin. Two month, then I quit again. You want?

No me. Thank.

Katherine inhales from the mouthpiece, breathes the smoke from her nose. They should have bar here. Booze, not just chicken.

Erin chuckles. Katherine goes on:

Maybe I sound naive, but honest? Before this week, thought I done bury family. That what told myself: I buried enough, no way more die.

God. Wish that how it work.

Katherine takes another drag. I lost my husband, while back. Then my son, Mike, three year ago. Now Irene. We had family once—happy family. Just me and Jacob left.

She returns the zing-stick to her purse, lifts out a worn hip flask. She watches the entrance as she ferries it to her lips. After a few swallows, she offers the flask to Erin.

This Erin does accept. She downs the liquor with a grateful grimace.

Katherine shakes her head. It bad idea I drink. Lot old student here tonight.

You teacher?

Was. High school.

Wow wow, Erin says in a thickened voice. She sips again, then returns the flask. What you teach?

Few subject. But history most.

Oh, that hard. History not my best.

Too depressing, right?

Well, yeah. War war war, kill kill kill. No want think it.

Mhmm, Katherine says. I heard that all time. I ever needed remind student: *Last generation had big nuke war, fifty million dead worldwide. Want that happen again? No? Then need know history.*

True. That true. Need know.

I hypocrite, of course. Since I retired, no want think it either. Today, I turned on news for sec: it all about HeatLeap. Lot refugee fleeing Global South—heat make their plastic leak toxin. I turned it off, put on *Candace Kooky Kitchen.*

The news . . . it all so blummo. I check every few week. No handle more.

The old woman smiles. We same, you me. No think, lot drink.

Erin laughs again, louder.

Katherine takes a final sip and drops the flask in her purse, where it clinks against a bed of buried items. She says:

Listen, it only right. Let me have you dinner soon. Least do, since you save my grandson life.

Ha! *Save* him? I just sit in car.

You hero, Erin, no deny. You help Jacob lot.

Well . . . thank. And sure. Dinner sound fun.

Shiny. Bet Jacob happy hear it.

Erin looks at the rear of the funeral home, where workers unload a shipment of coffins, rolling them down the ramp of a tractor trailer.

So Jacob, he live near here? He in college?

Katherine sighs. He live with me now, poor kid. And no, not college yet. In few month he turn twenty-one, so he study for National Aptitude Test. It very high stake this time. No want him get sent away.

That test no joke. I study night day, whole summer before. So much remember.

Katherine stares at the pine trees that edge the property, their peaks like arrowheads aimed at the smoggy moon. It just no fair him. He failed test in high school—some family stuff distract him. This time he studying great, and then . . . all this. I called NAT Board for extension, but they care? No, course not. "Rules are rules." But—but anyway. I best go back now. You visit more room tonight?

Might wait few minute first. Each room tough.

Katherine nods. Well, I tell Jacob you come dinner. Maybe he talk me then, she adds with a laugh.

The two women exchange their numbers, say their farewells.

Erin stands at the front windows, watching Katherine stride to the walkway with a tipsy gait, unsteady in her orthopedic sneakers. She rides down the hall to her daughter's hologram, where, after popping a breath mint, she opens the door carved with the windswept rooster. Through the doorway, Erin sees the rows of chairs, Jacob sitting along with his ragged square of fabric. She remains at the windows as the scene fades out, as if hoping the door will open again, offer her another glimpse of Jacob.

· · ·

In the final scene, set an hour later, Erin strides down an aisle of the parking lot, her visits at the funeral home completed. Behind her the smoke from the crematorium billows up through the branches; the cars sweep the night with their slow, spectral headlights.

When she reaches her sedan, she stops abruptly and stares down at her windshield. A small black envelope lies under the left wiper. She looks around at the other cars: no envelopes anywhere else. With casual movements, as though nothing is amiss, she slides it out and shuts herself in the car. She holds the envelope between her knees, unsealing it out of sight.

Inside is a slip of paper, a message printed on one side. In a minuscule font it reads: *Erin, you need log on Smartworld. Need go place with many mascot. URGENT.*

She does not read the message twice. Instead she folds the slip of paper in half and tears it into fragments. Then she rips up the fragments as well, until not a single word remains, only scattered letters on the jagged shreds. A few slivers fall to the floor mat; she bends down and quickly collects them.

Outside the car, a family of four comes strolling through the shadows. The wife pushes her husband's wheelchair; the son and daughter scroll their glowing phones, their young faces lit like apparitions. Before they reach her window, Erin lowers her head and stuffs the shreds of paper in her mouth. She swallows them down like pinches of salt.

# THE SMARTWORLD

The episode opens on Erin in an apartment building lobby. She stands in front of the elevator doors, her earbuds in her ears, listening to the cheerful whistles of walruses.

On the ceiling burns a bare striplight, casting a harsh glare on the rows of mailbox units. An ancient TV, bolted to the wall, plays the evening news: a picture of a wanted terrorist, a smiling college freshman in a Bride Barn uniform, her head circled in a highlight among a group of her blurred-out coworkers. She is accused of the bombing yesterday at a Gordon Wound Glue factory, thirty-seven employees dead, a hundred and two injured.

If any info, please call Terrorist Hotline, says the female anchor, her forehead pixelated from a crack in the display. 999-SAV-LIFE appears on the screen.

Erin stares at the hotline number, her plastic eyes alert in their sockets, like marbles set at the very edge of a table. The whistles resound from inside her skull, the tuneful warbles synched to a skittery beat.

The elevator chimes; the doors slide open. Erin steps inside and presses 9 on the panel. As the walls thrum around her, she opens PrayZone on her phone, then whispers a prayer from the Social Anxiety section:

*Oh Great Unknown, I want make good impression. It tough get know new people, not sure what best say do. May I remember they perfect, too, just like me. May we keep our mega chill, find lot peace together. May peace, loving peace, be our whole thing.*

When she taps *Prayer Complete,* a burst of seraphic confetti erupts on the screen. *Congrat on one-year prayer-streak!* the app proclaims. *Use code for free coffee+nugget at CODA Café!* An angel comes swooping down to her avatar on the hillside, carrying a silver wardrobe bag beneath its outspread wings. The angel zips the bag open, revealing a wide selection of tunic upgrades.

.        .        .

In the next scene, Erin sits at a kitchen table with Jacob and Katherine, each with a plate of boiled chicken before them. The apartment around them is cluttered, a space of cozy disorder, the main room stuffed with bookcases and an old rattan sofa, the table tucked in a corner by the galley kitchen. Books with unusual bookmarks—a twist tie, a bent paperclip—stand in stacks beside the sofa, many with raised dots along their spines. A chrome plaque on a bureau reads: YEAR BEST TEACHER.

The camera pans over to Katherine, gesturing with her wine-glass as she talks, the hinge squeaking between the segments of her arm. In a frustrated voice she says:

And I think church might do more. Not too "Christlike," in my opinion, all this murder. But I guess they scared like everyone. If Church condemned all terrorist—made big statement, like they should—then boom, they next attack. But no mean offend, Erin: I saw you blessed your food. You go church?

Yes. But it Church of Divine Acceptance.

Oh, CODA. I knew some student went there. You like?

Much. Lot better than reg church.

I heard no God at CODA, Katherine says, reaching for a bottle of Malbec on the table. She is dressed more casually tonight, in slacks and a wrinkled cardigan, her thick gray hair bunched back in a messy bun. She finds the bottle empty, then stands and creaks across the room to a wine rack among the clutter.

You can believe God if want, Erin replies. But it not require.

So it more like "self-help"? Not really religion?

Kinda both. Faith is technology, that their slogan.

Technology? Katherine asks, unscrewing the cap on another Malbec.

Erin nods. To help lead happy life.

Ah. Interesting.

Jacob, silent, pushes the tines of his fork into a chicken slice, the points piercing moistly through the limpid outer flesh. The camera frames him in a close-up as he lifts the fork to his mouth, as he scrapes off the slice between his teeth, a sound like a snail being pulled from its damp shell. He lowers his head as he chews, his long hair mingling with the drawstrings of his hoodie.

The pocket of Katherine's cardigan starts to buzz. She takes out her phone, looks amusedly at the screen.

Jacob smirks. It Dave?

My *boyfriend,* quote unquote, Katherine says to Erin. When old, get booty call six fifteen p.m.

Please, Jacob says. I eating.

She chuckles, setting the wine bottle on the table. Excuse moment.

Katherine strides to the balcony door, pulling open the glass panel as she answers the call. *What want old fool?* she teases as she seals the door behind her, then gives a muffled holler of laughter at his reply. Jacob laughs as well, his hand rising to cover his mouth.

He and Erin grow quiet at the table. In the silence he lifts his napkin and thoroughly wipes his plastic lips, as he has at several points throughout the meal. Erin sips from her glass, watching him over the rim.

*It's a bad idea, me being here tonight,* says her narration. *Getting this crush, indulging these feelings . . . it'll only end in rejection. When Jacob finds out about my past—that I changed my last name in high school, that my sister is Fiona Reynolds—he'll be done with me in a second. And that's assuming he likes me in the first place. I'm making bad choices again, like I did with Patrick.*

Jacob spreads his napkin back on his lap, taking care to drape it evenly over his thighs. He says:

So, how Owen doing? He back home now?

Oh, nice you ask. He just get out hospital—thank God. They save his leg, so that major. But he get depressed sometime.

Course. It sound like hell.

Thing he hate most, all the pain pill. In fog most time. He prob on disability few year.

How 'bout you? Jacob asks. You go back work?

Not for couple month. Store bad damage.

Must lot free time then.

It weird weird, Erin says. Like summer break or something. It nice at first, but then just bored. Think I hate Tablet Town, now want go back.

Jacob smiles. You me dif that way. I ever stay home could.

She takes a longer sip of wine. Your grandma say your NAT soon. How study go?

Same old same old. But yeah, not that long now. It pretty scary, if honest.

Def. Morning of test, I get all stomach sick. Barely make appointment.

He runs a worried hand through his hair. So many date, fact, statistic . . . it nightmare. Feel like my head go boom.

Me? I put sticky note all over bedroom. Few hundred.

I make lot voice memo, Jacob says. Listen while fall asleep.

That smart.

He shrugs. It just piss me off, you know? If I pass, my life go one way. If I fail again, another. Such bullshit, one test decide whole future.

I sure you pass this time. You be surprised—few month after? Like NAT never happen.

That the dream. Pass this blummo test, then forget it ever exist. I very political, Jacob adds with a laugh.

He forks another slice, but doesn't lift it to his mouth. Wish I could just . . . calm down, you know? Focus on test. Those terrorist, those fucker, they *such*— Never mind. Sorry.

No, it make sense. I no imagine study right now. That attack—I still lot flashback.

Shit. Sorry hear.

It is what is, Erin says. She sips her glass again.

Jacob raises the slice and chews, using the time to gather himself. Finally he says:

Flashback, I have all day. Not every minute, but . . . much. I have good therapist, some meds. But it only help little.

Yeah. Just need live through it. No easy way.

Last birthday, my mom get me Smartbody. Not cheap—she take out loan. But damn, I so glad have it now. It big big help relax.

Oh, she says. Amaze. What model you have?

SilkStream. She buy refurbished.

That good one. So glad it not DreamSpree—there lot on used market. Cost less, but super glitchy.

Jacob grins. Right, you work Tablet Town. You play lot demo at work?

I *run* them. I have Body at home, too.

Really? he says. That so qunky. We need meet up in Smartworld.

Def. Maybe a MoonPark?

Sure, yeah, hear they shiny. What it like? You float whole time?

Erin chuckles. No, no. Can set gravity however want.

The figurines start to discuss their favorite Smartworld Domains: DazzlePort, CityCity, WowQuest. They talk in eager voices, the shyness gone from their glossy faces. She laughs as he describes his first time flying through CityCity, how some rich woman had lassoed him from the bedroom of her cloud palace, where, after she yanked him through the window, he found three users in a state of complete undress.

Oh God, Erin says, giggling. You need be careful in CityCity.

I know! I tell them no thank—then jump out window.

The figurines talk further, Erin pouring herself a glass from the new wine bottle. There are only occasional flickers of anxiety in her eyes, as if at a danger she refuses to acknowledge, a caution she refuses to observe. She slips out her phone, opens her photo app, and zooms in on Jacob, so that, in the rectangle of the screen, he seems to be mere inches away as he speaks to her. She thumbs the soundless shutter button once, twice, again.

.        .        .

In the final scene, set back in the lobby, the elevator bell gives an echoey chime. The doors slide open and Erin steps out onto the tile, her legs a bit unsteady from all the drinking. The television now plays a reality show, *Coast Kings,* about a group of male survivalists who've purchased an abandoned town on the ocean-flooded coast. On the screen two heavily bearded men stand in a ruined country club, holding out *voilà!* arms toward a table of taxidermied crocodiles. The reptiles, bent at unnatural angles, sit in chairs around a frilly tea service. Each crocodile webs a teacup, tilted at its teeth as if to sip.

The camera follows Erin as she totters out to the parking lot. Her articulated body looks at odds with itself, her torso rigid while her legs wobble below her. Her shadow sways between the streetlights; her feet stumble over lumps in the rucked pavement.

After she climbs into her sedan, she taps her phone and opens her DriveSafe! app. On the screen appears Billy DriveBest, a stoic boy in suspenders, standing with his arms crossed beside a car wrapped in chains. She puts the phone to her lips, exhales into a hole in the casing.

Billy wags a stern finger. *You need to stay—no drive this way!* he sings like a church cantor.

Malbec, Erin mutters. She reclines her seat and looks up through the windshield, gazing at the old concrete building with its jutting AC units, at the barred windows of Jacob's ninth-floor apartment. The sounds of traffic murmur beyond the building, a distant gossip of horns and rumbling engines.

The camera films her from the passenger seat, showing her face in profile as she stares at the balcony doors, the vertical blinds giving a partial glimpse of the living room. After a long moment, she turns her head and looks into the camera. She narrates out loud:

So Jacob owns a Smartbody . . . I couldn't be more surprised. After dinner he showed me his bedroom: the floor lined with padding, a harness on a support beam, his Body parts stored on a shelf—a VR setup more pricey than a year at a top college. Whatever his issues with his mother, she spared no expense on his Smartworld life.

On his nightstand was a ViewPoint Smarthead, a helmet designed for blind users. These Heads aren't effective for everyone—I've had customers return them at work—but for Jacob it was a match, letting him see the simulations with a flawed but functional sight. This helmet has no internal screen; instead, its SeeBreeze transmitter sends frequencies to the polymers in his eyes. I can't help but wonder: What will he think when he sees me in Smartworld? What might that change?

In any case, we planned to meet in MoonPark this Saturday night. I can't believe I'm doing this, going back into the World, facing the memories I tried to leave behind there. Memories of Patrick most of all.

He was the reason I bought a Smartbody in the first place. In high school, I'd stood helpless while I watched him die in front of me, his life cut short one summer afternoon, gone before we had a chance at a future. It was a few months after his death, as I scrolled aimlessly online, that I noticed an ad for a Smartworld program in my feed. Its name was EZ Pal, and its slogan read: *Never Say Goodbye*. Though I didn't own a Smartbody—couldn't conceive of affording one—I clicked on the ad at once. I watched the demo videos for hours, hunched at the desk in my bedroom, dreaming of the perfect life I could lead in this program. When I finished, I knew I'd buy a Body one day, no matter the price. It was the closest I could ever get to Patrick again.

I imagined this wouldn't be soon, perhaps in my late twenties, when I had a career and some savings. But I had no idea in high

school what the next years would hold for me, what a different life
I'd be leading after I graduated. At nineteen, I found myself alone in
the house, my sister vanished, my father buried, my name on my first
savings account, the sole recipient of my father's will. I'd promised
him to save the money, to use it for my education, and I'd meant those
words when I'd said them to him at the hospice. But after he passed,
after I'd lived inside a house filled with his absence—hearing his
voice in the silence, sitting across from his empty chair—I felt far too
lonely to restrain myself: I went online and ordered a high-end Body
and harness. Now that I'd lost my closest relatives, now that I had no
interest in college, now that the terror groups had ramped up their
attacks across the country, no public place safe from their assaults, it
seemed wisest to flee the real world with my Patrick.

I'll never forget my first EZ Pal session. Unlike many users, I
wanted no mansion or castle, no fantasy realm in the sky, and so I
emerged on a replica of my own driveway, looking out on the snug
little street where I'd lived my entire life. There were differences,
of course: no smog, no barred windows, no risk of shootings or
bombings. I could control everything here, even the temperature of
the rain. I strode up the path and into my house, marveling at the
exactness of the replica—the poppies on the wallpaper, the tulips in
the dining room, the crashing wave in the lighthouse painting—until I
stopped at the closed door of my bedroom.

I held the knob for over a minute. Part of me sensed this was a
mistake, perhaps a huge one. Finally I inched the door open.

Patrick sat on the edge of the bed, his sneakers just above the
carpet, as if I'd stepped inside the most vivid of my daydreams.
The designers had captured every detail: his hair fell messy to his
shoulders, his face was thin and birdish, his left ankle nicked where I'd
specified. He wore the T-shirt in which I'd first seen him, a counselor
shirt from Camp Crazy Canoe. As I stepped inside he smiled at me,

his eyes gentle and inquisitive, which I'd stressed in the design forms. But by then I'd forgotten the program: I was with Patrick, my beautiful Patrick, my love at last before me in living polymer. At great cost I'd brought him back to life, even aged him two years to make up for lost time. I was so overwhelmed I knelt before him and wrapped my arms around his legs.

"Little hungry," he said above me in an upbeat voice.

I rose on my knees, gazed into his eyes. A smogless sun blazed through the window beside us.

"Why cry?" he asked in a quieter voice. "You sad?"

"We go fridge," I said, wiping my eyes. "Maybe some chicken there."

And so began my years with this virtual Patrick. To myself I seemed happy, a convincing version of happy. Most nights after work I'd drive straight home and boil my love his dinner, then spoon him on the couch while we binged our favorite shows. Other nights we swung on vines in *Jungle Jam,* or screamed on rides at FaceMelt Mountain, or even just played some badminton out on our lawn. He excelled at all games, and seemed to truly enjoy them, pumping a fist when he won, pouting ironically when he lost. Though he wasn't truly sentient—not aware of his own existence—his AI helped me forget this, asking me questions about my coworkers, remembering the places to rub my back, telling me stories from his fake photography job. On date nights I'd take us to *History Tryst,* then lean against my Patrick as we were rowed through Renaissance Venice, fanned with palms in ancient Rome, flown over Versailles in an early hot-air balloon. Some date nights we stayed at home, sat hand in hand at our pine tree, pointed up at shooting stars as they coursed through the virtual sky.

In bed I lay beside him, stared into his caring eyes. I often talked to him for hours there, about anything under the sun: my past, my future, my anger at my sister, my daily grief for Dad. Patrick nodded and asked me questions, listened with a face of warm compassion. Whenever I wept, he cupped my cheeks and kissed away my tears.

Deep down, of course, I knew he wasn't real. Deep down I felt only loneliness, the same loneliness that had led me to this virtual home. But night after night I ignored this feeling, pushed it off into the shadows around our bed. When I'd talked myself to silence, I cuddled close and slipped my arms around his shoulders. Then, at my voice command, Patrick took complete control, undressed me and made love to me with a tender, focused roughness, my authority gone as I moaned his name inside my padded Smartroom, where, alone, I lay in midair among the cords that held me, his ardent thrusts nothing more than the pulse of my Lady Insert. When he climaxed there was no cleanup. I fell asleep in his arms.

The next day at work, on bathroom breaks, I'd splash water on my face until I looked less giddy and elated. I worked with Owen at Tablet Town now—I'd needed a job for my data fees—and I intended to keep my new life with Patrick a secret. Sometimes I longed to tell Owen everything, just like I'd longed to tell Dad in high school, when I'd kept the real Patrick a secret from my father, my sister, my friends. But Owen might urge me to leave the program, might question if this was happiness or just a way to evade my grief—a question I never allowed myself to ask. So I kept my secrets safe, the only happiness I could trust.

After almost two years together, I took the next step with Patrick: I signed up for some overtime shifts and bought us a Pregnancy Upgrade. I wanted to have a daughter with him, to see us both in our child, to watch her grow older in the rooms of our perfect home. I opted for a nine-month pregnancy, realistic except for any pain or discomfort.

The first months were some of the best I've ever known. My breasts swelled, my stomach grew, my face glowed with a fresh maternal light. At night I'd stand in our bathroom and admire myself in the mirror, seeing a joy in my eyes that was not a trick of the program, a joy that bore no trace of all my losses. I'd gone through so much since high school—but now, as I smiled back at my nude, expectant reflection, my loneliness seemed to have faded. This was a new kind of happiness, visceral, embodied, extending into the future, remaking the past.

Then, seven months into the pregnancy, the loneliness returned.

Hard as I tried, I could no longer push the feeling into the shadows, as if it had gathered strength throughout those blissful months. It plagued me wherever I went, even swimming in the sea with Patrick, even gripping his strong shoulders as we made love. As I watched my stomach blossom, as I felt the fetus shift, as I grew teary-eyed at the baby ads that popped up in my browser, I could see the self-deception behind my bliss. My emotions were real, that much was true, but the rest was forged, synthetic. I had wanted too much from my fantasy, had tried to shut out the real world entirely, and now, it seemed, my mind was rebelling, reminding me that I wasn't a mother, that this was all an expensive illusion.

I began to be cold toward Patrick, to sit apart from him on the sofa, to skip our date nights. I'd exit the program abruptly and lie on the bed of my actual bedroom, angry, confused, and missing the weight of my daughter against my torso. As I boiled his dinner one night, a sudden rage swept through me: I grasped a plate and hurled it against the wall, the porcelain shards strewing around my feet. I rushed from the kitchen and locked myself in the bathroom, scared I might slap him or punch him if he came near me. Patrick knocked softly on the door, whispered, "You do okay, my love?" I didn't reply.

The upgrade had also increased his tenderness settings. Hoping they'd ease my loneliness, I didn't lower them. He'd shake his head in wonder as he placed a hand on my belly, nuzzle my neck like a puppy until I winced and pushed him away. Sometimes, after making love, he'd whisper into my ear, "What want name baby?" The name I liked was Patricia, but I felt too unnerved to tell him. He might start embroidering the name on a blanket, a new hobby the upgrade had given him.

One night, while we watched a show in bed, he rested his hand for the thousandth time on my stomach. "Just kick," he said, "you feel?"

"Course," I replied irritably. This was a conspiracy between the program and Patrick: every time he touched my stomach, the baby stirred. At first I'd loved this feature, this vital connection between father and daughter. Now it felt manipulative, almost mocking.

"Baby here so soon," he said, his eyes damp with tears, as they often were these days. "This dream come true."

I started to lose my temper, even worse than that night in the kitchen. Before I could restrain myself, I gripped his hand on my stomach so hard he gasped.

"I do wrong?" he asked in a penitent voice.

*"Pause show,"* I snapped at the television. I pulled off the blanket, strode quickly from the room.

I stood in the kitchen, struggling to catch my breath. I kept thinking: Is this really the life I've chosen? A fake husband in a fake house, a fake child in a fake womb—a daughter who, for all of my love, would never truly know me, never even know herself? At the same time, it was clear I'd never leave EZ Pal, not while this lifelike Patrick haunted my virtual home. I loved him too much, had loved him too long, to abandon the ghost of his presence. My daughter kicked again, a persuasive shifting of her unreal body. And that's when I lifted my head, when I saw the block of kitchen knives, their handles deep in shadow below the cabinets.

I made no conscious decision about what happened next. More than anything, I watched myself. I watched my hand rise into view, my fingers grip a handle, the carving knife slide out from the block.

I watched myself turn and stride back to the bedroom, the length of the blade swinging beside my knee. "Feel better?" Patrick asked me as I stepped inside the room, as I watched my shadow darken in the lamplight. I nodded. In a numb, spare voice, I ordered him to lie flat on the bed. As always, he obeyed. My free hand lifted a pillow, set it down over his face. Then, for some reason—maybe the fabric tickled his nose—Patrick let out a gleeful laugh. At this, my anger took over completely.

I clenched the pillow around his face, pinning him to the bed. I said, *"No move, stay still,"* when he stirred with confusion. Even in this state I couldn't bring myself to stab him, so I angled the blade across his neck, pressed it down hard against his plastic. I pressed harder, not relenting, when he screamed into the pillow, when his surface buckled and cracked apart in a thin, ragged line, when his beloved body spasmed and ceased to stir. I pressed the knife down deeper, widening the wound, causing stray reticulations all along his lovely neck, until I realized that he was dead, that it was over. For a minute I just stood there, staring down at the fissure, the dark glimpse inside his hollow body. Then I dropped the knife to the floor and lifted the pillow.

It was the second time I'd seen Patrick dead. He stared up at me with a face more shocked than frightened, his lips contorted open in a silent scream. His panicked eyes, his lifeless hands, the garish wound in his throat—the program had made this real for me, too: a murder.

I should have left that grisly program then, left and never returned. Instead I crawled back into bed with him, pulled the blankets around us. I gathered his broken body in my arms.

The next morning I called in sick to work and paid for the program to bury him, a simple granite stone beside our pine tree. I sat there at his graveside, my knife hand trembling on the grass. I knew that, in reality, I hadn't killed my love: what I remembered as a murder were just movements of my Body, a pantomime of violence in my Smartroom. But I could still hear his muffled scream, still feel the blade cracking through his plastic. I still saw his face as I raised the pillow—the death that I'd created.

As I sat before his grave, I tapped open my Pregnancy Menu. I needed to fill out several forms before I reached the screen that asked: *Sure Cancel Pregnant?* I tapped *Yes*. I looked down and watched my stomach sink, my broadened waist recede, all without the least physical sensation. Once this virtual abortion ended—it took less than fifteen seconds—I lay down in the grass beside his headstone. I traced my finger along the carving of his name.

Later that day, I'd call Owen and tell him everything about Patrick. I'd start the story back in high school, when I met the real Patrick, when I lost him the first time; I'd break into tears as I finished the story, when I pressed the knife to his simulated throat. But for the moment I was far too tired for confessions. I curled up on the lawn, tucked my knees against my chest, and went to sleep beside my twice-dead love.


Erin falls silent in her sedan. She looks away from the camera, staring out at the dim pavement of the parking lot. Scraggly grass struggles from the cracks in the sidewalk; the streetlamps crane like long-necked birds above their puddles of light. Then she raises her phone and exhales again in its breathalyzer.

*Not yet!* sings Billy DriveBest, tapping his oversized watch. *To travel safe, you need to wait!*

Erin leans her head against the window. She says: Carla, play *Patrick Video #11*.

Playing *Patrick Video #11*, the phone replies.

The screen switches to a video of a garden path, packed with figurines in Hawaiian shirts and sandals. Hundreds of butterflies perch on the foliage, or flicker about in a fluttering flight, their beating wings a blur of speckled color. In the foreground stands

Patrick, a little boy of eight or nine, dressed in shorts and a Super Rooster T-shirt. He gazes down at a silvery butterfly, which suns on a low hedge directly before him. He reaches a hesitant hand toward the hedge, where, miraculously, the butterfly stays quiescent for several seconds, allowing the boy to stroke its lambent wing. Then the butterfly draws its wings together and flitters from the frame.

Erin, her finger aglow from the screen, rewinds the clip and watches it once more. This time she pauses the clip near the end, when his fingertip first settles on the wing, when his expression changes from caution to fascination. Her glassy eyes repeat the image in miniature.

# A TRIP TO THE MOONPARK

The episode opens in Erin's bedroom that Saturday night. The camera follows her as she enters the room and reaches below her bed, grasping the domed top of her Smarthead. She carries the helmet into the hallway, past the row of missing pictures, to a closed door at the opposite end of the hall. She hesitates a moment, the camera zooming in on her anxious face. Then she turns the knob and says: Smartroom light on.

The room was once her sister's bedroom, but the space is now remade: the floors and walls concealed in padding, a network of runners spread across the ceiling. A harness hangs down from the central runner, suspended at chest height with thick elastic cords.

Erin removes her robe and slippers, steps barefoot to her Smartbody. It sits in pieces on the padded floor, lined up along one wall: the blocky Hands and Feet, the pipelike Legs and Arms, the turtleneck of the Torso. She pulls them onto her plastic figure with fluid, practiced motions, each part custom-fitted to her, snug but never tight. She pulls on her Smarthead last, hiding her nervous face with the bare slope of rubber. In the Body the figurine looks like a different order of being, an eyeless android with a thin, immobile mouth.

Smartbody on, she says after strapping into the harness. Open MoonPark 6.

The scene in her Smartroom vanishes. Erin, now dressed in a white sundress, stands on a glowing footpath, a trail of pearl that threads its way across an immense moonscape. The plain of stone stretches for miles, rolling out to the far horizon, where a long-tailed comet snakes its way across the starred enormity of space. She follows the path up a slight incline, her low heels clicking against the radiant pearl.

The MoonPark rises into sight as she crests the slope, a pastoral landscape set on this stony vista. Here songbirds wing from tree to tree above the forest trails, flying over the running paths, the scenic lookouts, the rustic bridges, all teeming with figurines in their twenties who enjoy the park in summer clothes, many shirtless in the swimming pool beside the volleyball courts. Others toss Frisbees across the common with a jerky chop of their forearm, or dance around a blazing bonfire, or flirt beneath the pines on marble benches. They are slim, attractive, flawlessly groomed, their plastic of various shades, their clothing of countless cuts, none injured or unhealthy-looking, no chipped surfaces or prosthetic limbs in sight. An icy light illuminates the entire improbable scene.

At the entrance to the park stands a soaring glass archway, gleaming four stories against the star-strung sky. A sign in cursive floats above the arch: WELCOME TO MOONPARK 6! SPONSORED BY FAT CAT INVESTMENT APP!

Erin glances uneasily at the park, as if looking for signs of danger: the sparkling lake where Jet Skis slice a path through the gelid sunlight; the unicorns who graze in pairs among the many gazebos; the go-karts buzzing around the echoing speedway. There are product mascots everywhere—Glossy Gals and Study Buddies, Flippin' Chickens, Fred the Meds—the cheerful bots posing in tableaus throughout the park. Her gaze lingers longest on these animate advertisements.

Under the archway, waving a plump forepaw, the mascot of Fat Cat Investment App greets the new arrivals. The portly Persian wears a tailcoat tuxedo, a glistening pocket watch chain, his head swiveling to give each guest a smile of fiscal sageness. *Meow, meow! Invest now!* he exclaims as Erin passes him. She shoots him an edgy look and quickens her stride.

Erin follows a bending fork in the path, heading down a shaded lane of benches. Here the figurines sit in pairs—men with men, women with women, various hetero pairings—some chatting with ease, others struggling for conversation. A woman fidgets her bracelet as her date explains his daily vitamin regimen; two young men toe the pebbles as they volley awkward questions about their families. Now and then, causing no surprise, a figurine grips the top of their head and gives an upward tug. They disappear at once, gone from their bench in an instant, as if they never wooed on the wooded moon.

Midway down the lane, Erin sits at a bench and smooths the lap of her dress. She taps the air to open her user menu, a glassy panel that hovers before her face. Carla, play *Nuclear Family,* she says, and then watches a scene while she waits for Jacob.

In "Uh-O," Max and O are now fourteen, high school freshmen. One winter night, on a sleepover, they sneak some beers to the waffle's basement, where, new to drinking, they find themselves drunk after their second bottles. Soon they are talking in slurred voices, confessing their longtime crushes on each other;

the scene fades out on their first clumsy but passionate kiss. The next morning, however, when Max wakes up hungover—his shirt on the floor, O's rubber arm draped across his chest—his eyes snap open with a look of total panic.

Hearing footsteps, Erin raises a finger and drags the screen from her eyeline. She sees Jacob rounding the corner with a brisk gait, his persona a perfect replica of the plastic man. But here he strides without a cane, his hair swept back from his face, his eyes uncovered as he gazes down the path. He looks both eager and anxious, like so many in the lane of benches. Erin waves to him and he gives her a skittish smile.

Sorry late, he says as he approaches. My stupid NAT class went long.

Oh, no notice even. Just get here, too.

Jacob lowers himself to the bench, his virtual hinges bending. Even in the Smartworld he wears a hoodie, his usual cuffed jeans and canvas sneakers.

This place shiny, he says. Great recommend.

Thank. MoonPark 1 or 2 better. But much crowded.

Lot Smartworld like that. Qunky place, but way way people. You ever go *Hurtling Void?*

No, Erin says. What that?

This friend from CityCity, he take me. Like thousand people there, all float in empty space. Then big wind come from nowhere, start throw us all around. Idea is meet new people. Crash into them, say hi.

Oh God. Not for me.

This one girl hurtle into me. Try stuff her number in my shirt.

What you do? Erin asks.

I panic. Pull off my Smarthead.

Good move.

Jacob laughs. Well. Sound like we both antisocial.

You no idea, she says with a smile.

Across from them, in a huge advertisement, dozens of Fat Cats bustle about an outdoor Stock Exchange. They jot down quotes from the ticker display, purring with pecuniary delight. Slogans scroll across the ticker: THE MARKET NEVER PAW-SES! INCREASE YOUR CAT-PITAL GAINS! When a figurine passes near them, the Fat Cats turn as one and exclaim: *Meow, meow! Invest now!*

Erin's smile fades as she watches them; the worry returns to her eyes.

Want stride little? she asks Jacob.

The camera follows them as they stroll along the benches, their stiff hands almost scraping in the narrow lane. Beyond the final benches spreads an open plain of moonscape, and there the lucent orb of Earth hangs small on the horizon, suspended against the starlight with its continents and oceans, its overlays of clouds, a sliver of sun peeking above its rim.

I keep mean ask you, Jacob says. Where you live in town? Apartment like me?

No, in house. House I grow up in.

Oh. Not sure why, but no think you live with parent.

I don't, Erin says. Live alone.

Jacob slows his pace on the path, absorbing the meaning of these words. It lonely there?

Sure, yeah. All time. But lonely get normal.

Right. It weird weird what get normal.

The benches fade behind them as they stride into the park's forest area. Birdsong replaces the chatter of couples; slants of sunlight angle through branches; two doves sit cooing on the roof of an ancient grotto, rubbing their ivory necks together like

wind chimes. Erin and Jacob sit on the bench in the grotto, art-
fully cracked as if by the passage of time.

So what it like, live with Katherine? she asks. She seem like
pretty qunky grandma.

He gives an uneasy shrug. Light dapples his face from cracks
in the domed ceiling. It fine, he says in a lowered voice. Not
great.

You worry she listen at door?

She prob not. But it small apartment. No want hurt her
feeling.

His voice stays lowered as he describes his life with Katherine. He's grateful to her, of course, for taking him in when his
mother passed, for giving him time to study, not rushing him
into a full-time job with the date of his NAT so near. If he has
complaints about her, then she could "def" complain about him:
he's broke, spends all his time in his Body, barely covers his data
fees with some online admin work. But that doesn't make her an
easy roommate—his grandma drunk most nights after dinner,
trying to drag him into conversations, so that, after eight p.m., he
waits in his room and listens for her bedroom door to shut, her
faint snores. Before then she stumbles around the kitchen, or
sits muttering on the sofa, or, if the mood strikes her, invites over
her off-and-on boyfriend, Dave, a retired teacher and a decent
guy, but a big drinker as well. Their visits can end in arguments,
Dave grabbing his coat while Katherine tells him to get his "old
ass" out.

Jacob understands why she drinks, the deaths and losses that
haunt her. Whenever he feels resentful, he tries to remember
what his mom once told him: that, for most of her life, Katherine was a very different person, an upbeat wife and mother, a
devoted teacher who lived for her students, never drinking much

except on special occasions. That only changed later in life, when her husband, Jacob's grandfather, died in an airplane hijacking. Then other losses followed.

He real nice guy, my grandpa, Jacob says. Just know him when kid, though.

My father kinda like Katherine. Not much drink. But he haunted.

Hope we no get like that.

Erin chuckles. Think I am already.

Jacob considers this. Yeah, me too.

She asks him about his future, what he'll do when he passes the NAT. *If* I pass, he says, and then tells her his next goal is college, that he'd love to study psychology, become a therapist for young people, because a few gifted therapists have really helped him over the years, and he'd like to do some good in the world before a terrorist kills him—though he doesn't mean to sound negative, and maybe he's talking too much?

Not at all, Erin says. Go on.

Could be programmer or something. Def make way way money. But, dunno, just love think people. Maybe dork, but that my fav.

Could see you as therapist. You good listener.

Ha! Nice you say, after talk myself half hour. And what about you? You go back Tablet Town? Think it safe?

Erin shrugs. Prob safer now, after attack. Most group like attack new place. Spread more fear.

Shit. That true.

This fun world we live in, huh?

Jacob laughs. Just the best.

An hour later they leave the grotto and continue down the path, chatting as the forest thins around them. They stroll past a row of tennis courts, past a meadow where women on pogo sticks bounce hundreds of feet in the sky, showing off their spins against the panoplies of space. They pass an archway with a blazing sign, CLUB MOONFIRE, where, in a crater with laser lights, hundreds of figurines with glow sticks dance around a roaring pyre, shaking their rigid posteriors to a Rhythm & Noise electro song: heavy drum and bass with rhythmic meows. Some flail their limbs in jerky patterns, some shimmy their torsos from side to side, their dances constrained with bodies only flexible at the hinges, limiting them to lurching moves among the lasers.

Erin and Jacob talk about music as they pass the crater: their love of mellower Rhythm & Noise, their deepening interest in "Splice"—the most popular genre of the last generation—where snippets of music from all eras are stitched together over a catchy beat. A troupe of Nightclub Glossy Gals dance in the sky overhead, their sequined dresses swishing below the slogan DARE TO DAZZLE!

Soon they are sharing funny stories from their childhoods. Jacob tells her about sneaking out in a snowstorm when he was six, lying still on the lawn for an hour while he pretended to be snow.

No get bored? Erin asks.

Sure, but try not think it. Snow not bored. Just snow.

That hilar.

Mom find me at last, Jacob says. She super scared. I no talk, no move.

What happen?

He shakes his head. I melt? No remember.

Beside the path, two girls in clown makeup sit on floating carpets, quizzing each other with NAT study questions. One asks: How much Ground-Up-Bone we burn nineteenth century? Her partner replies: God, another GUB question? This way way depress.

As she rounds the corner, something catches Erin's eye from a Fat Cat ad in the distance. One of the Cats has left his commercial, no longer doing a backstroke through a pool of platinum coins, but rushing on all fours down the path in Erin's direction, as fast as he can in his comically tight tuxedo. His face still wears its sage expression, but his hurrying body betrays this calm, as if some other being has taken possession of the mascot.

So, that most of MoonPark, Erin says abruptly. Want go somewhere else?

Jacob notices the mascot as well. Damn, that Cat bonker. What wrong you think? Bad code?

All these ad . . . so annoying. Mind if we leave?

He hears the anxiety in her voice. Def, yeah. No prob.

You ever play, uh, *Jungle Jam?* she asks.

Only every day. Well, not every day. But lot. *Love* that game.

Perfect. I just get—get some water first. Then meet you there, okay?

Jacob taps at his menu. See soon. We show those alien who boss.

He disappears from the path, a few seconds before the Fat Cat bumbles beside her. Erin stares at the fiscal feline, his white bow tie askew from his run, his pocket watch trailing behind him on its chain. He pulls out his notepad with a hasty paw, tilting the page to show Erin what he writes. With his fountain pen he scribbles:

*Erin—message for you. Need listen me. There bad bad attack soon.*

I not doing this again, she says in a fast whisper. You hear me? If my sister send you, tell her I no want this. Stop follow me. Just stop.

The Fat Cat has continued writing. *This attack much dif than other. It—*

Erin glances away from the notepad. Carla, set Gravity to zero.

This sends her soaring at once from the surface of the moon. In seconds she rises higher than the tall glass archways, the mini-golf course shrinking below her, the dancing Glossy Gals above the bonfire. The Fat Cat is helpless to follow her flight, his whiskery face gazing up at her, his notepad dangling limply from his paw.

Erin swivels her body as she ascends, facing herself toward the depths of space, swimming into the void with a swift breast-stroke. When the moon is far below her, the park a grassy pinpoint, she taps her menu and stops her rapid climb. Floating in the night, she stares out at the sea of virtual stars.

On the soundtrack plays an acoustic guitar, a kick drum thudding below its picking pattern. A spotlight pierces through the dark and illumines Erin where she hovers, its beam like the dust tail of a comet. She sings into the void:

> *The day I dropped a fist of dirt*
> *Inside my father's grave,*
> *I envied him below the earth*
> *Where all his pain could fade.*
>
> *That day I bought a VR suit*
> *To lose myself in dreams,*
> *To flee the sorrows of my youth*
> *Behind a Smarthead screen.*
>
> *I thought no one could track me there*
> *But someone must have been aware:*
> *Just when I'd put my past behind me,*
> *The mascots showed up to remind me.*

In the vast sky, the thousands of stars glide from their fixed positions. They swirl out and re-form themselves into images of a family: three figurines composed of starlight laughing on a picnic blanket, then riding on a starry carousel, then strolling down a shoreline made of stars. From far below, the group of Glossy Gals flies up from the bonfire, each with a pearl microphone held to her mouth. They hover behind Erin, their sequins shimmering as they sing along with the chorus:

> *Why must all*
> *The light I touch*
> *Crumble into stardust?*

> *Why must all*
> *The love I trust*
> *Burn up like stars and die?*

> *With my fake last name*
> *I dream in vain*
> *That a man like Jacob will remain*
> *When all this stardust stains*
> *The hollow sky.*

As the song ends, the starry family shatters into shards of light; the thousands of stars slide back to their positions. The Glossy Gals blow the camera a kiss and float down to the fire. Then, with a soft chime, a message appears on Erin's menu.

*Hey, you coming?* Jacob asks. *These UFO no blow themself up!*

Erin starts to tap a response—*Sorry, feel blummo all sudden. Maybe* Jungle Jam *on dif night?*—but then deletes this with a swipe of her finger. Instead she messages: *Be right there! Excited!*

Before she leaves the sky, Erin opens the Security panel of her menu. Darren the Hacker Defeater appears on her screen, a knight in full medieval armor, his visor down, his sword raised in front of Firewall Fortress. She scrolls to *Max Protection Plan* and pays for the extra encryption.

# 7

# THE CHURCH OF
# DIVINE ACCEPTANCE

The episode opens on a wide shot of a holographic Moses, his bearded face bright with a welcoming smile.

The prophet stands inside the atrium of a busy shopping mall, his humble robe draped down to his sandals. He holds up two enormous tablets, one made of stone and the other a digital screen. The word FAITH is chiseled into the stone in bold, archaic letters; the word TECHNOLOGY glows in a sleek font on the display.

A crowd in the hundreds is flowing past him, striding past the stores that line the long, echoing passages of the mall. The stores have names like Heaven Scent, Pram of God, Shroud of Purrin'—this last a Bible-themed pet café where puppies and kittens nap in a miniature manger. In the crowd are young families and elderly couples, middle-aged singles strolling alone, rough-looking men in torn jeans and professional women in pantsuits, congregants of all ages leaning on their canes or swinging on crutches. A teenage boy, egged on by friends, steps inside the

Moses hologram, extending both arms to mimic the Lawgiver's posture.

Erin pushes a wheelchair past the hologram, the thin tires gliding along the tile. In the chair sits Owen Foley, a thickset man in his late fifties, his chipped hands folded on the stomach of his olive sweater, a plaid blanket spread across his lap. His right foot is absent under the blanket's tasseled fringe.

*It took a few weeks of recovery,* Erin narrates, *but Owen called me last night and said he felt good enough for the service today. He was chatty when I picked him up, but he warned me he'd taken some pain pills, that he might get groggy soon. I'm just glad he's here, that some parts of his life can resume.*

*I haven't known Owen very long, only the last few years, but at this point I couldn't imagine my life without him. Those years were strange and painful, and working with Owen, going to CODA, meeting up to binge bad TV shows . . . when I look back, that was what got me through them.*

The camera dollies beside Erin as she follows a bend in the hallway, her blouse glimmering under the emerald skylights. More stores slide past on either side: a used guitar shop (The Second Strumming), an eyebrow salon (Blessed Are the Fleek). Actors dressed as Bible characters stand between the stores: a Peter perched on a boulder, a Dreamcoat-wearing Joseph, a troupe of Wise Men posing under a holographic star. Parents swipe their CODA cards, photograph their children with the legends of the faith.

Above them, on the mall's second level, there are no stores or actors. Here security guards in combat gear stand along the railings, their faces bored but attentive as they gaze down at the masses, their assault rifles strapped across their shoulders.

Owen turns partially in his seat, speaking to Erin over his shoulder. His weak voice strains against the crowd noise.

So. Your big date last night?

Erin leans forward to hear him. Yeah. We meet up at MoonPark.

With . . . Jacob, was it?

That right. Jacob.

He shakes his head. These pain pill. Tough remember anything.

Not sure if "date," though. Maybe only hang.

Owen reaches back and rests a hand on Erin's. It fun?

Sure, def, she says after a pause. Not sure how he feel, though. Jacob—he little shy. I need wait see.

You really like him, huh?

Erin laughs. It that obvious?

Just coz know you.

They roll past the window of the Smartworld arcade, Sacred Simulation. A screen plays videos of the VR games on offer: a user slinging a rock at Goliath, steering a raft inside a whale, flying a pale horse through a burning city. In the game *Pharaoh's Court*, a user plays tennis against the ancient monarch, surprisingly agile despite his hulking headdress.

You plan second date? Owen says. Or, sorry—hang?

On Tuesday. It just . . . it much confusing. Not sure what wear: if it date, one outfit; if not, another. It no fair for woman. Guy, they just throw on whatever.

You take some FirstLook photo?

She laughs again. Way too many.

Erin hands him her phone. On the screen is a picture of her Smartworld persona, standing in a green sheath dress on a wide shelf of beach rock, a sweeping view of the ocean at sunset behind her.

Dramatic backdrop, he says.

Yeah. I better in low light.

No say that, sweetie. You beautiful.

Right, and you no bias.

I not! he says.

Owen begins to scroll through the outfits: Erin dressed in skirts and jumpsuits and rompers, blazers and blouses and halter tops, a few pictures of her smirking in elaborate ball gowns. Finally Owen scrolls back to a shirtdress with a slight flare to the skirt, a belted waist.

Here, this one good, he says. It pretty, but fine if not date.

Def, put bookmark. You just save me two hour.

After another bend in the hall, they enter the Worship Wing of the campus. The entrance area is four stories high, vast as an airport terminal; the crowd of congregants swells here to the thousands. A group of guards dressed as apostles—their helmets painted with halo rings, their shepherd staffs equipped with tasers—usher the crowd through a bank of body scanners.

THIS WAY WORSHIP WOW! ARENA, reads an emerald sign.

·         ·         ·

The next scene opens on an aerial shot from the top of the arena. The seats are filling at a rapid rate, from the VIP section in front of the stage to the distant skybox windows, where figurines in recliners order chicken and drinks from the waitstaff. The jumbotrons above the stage play ads for the church's sponsors: one for a musical boiling pot, one for a crackle concealer, one for the Hush Helmet, a head magnet that promises happier dreams.

Erin rolls the wheelchair to the end of a mezzanine row. She locks the wheels, then takes the seat next to Owen.

It sad admit this, she says. But last night? That my first date ever. If it *date* at all.

Really? That true?

Well. Except with Patrick.

Owen is silent for a moment. You never went school dance?

She gives a rueful chuckle. Almost. This guy, Albert, he ask me junior prom. But he cancel of course, right before dance. Because, you know, that when Fiona . . .

Right, right. Damn. That happened your junior year.

It awful time. Even if Albert want go, I prob skip anyway.

Owen adjusts his lap blanket, a sheen of moisture coating his lowered eyes. He sighs and wipes them clear with the back of his hand.

Shit, Erin says. Sorry that.

It nothing. Just these pill. I get all blummo.

You no worry for me, okay? Doctor say you need relax.

Owen wipes his eyes some more. Listen, this Jacob? If he no like you, he idiot. You deserve best guy. Very best.

I tell him you say that.

I serious, sweetie. You no value self enough.

Erin leans over and kisses his temple.

Need pull myself together, he says, now dabbing his cheeks with the blanket. This no good.

It okay cry.

Sure. But if start, might never stop.

Across the arena, the jumbotrons play an ad for Gordon Wound Glue. In the ad a smirking boy in overalls—the cartoon mascot, Gordy Glue—skateboards into a bullring where a matador lies fallen in the dust, a deep crack running along his wrist. The boy bends down to the bullfighter with a giant tube of glue, and then they both turn their heads and sing to the camera: *Got Crack in Plastic? Wound Glue Fantastic!*

Screw you, Gordy Glue, Owen mutters.

Erin, lost in thought, stares blankly at the ad. She says:

If Jacob ask my past, I no idea what say. He think I Erin James, rando Tablet Town employee. Not Erin Reynolds.

He gives her arm a squeeze, her surface firm against his fingers. Just try have fun, sweetie. You deserve some fun.

It be like Albert if I tell him. He no want see me again.

So what then? You *never* go on date? You never get have life, because what Fiona did?

Erin looks out at the crowd, the couples and families of every cast gathered here to worship. Some joke about the jumbotron ads, some read the CODA bulletin, some bow their heads together, saying a quick PrayZone prayer before the service begins. They speak in easy, offhand voices, immersed in the routine intimacy of their lives. Erin glances down, folds her hands in her lap.

Above her the arena lights go dim. GET READY TO WOW NOW! appears on the stage curtains, projected in glittering letters. Then the strum of a lone electric guitar comes flooding out over the audience, thousands of whom now rise to their feet, a colossal creaking of hinges across the arena. The curtains begin to part, revealing a six-piece band onstage, drums and bass and piano, the sawing bows of a cello and violin. A choir in emerald robes claps to the beat, their forearms swinging on their elbow pivots, their hollow palms resounding. They launch into the first song, "Perfect," the crowd singing in a single voice:

> *When I low*
> *Nowhere go*
> *CODA know:*
> *I perfect!*
>
> *When I no*
> *Make much dough*

*They say, Whoa:*
*You perfect!*

*Future bright!*
*Love my life!*
*Dance all night—*
*I perfect!*

*Have lot fun*
*And when done*
*Sing to sun:*
*I perfect!*

*Perfect—whoa, whoa!*
*Time to love and grow!*
*Perfect—whoa, whoa,*
*Ever CODA know!*

The song cascades into an instrumental section, the guitarist perched at the lip of the stage, his head thrown back as he plays a fervent solo. The crowd responds with ecstatic cheers; a swarm of spotlights sweeps their radiant faces.

A man near Erin has set his daughter on his shoulders, the little girl brightening and darkening from the spotlights, waving her rubber prosthetic hands to the beat. Erin glances at them throughout the solo, then leans down to Owen's wheelchair.

I need bathroom, she says. Maybe few min. You be okay?

He sees her troubled face. No rush. I fine here.

Thank. I . . . I back soon.

The camera follows Erin as she strides to an exit sign, her silky blouse flashing as the spotlights stream across her. Out in the corridor she passes a series of posters—an ad for Pastor Mark's podcast, *Born to Chill*—each with a picture of the goateed preacher in a different relaxed tableau: reclining in a hammock between two palm trees; playing passionate bongos in a room filled with lava lamps; sitting in a lotus pose beside a grassy mountain road, the sunset glistening on the motorcycle behind him.

Erin pushes open the bathroom door and clicks down the emerald tile, then shuts herself inside the last of the stalls. She hangs her purse on the jacket hook, begins to catch her breath. The immense room is empty save for a woman at the opposite end, humming the tune to "Perfect" while she flushes and washes her hands.

Soon Erin is alone. She looks at the camera and says:

Last night, after I logged off with Jacob, I sat alone in my Smartroom for over an hour. The night had gone well in the end, but the anxiety . . . it was overwhelming. I'm not just nervous about my secrets, what to tell him about my past—it's all the normal stuff that baffles me as well: how to date, tell someone you like them, be their girlfriend. I've never kissed a man other than Patrick, never fallen in love with anyone else, never worried I'd scare away someone I like. With Patrick I had nothing to hide; he knew everything about me already. Even before EZ Pal, before our virtual life, he accepted the best and worst of me, knew every thought that passed through my mind.

I still remember the first day I saw him. The first instant that our eyes met, the first time the world froze in place and left us alone in that cell of silence. So much has changed since that afternoon—my father was still alive; Fiona was still in college—that the day seems more like a dream to me, a dream more real than life. I suppose the past is always a dream, of sorts. I was seventeen when our eyes met, innocent, unsuspecting, just a high school kid at an aquarium with my father.

Erin sits down in the stall, her waist bending at its hinges. The camera shows her from a side angle, her body a stiff *L* at the edge of the seat. She continues:

Meeting a boy was the last thing on my mind that August day. I can still see myself that morning, sitting with Dad in his station wagon, the highway streaming past my window, the stereo playing an old Charlie Parker song he loved. Dad worked at a local college, a professor of oceanography, and spent his summer months on research and writing articles. A few mornings each week, he'd wake up early and drive the hour to Brunell Aquarium, where, surrounded by aquatic life, he could stroll and think and tap away at his laptop. As a kid I'd loved the aquarium as well, but I hadn't gone in years when I asked to tag along that day.

"You no swim this morning?" he said to me in the kitchen, where I'd found him spreading hummus on a bagel. It was toasted to the dark crunchiness that split us as a family (Fiona also loved hers burnt; I thought it tasted like tree bark). He wore shorts and a plaid shirt, the sleeves rolled up to the elbow, so different from the three-piece suits he wore to teach.

"Eh, can skip one day," I said. "I get in workout later."

Dad looked at me, intrigued, as he bit into the bagel. I hadn't gone on this trip since middle school, when I'd followed Fiona's lead and lost all interest in the aquarium, called it *boooring* like my qunky high school sister.

"Sure then. Amazing," he said. "They just finished new coral reef tank. Think you love it."

"Wow wow! Bet lot new see. This shiny."

I was faking my enthusiasm, of course. I needed a favor from
Dad—a fairly expensive favor—and I wanted him in a generous mood
when I asked him. This was one of the only times I'd manipulated
my father (the last was a weeklong campaign to let Fiona take me to
NoiseFest, where I'd scraped my knee at the Klacky Klack concert
and bled through my favorite jeans), but, like any teenager, I had an
instinct for deception when required. In the car I tapped my foot
to his jazz songs, made appreciative sounds at the solos, asked him
how he'd discovered the genre in the first place. He told me about
an afternoon last spring, jogging on a treadmill at the campus gym,
listening to a Splice song that featured a stunning saxophone snippet.
"The way he played, it made my heart glow. It so beautiful," Dad said.
He'd stopped the treadmill and dripped sweat on his phone as he
found the player, John Coltrane, in the credits.

"Ewww," I teased. "Stop talking your sweat."

He laughed. "Not gross. Everyone sweat."

"Swimming a clean sport. It all wash off."

Soon I was asking him thoughtful questions about the career
of John Coltrane. Dad went into full professor mode, putting on
Coltrane's "most way way" album, *Ascension,* explaining "avant-garde
aesthetics" to me while the wild, tangling horn lines soared from
the speakers. But then, mid-sentence, his forehead wrinkled with
amusement. "Ah. I see what happening here."

"What mean?" I asked, all innocence.

He chuckled. "You sure know your old dad. You go aquarium with
me. Ask about jazz."

"This music real qunky. I like it."

"Uh-huh."

"I serious!" I said, feigning offense.

"Hmm. And there no *reason* for all this?"

I'd worried this might happen. It was Fiona, not me, who chatted
on car rides, who'd get conversations going while he drove. More

often than not, I'd spend our rides lost inside my phone, checking posts on the *Nuclear Family* message boards, reading the latest FamFics.

He added, "Look, I having blast. I glad talk jazz whole ride. But, y'know. You not exactly subtle."

I frowned down at my sandals, at some flakes of dead skin around a toenail. "Well . . ." I began. "There something, yeah. Something I want ask."

"You can pierce nose if want. *One* nostril. But no tattoo."

"Like I could pull off nose ring."

He laughed. "So what then. You want join cult?"

"Before I tell you, I just one question. You like when we hang out, right? Me you have lot fun?"

He raised his eyebrows. "This your sales pitch?"

"Just answer question."

"Def, little fish," he said. "Love spend time you."

"Then imagine whole weekend together. Father-daughter getaway. Just us two, since Fiona away at school."

"Getaway?" he asked, interested but wary.

I felt my pulse tick up. A few days before, my message boards had exploded with major news: *Nuclear Family* had just announced its first convention ever, "FamCon," a chance to meet the creators, the writers and voice actors, not to mention the many "FamFans" I'd befriended on the boards. You could see the stop-motion sets where they'd filmed iconic episodes; you could pose some moveable figures yourself and shoot a short video—like filming your own FamFic. Fiona, a huge fan as well, would have driven us there in a heartbeat, but she was overseas right now, gone until December in a study abroad program. If FamCon was in my future, I'd need Dad as my chaperone this fall. He wasn't a strict parent, but he'd never send his high school daughter alone to some distant city.

I started to make my case, a vein throbbing in my neck. I told him the trip would be wow wow, that there were wonderful museums in the area, that, when the con wrapped up for the day, we'd have lots of time together to bond at night. Yes, it was a whole region away, an eleven-hour drive, and yes, we'd need to pay for a hotel, but I could get an after-school job to cover those expenses.

"Really?" he said. "You want go that bad?"

"Sure, I def find job. This the first *NF* convention. It historic."

So far I'd managed to avoid a job, even a part-time job, that summer. Dad agreed I should focus on my swimming, on getting ready for college recruiters, not waste those months at some pizza place when I could be perfecting my flip turns. But with my friends all working, I was left with hours alone each day on the *NF* message boards, which soon became my main social outlet. That was probably why this convention felt so life-and-death to me now.

Dad said, "Here what I no get. This show, it all stop-motion—no people in it. At convention, it not like you meet anyone in show."

"Yes will! Meet *voice* actor. Plus meet creator, set designer. Plus get exclusive merch."

"Oh. 'Exclusive merch.'"

"Could be worth lot someday."

He sighed. "What date they have this?"

"It start November thirteenth. All weekend. You only need one day off teaching. It best time ever."

"I amazed there whole convention," he said. "No mean to criticize, but that show so . . . limited. Every episode set exact same time: first year after war. None of the character ever get older, develop as people. Not much story there."

Dad wasn't a fan of *Nuclear Family,* which made sense to Fiona and me. The war had made his family refugees, killed his parents in a labor compound; he couldn't enjoy a sitcom that took a surreal approach to that era, that had talking waffles and robots and musical numbers. But nor could Fiona and I resist its zany characters, or how (unlike in school) it used humor to make the history come alive, a history Dad would never discuss with us. We even enjoyed its old-fashioned dialogue, hearing how people talked in the last generation, those long, baggy sentences so different from how we spoke now.

I decided on a different approach. "If we go, we talk jazz whole ride, both way. Promise. No talk anything else."

He laughed. "That what think of me? I force you talk jazz?"

"This might be only convention. If miss it, I never forgive self."

Dad rolled his neck, its wrinkled skin stretching taut, relaxing to a slight sag. He'd cut himself shaving that morning, and a dot of tissue clung to his Adam's apple, a pinpoint of blood at its center. A billboard for the aquarium passed in his window.

"Okay, I give it some thought," he said at last. "But . . . guess I should tell you. This fall, I might need travel little. Maybe November, not sure. I looking for new job."

I tilted my head. "But you just get promotion."

"No worry—I stay till you finish high school. Just exploring option, that all."

This wasn't a huge surprise, though I acted that way for his sake. Last year, Dad's college had finally offered him a tenure-track position, incredible news after decades of adjunct teaching. Until, that is, some drama with a colleague soured him on the school. It was nothing all that scandalous: just a brief affair with another professor, Brad Taynor, which ended when Brad moved away to save his marriage. I'd heard the story from Fiona, whose friend Rob attended Dad's college, and who'd once seen the two men kissing in a stairwell after hours. Despite the mess of the affair, we were glad Dad had found some love for himself, if only for a short while. He had been single for so long, ever since his husband, Owen, left when we were small.

I never discussed the affair with Dad, of course—he'd be mortified. Whenever Fiona and I said he should date—that we'd love it if he had a boyfriend—he'd blush and change the subject. "You two my life," he'd tell us, "no worry all that." For a man this private, the gossip at work must have been acutely painful. Painful enough to consider leaving his job, to relocate in his fifties.

But I still had other matters on my mind. As we took the exit for the aquarium, I said, "So you look for new job. That great. Maybe there college near convention?"

"I let you know. Give me month or so."

"I need wait *month?*"

Dad smiled. "Fine, fine. Two week. You drive hard bargain, little fish."

As always, Dad handed me a bottle of sunscreen when we stepped into the parking lot. I was fair-skinned and could burn quickly, even if much of the aquarium was indoors. I smeared on the lotion for thirty seconds or so—sunscreen made me impatient—then turned to face him. "Little on cheek," he said, and I rubbed it into my skin as we walked to the entrance. Dad breathed raggedly beside me, then took a hit on his inhaler: his lungs had never been strong after his years in the refugee compound, working long hours in a factory with poor ventilation. Through the windows I could see the vast, open lobby of the aquarium, the whale skeleton that hung below the skylights.

When we were younger, Fiona and I would visit the aquarium with him several times a year. We adored the haughty sea lions, the starfish we could pet, the glass-ceilinged rooms where sharks swam thrillingly close above our heads. We loved the sugary funnel cakes, sold at a stand near the otter enclosure. We even had names for our favorite penguins, though it's doubtful we could tell them apart; there was probably a new Doris or Fred on every visit. As Dad and I walked into the aquarium now, as we started down the mazy halls past tanks I hadn't seen in years—the squids and bat rays and amphipods, the jellies and barracudas—I felt a wave of nostalgia for those days. A seahorse bobbed in a tank to my right, so cute that, before I could stop myself, I let out a little squeal.

Dad laughed. "See, it not so *boooring* here."

I blushed, felt the blood hot in my cheeks. "Yeah. It okay."

Before we bought our funnel cakes, Dad stopped at the bathroom in the outdoor food court. I waited on the hot sidewalk, my T-shirt stuck to my back, wishing I'd worn a hat to block the glare. Hundreds of patrons sat eating their lunches at the tables around me, burritos and falafel and beef lo mein, salads buried in snowfalls of cheese and bacon. Some young men stood in line at a food truck, Flo's Calzones, all dressed in the same green T-shirt, *Camp Crazy Canoe* printed on the back. That was when I first saw Patrick.

I wish I had taken his picture then, pulled out my phone and captured his image forever. But something about his appearance made me forget my phone, forget myself entirely. He was a skinny, bird-faced man a little shorter than his friends, dressed in the camp T-shirt and a pair of cargo shorts, his long hair haphazard on his shoulders. He didn't talk to the others in his group but wore a far-off, thoughtful expression, staring out at the log-covered stream of the otter enclosure. He had a scratch on his left ankle, a thin slice among the downy hairs. He rubbed an eyelid with the back of his knuckle. He was beautiful.

I'm not sure how long I watched him. Probably less than thirty seconds. Then, to my surprise, he turned his head and saw me.

A few years earlier, I would have blushed and looked away if caught like this. But I'd become more confident this year, when, as only a sophomore, I'd won a few first-place trophies at regional swim meets, earning me a story in our local paper, some unexpected attention at my high school. I was still lanky, self-conscious, a loner at times—not blessed, like Fiona, with the confidence for a large friend group—but I was no longer the shy freshman who kept her head down in the hall, who ate lunch with a few other bashful girls who barely spoke to each other, huddled together more out of fear than friendship. These days I had actual friends, I'd get invited to parties, and, when I wanted, I could hold the gaze of a man who looked at me.

The world froze around me as our eyes met. His gaze was sincere, inquisitive, as if, to his own surprise, he'd met the eyes of someone intriguing, someone he'd like to know more. It might be my imagination, my projection onto the past, but, as our eyes lingered, as a smile found his lips, it seemed like he was debating whether to leave the line and talk to me, maybe ask me for my number. There was a boldness to him as well, I could sense it. A second before the attack began, he lifted his hand to wave.

I saw the bullets hit him before I heard the shooting. That at least is how I remember the moment, how my memory has pieced it back together: first the sudden punctures in the chest of his T-shirt, then the deafening report of the machine gun, a sound that rattled my rib cage, seared up my spinal column. As the crowd began to scream, as they ran or ducked under tables, I watched him crumple to the sidewalk with a strange, disjointed looseness, like every bone in his body had gone gelatinous. His shot-up shirt, his outflung arms, the puddle of blood spreading beneath him—I remember staring at him for a long time, maybe a full minute, but, in reality, it must have been only seconds, because Dad was already out of the bathroom when he heard the gunfire. He ran and tackled me down to the pavement, covering my body with his own.

From the sidewalk I stared at the beautiful man, my head now level with his. Sneakers raced between us, another body fell, but I didn't look away. His thoughtful face had slackened into a blank, indifferent mask. There was no curiosity left there, no depth to his widened eyes.

Though I stayed on the ground, pinned to the pavement, I could feel a surge of movement inside me, a door swinging open, a spirit rushing inward. This young man was gone now, dead, that much was clear. But I could somehow feel his final thoughts, the mixture of panic and disbelief that had followed him out of this life, that had sped between the fleeing sneakers and found a home in my body. I could feel the bullets pierce through his lungs, the flinch of his tibias, the down-sweep of darkness, death coming fast, too fast, no time to think. It was as if we were one person, as if a part of me had died in his body as well. That void in me became his new dwelling.

From then on—before I even knew his name, before I saw it that night on the news—Patrick was with me. He was my secret, my sacred, the windowless cell where I lived. In under a minute the gunfire stopped, showed no sign of resuming. My father, crying, asked if I was hurt.

In the bathroom stall, Erin takes her purse off the jacket hook. The camera zooms in on her face as she shuts her eyes and swallows a SettleSelf capsule. The overhead lights sheen her molded features, her hard eyelids. Then she closes the bottle and strides from the emerald bathroom.

The music of the worship band still echoes down the corridor, a pop-rock song with a bubbly acoustic guitar riff. The crowd croons as one:

> *I body no soul,*
> *No think ever whole,*
> *Till CODA let see*
> *Each day blessing me!*

Erin does not return to the arena. Instead, her stiff arms swaying beside her, she wanders back to the shopping mall. The stores all sit deserted with the service underway; the sunlight pours in sea green columns through the skylights. An Angel Gabriel, on break, strolls past her reading his phone, two massive wings sprouting from his back.

At the end of the next hallway rises the dark, solemn facade of Ancient Cathedral. Here an entire three-story wall mimics the front of a Gothic church, its gargoyles glowering under the cornice, its saints in shallow niches, its round rosetta window flush with light. A high, haunting plainsong wafts from within. Erin lowers herself to a bench, then sends a text to Owen: *Let know when wrapping up. I come get you.*

She takes out her earbuds, pushes them into her ears.

Carla, play "Seal Serenade," she says.

Playing "Seal Serenade."

A baying bursts from her earbuds, a chorus of seals calling out to a dubstep beat. Seagulls are heard in the background, a faint lapping of waves.

Erin exhales as the aquatic music reverberates from her skull. On a pedestal beside her shines a hologram of the *Pietà:* the Virgin seated with the lifeless Christ draped across her lap, gazing tenderly at her Son's translucent face.

---

## 8

Side by side, the branches rushing past them, Erin and Jacob swing on vines through a dense tropical forest. The trees around them explode into flames, or topple over with a momentous crash, sliced in half by the red-hot lasers that scorch through the jungle canopy.

The lasers burst from UFOs that swarm through the sky above them, visible in the gaps of the burning foliage. As Erin and Jacob swoop through the jungle, they lift their crossbows and fire bolts at the alien invaders, the tip of each bolt a cherry-red explosive. The metal saucers ignite at once when struck, then plummet and come smashing through the canopy, perilously close to the figurines if they don't swing fast enough. An alien pilot ejects from the top and speeds away on a jetpack; extra points are awarded when a player explodes him, splattering the leaves with a rain of cartoonish gore.

Erin and Jacob have just released their vines and are soaring toward the next ones, so high at the top of their arc that they clear the treetops, when Erin tosses her crossbow away and throws an arm around Jacob, their bodies flying off course through the sunny air. She taps her menu as they plunge, turns off Death by Falling. They land on a hillside and roll down laughing, bouncing off an occasional boulder, their hollow bodies sonorous with each impact.

At the end of their long tumble, Jacob lies on top of Erin, his breathless face regarding her from above.

Well, we lose that round, he says.

Worth it.

So much for defeating invader.

Eh. Planet doomed anyway.

Which side you on? he asks.

She lifts a finger, bops his nose. I never tell.

Jacob smiles down at her, his long hair draping her face on either side. There is an eagerness in his smile, a suppressed yearning.

*Kiss him, you idiot,* she narrates. *Just pull him down and—*

He gives an awkward laugh, then his hinges murmur as he lifts himself off her.

So . . . what want do now? she says, a slight strain in her voice. Blow up more alien?

Nah. I prob *Jam*-ed out today.

My beach?

Sound good, he says. Want fly?

Def.

Both tap at their menus. In an instant they hover above the fiery forest, their arms replaced with eagle wings that softly beat the sky. They shrink into the distance, the lasers still slicing through the jungle behind them.

---

Jacob stands shirtless in the shallows near the shoreline, submerged up to his waist in the rolling tide. The sunlight sparkles off the waves that shape themselves around him, so that he seems to stand less in water than in a pool of flashing, iridescent light. His eyes are shut, his face attentive, listening.

Marco! he calls.

Erin, farther from shore, backpedals deeper into the light. Polo! she responds.

He wades toward the sound, the waves sloshing his navel. Erin darts to her left, then to her right, then to her left again, but he follows these redirections as if drawn to her by a magnet.

This no fair, she says.

Marco! he repeats.

Behind them curves the crescent of a small private beach, its sand smooth and luminous, a tilted umbrella shading a striped blanket at its center. A beach house sits above the sand, its tall windows a mirror of the sea and the horizon, where the sky and water melt together like the sound of cellos playing the same note in unison. Seagulls circle in the glass with silent wingbeats.

After a few more dodges, Jacob slides in front of Erin. Laughing, he slips his arms around her, pulls her close against him.

Let you win, she says flirtatiously, pressing against his chest.

Sure.

Her lips angle up toward his. Call liar?

Maybe.

They grow quiet; the waves whisper around them. All teasing gone from his voice, he says: I like you lot, you know.

Like you, too, Erin answers.

No, but I mean, I *like* you. I . . . crush. It stupid word, *crush*. But it true.

Feel same way.

Jacob lets out a held breath. I hoping you say that.

You no tell? I big big crush. Like, it hurt so big.

The anxiety leaves his face. His expression opens with a new depth, a gentle swell of music without sound.

Erin presses closer to him, their legs entwined below the skeins of sunlight. Then, with a sudden laugh, she drops herself below the waves and pushes her feet off the ocean floor. She swims away with rapid strokes, her hair rippling above the surface like a sea anemone.

Jacob, startled, watches the spray around her kicking legs. Where you go? he calls.

Erin does not respond, her hinged arms pumping like pistons in the sea-shine. Midstroke, she taps the air above her head and vanishes. He looks out at the empty ocean, the water still troubled around her absent shape.

Hey there, she says behind him.

Jacob swivels around and she splashes his sparkling chest. She is grinning, exultant.

Why leave? he says.

She runs a palm along the water, her eyes following its movement. Dunno. Just happy.

You run away when happy?

Sometime, she says, stepping closer.

Erin cups his face between her dripping hands. Their hard lips graze each other's, a scratchy sound of plastic brushing plastic. Then she wraps her arms around his waist and kisses Jacob fully, silencing their lips in the firmness of the contact. Their shining, sun-wet bodies move as one.

A few days later they lie on the beach, spread out on the striped blanket, the virtual sunlight unchanged above the shore. They speak in soft voices, their faces close in the shadow of the umbrella.

And that last time you talk her? Erin asks. Her hand lightly strokes his lower back.

Yeah. We in Tablet Town parking lot. I tell her hurry up, get new power cord for Smarthead. I total jerk that day. Total prick. So dumb.

But you think normal morning.

I just bad son, just asshole, Jacob says. She struggle much, my mom. But I ever take for granted. Ever headache her.

I doubt.

He stares past her, toward the pine trees that sway at the beach edge. There good time, too. Much good time. Just, look back, it hard remember. Tough explain.

No, I get. It same with my dad. Hard remember him healthy, alive. When life still good.

He professor, right? You no talk him much.

Dad teach oceanography. Teach it long time, Erin says. She doesn't elaborate, goes on stroking his back.

High above them, in the smog-free sky, an ancient red propeller plane flies back and forth below the clouds, its rudder trailing a long, flapping banner: GOT CRACK IN PLASTIC? WOUND GLUE FANTASTIC! In the cockpit sits a goggled Gordy Glue, an aviator scarf streaming from his neck. As he nears the circle of seagulls, he raises a giant water gun and squirts some Wound Glue at them.

And then what happen? Erin asks.

Then?

At Tablet Town. After your mom leave car.

Well . . . then I hear explosion. Then I sit there, wait. Phone tell me right away, Mom in blast zone. And I just know. Just feel. She gone.

God. I remember that. You know somehow.

Whole time, so much shooting. I get on floor back seat . . . figure I die too now. By time I get your message, everything feel like joke. I laughing when I text you back. That weird weird, huh? I laughing.

She presses her lips to his sun-warmed forehead. Jacob shuts his eyes and exhales slowly. He continues:

We fighting lot, last few year. Mom and me. It not even fight, not really—she no fight back. I just mad at her all time.

What happen? If okay talk it.

It not fair, how I treat her. She make mistake, sure. But I so mean—she no deserve it.

Jacob begins to explain. The trouble had started two years before, in his last year of high school, when his grandmother, drunk at dinner, had cracked a very unexpected joke. He and his mother were at her apartment, laughing as Katherine recounted a funny story she'd heard on the news, all about some zinged-out employee who had shut off the fridge at a sperm bank, destroying hundreds of viable specimens when he left for the night. Katherine, chuckling, had turned to Jacob and said, "Imagine that happen your dad sperm. You no be here!"

For his entire life, Jacob had heard a very different story about his father. Irene had said his name was Steven Neibur, a young doctor drafted overseas in the final year of the war, sent into battle as a combat medic, killed in a skirmish while carrying a soldier to safety. According to her stories, Irene was engaged and three months pregnant when Steven received his draft notice; Jacob was born not long after his death. In truth—as Jacob would soon learn—his mother had never wanted a husband, not after some disturbing experiences with a college boyfriend. ("Ralph," Jacob says to Erin. "Real sociopath, that guy.") So a sperm bank had seemed the best idea when Irene decided on children, not planning then to invent some mythic father for her son.

But Jacob was born blind in a bleak era, and Irene had decided her son shouldn't feel even more different from others, that instead he should have a father figure who represented the best of manhood—a father figure that she, Irene, could create for Jacob from scratch. This might even make Jacob less toxic than other men, not self-absorbed or controlling like so many she had known. Katherine disapproved of all the lying, but she agreed to go along with her daughter's wishes. The myth of Steven continued for almost two decades.

At dinner that night, Irene jumped in right after Katherine's joke. "Wow wow, Mom," she said with a stilted laugh, "you much drunk. Why bring up Steven sperm?" Katherine mumbled "fuck" beneath her breath, sober enough to see her mistake but not to conceal it. She tried to backtrack her comment—"Well, you know, if Steven sterile, then you no get pregnant. That all I mean. Good he not sterile"—but Jacob could hear the note of alarm in her voice. By the end of the meal, he'd made them admit the truth to him. He went quiet for a few minutes, saying nothing as his mother tried to explain. Finally he stood from his seat and muttered, "I want go home now."

That night shattered his sense of self. He was a lonely kid in high school—never many friends, rarely invited to hangs or parties—but his father's memory had made this bearable, let him remember he was the son of a selfless hero. He'd asked his mother countless questions about this brave, inspiring doctor, who, despite his physical absence, felt ever-present to Jacob through her stories. Irene had obliged her son, dreaming up a tapestry of lies: Steven's habits and hobbies, his political beliefs, his marriage proposal while parasailing ("he almost drop ring!"), his whoop of joy when he learned Irene was pregnant. Steven had lost his own family at the start of the war, when the first warheads fell along the coastline, only spared that fate himself because he'd gone out west on a skiing trip with friends. He was an orphan who'd worked hard in school, who'd never given up hope, who'd devoted his life to others until the end, and who would be so, so proud of Jacob if he knew his son today. Onto these stories Jacob had mapped his entire identity.

Now, in a single meal, he'd learned that Steven was a lie, that the people he trusted most had deceived him for eighteen years. Though he started talking again in the days that followed—even said he forgave his mother—he stayed in his room as much as possible, avoided his friends from school, struggled to finish his homework or study for tests. He'd been an excellent student before this, had even learned braille in grade school, and, in his NAT class, had seemed on track to pass the test that fall. But he barely slept the night before the NAT, kept forgetting his mnemonic devices, and ended up with a score fifteen points under passing. Now college would need to wait until his second, final attempt when he turned twenty-one—and who knew if he'd pass then? He might just fail the NAT again, get sent to a government training camp, then assigned a job he hated for the rest of his life. Despite his weekly trips to therapy, he fell into a deep depression.

Around this time, Irene took out a personal loan and bought her son a Smartbody. This came as a complete surprise to him: he'd never asked her for such a gift, never even expressed an interest to her in the Bodies. They'd only talked about them once before, in sophomore or junior year, when he'd listened to some early user reviews of the "ViewPoint," a Smarthead built specifically for the blind. Instead of a screen, this helmet used a See-Breeze transmitter, sending frequencies directly to the polymers in the eyes. The ViewPoint worked best for users with partial sight, but it had also worked for users like Jacob, users with total blindness. "It not perfect," said one such user. "It mostly basic shape and color, like little kid do drawing. But know what? The people I meet in Smartworld, they no *clue* I see dif. First time ever, I fit in with sighted people. Love my ViewPoint."

This Smarthead cost so much, however, that Jacob had never imagined owning one, and, in any case, he felt no need for an alternate experience of the world. He'd known people who lost their sight in childhood, but Jacob, born blind, never felt he was "missing" something; his lack of sight was not an "absence," just the way he'd always lived, a fact about his body, like the shape of his nose or the way his voice sounded. It baffled him why people treated him like he came from some other planet: why they spoke louder as if he couldn't hear them, or addressed him through his mother as if a blind person needed an interpreter, or said things like, *It must be so hard* or *You so brave,* as if this single fact about his body defined him, as if his life was some unrelenting hardship. Yes, his life might be different from theirs, but everyone had different bodies, everyone had struggles—it wasn't like he had a terminal illness or something. The older he grew, the more he realized: for him, the hardest part about blindness was not his lack of sight, but sighted people.

So when, out of nowhere, his mother knocked on his door one night and said she had a surprise for him, when she presented him with a Smartbody and a ViewPoint, he took this at first as an insult—she, of all people, should know he didn't crave a "cure" to his "condition," that he'd resent the implications of this gift. Nor was he in the mood for gifts from his mother: the rift between them was far from healed, and he'd isolated himself even more after failing his NAT. "Why buy this thing?" he asked her. "I no want it." "Just give it try," she replied. "See if like. They have return policy."

Later that night, he put on his ViewPoint for the first time. He heard the SeeBreeze hum to life in the Head, and then he found himself transported to what would become his favorite Domain: CityCity. He stood in a rooftop garden, a crimson sunset spread before him, a view of skyscrapers that stretched to the horizon. It was a world adorned with visual details, an added layer of sensation that enfolded sound and touch, opening a spatial depth around him, a riot of shapes and colors. He looked down at the churn of dancing bodies in the block party below him, looked up at the dozens of sky surfers riding their boards through the sunset. He looked behind him and saw other new users mingling in the garden, eager to chat, to explore the Domain together.

It was new and strange to have vision, but what drew him most to Smartworld was escape, the chance to leave a life where people kept him on the outside, where his own mother had invented a father for him out of pity. Here no one ever asked about his vision; here he was treated the same as anyone else. They didn't know that the Smartworld he saw was blurred and blocky, with flickering edges and faces that often looked exactly the same, so that, whenever he met someone new, he tapped his menu to make their name float above their head. They didn't know the ViewPoint sometimes gave him headaches, even nausea if he ignored the headache too long. No: they thought he was just like them. He was finally free from the pity, the false assumptions.

In the end, Jacob was grateful to his mother. He was fighting less with her, putting less distance between them, when they drove to Tablet Town the morning of the attack.

For days after her death, Jacob sat numbly alone in his bedroom, unable to face his grief and regret, the shock that still echoed through his hollows. He was desperate to log onto Smartworld, but he lacked the power cord he needed, and he couldn't bring himself to ask his grandma or buy it online. He knew he needed to study—the NAT almost never granted extensions—but he could barely eat the meals she brought him, barely speak to the trauma counselor they visited. Then came the wake at Flippin' Chicken, Jacob too rattled to talk the entire night, haunting a back row like some cousin of the deceased, not Irene's only child, the son who mourned her.

That day, all day, I awful to my grandma, Jacob says to Erin on the beach. I so angry her, no help it. Night before, she get so drunk, she come my room like two a.m. She sit next to me, start tremble, mutter, cry. I no want seem awake—if do she make me talk till dawn. Then Grandma shake my shoulder: *Jacob, you awake? Jacob, I want talk you.* I sit right up, start yelling her face, *Get out! What wrong you? My mom just die, what wrong you?* Grandma leave real fast then. Hear her vomit bathroom.

Oh, sweetie. That rough.

Next day, at wake, everyone think I sad. But I angry. Super angry. Whole time I think, *This my fucking life now? Trapped with drunk grandma?*

You just lose your mom. It okay feel angry.

Not these day. Not when terror attack any sec. Then people you love gone—and last thing you tell them? *Hurry up.*

Your mom know you love her, Erin says. I sure that.

He sighs. When war start, my mom just teenager. She grow up awful time. But I never think it much, you know? Not till after she gone. I just mean to her, criticize her. Point out her mistake.

That not all you do. You say lot good time.

Yeah. Yeah, guess so.

Jacob rests his face on her shoulder, his nylon hair spilling down her chest. He says:

I just ever feel so selfish. Like right now. Here with you.

What mean?

My NAT. The test next month—I maybe fail. Then I get sent

some training facility, who know where. If I better guy? I wait, pass my test, *then* I tell you crush. But I no help it.

That not selfish, Erin says. That romantic.

I just no hide it anymore. It hard study, want tell you so much.

She kisses the top of his head. Me, I take test bad time, too. Feel blummo whole morning. But I pass.

Bet you never even fail practice test. I fail two this week.

She waves this away. Few bad practice test—that nothing. You still some time.

Jacob nods, unconvinced. Okay if I put on music? Help me calm down little.

He taps his menu and turns on a song, "Cruising Altitude," a soft cascade of corks over the cabin hum of an airliner. The figurines fall silent, their hands clasped on the blanket, the aerial music lulling their eyelids closed. The propeller plane chugs above the ocean, Gordy's goggles streaked with sunlight, his long scarf rippling behind the cockpit.

When the song is over, Jacob reaches up and strokes the firm surface of her cheek. Well, guess better go. Need wake up early, hit ground running. Want hang after dinner?

Anytime, just text. Maybe play *Tornado Town* tomorrow?

Shiny. I should study more, but I ready snap by dinner.

She chuckles. You doing great. Really.

Jacob runs a finger along her jawline. Miss you already.

They share a lengthy kiss. Then he grips his head with both hands, pulls upward and disappears.

The impression of his body rises slowly from the blanket, unwrinkling at the edges of his outline. With a faint smile, Erin rests her palm inside his fading shape.

*I wish I could relax around him,* she narrates. *Stop worrying for a second, forget all the secrets I'm keeping. And the most stressful part of all? It's how happy I feel with Jacob—truly happy for the first time in years. I know how to grieve, how to keep myself hidden, but what can I do with happiness, so dangerous if I trust it, if I count on it to last?*

*The problem is, happiness never feels like a bad idea. No, it feels wonderful: like this happier me was asleep since high school, since the day I saw Patrick die at the aquarium. Like I can finally feel her waking up, her weak pulse quicken beneath the skin.*

Erin taps her menu and puts on a peaceful WOBATS song: whooshing wind over bright bongos, a far-off clicking of tap shoes. The music mingles with the low purr of Gordy's plane. A seal leaps from the water, hind flippers flashing, and crashes back under the shine with a tranquil splash.

Then, with a sharp inhale, Erin sees that Gordy is no longer in the cockpit.

The mascot stands smirking on a wing of the aircraft, a hand shading his goggles as he watches her. When he sees that Erin has noticed him, he gives her a wave and hops off the wing at once. He plummets down through the sunlight, his smirk static, his bowl cut blowing, his scarf trailing above him like a cut puppet string. He falls at a gradual pace, as if choosing his own rate of gravity.

Shit, Erin mumbles.

Gordy finishes his slow descent, landing on the foaming crest of a wave. He does not sink but stands on the breaker as if on a liquid platform, the curl of water undented from his weight. The tide carries him to shore like a moving walkway, slides away and leaves him in the swash zone. He strides to Erin with a swaggering gait, unnerving on a child so young. She gets to her feet as the boy approaches, looks down at his freckled face.

The mascot wastes no time. He drops to his knees before Erin can speak, starts scratching hasty letters in the sand. His

expression is smug and mocking above the sincere swoops of his
finger.

*LISTEN,* he scratches. *YOU NEED LEAVE TOWN. YOU
NOT—*

No, you listen! Erin snaps back, a shade of desperation in her
voice. My life, it finally good—I no want this anymore. These
attack you warn me, they never happen.

*—SAFE HERE,* he continues. *CALL TERRORISM BUREAU,
BARB FULLER. SHE—*

He begins to scrawl the next word, but Erin crouches down
and grabs the straps of his overalls. With an angry jerk of her
hands, she swings Gordy around to face her. He tries to shake
free, but she grips the straps more firmly.

This *over,* she says. If Fiona send you, tell her: *leave me fuck
alone.*

The mascot's face has only two expressions: the first his smug
smirk and the second a playful taunt, his scarlet tongue stuck
out, his right eye closed. He switches these expressions faster
and faster as she restrains him, his tongue darting, his eyelid flapping like a camera shutter. At last he gives her a hard push and
tumbles onto his back. Gordy is on his knees in an instant, his
finger scratching frantically.

Erin lets out an exhausted sigh. As he scribbles a crooked
*TELL,* she pulls up on her head and vanishes.

# 9

Erin stands alone in her Smartroom, her hair mussed, her helmet on the floor beside her Feet. Her harness cords tremble as she catches her breath, still rattled after scuffling with the mascot.

After a moment, she starts to remove her Smartbody. She pulls off the parts with brusque gestures—the Hands and Arms and Torso, the Feet and Legs—and drops them in a messy heap on the padding. Then she slips on her robe and strides down the hall to her bedroom. An old beanbag chair lies under the window; distant streetlamps pale her closed curtains. Silhouetted in their glow, she looks less like a body than an absence in the light, a space through which a body might pass.

In the darkness Erin speaks aloud, not bothering to look at a camera:

I keep thinking about the aquarium shooting, the day I watched Patrick die. His face on the pavement, his bloodstained shirt, his spirit merging with mine. I'm not sure why, but that cryptic summer won't leave my mind since I met Jacob. I remember coming back home the night of the shooting, shutting myself in my bedroom, watching news clip after news clip about the attack. In calm, polished voices, the anchors presented the basic facts: the number dead, the number injured, some details about the shooter. They spoke in the past tense, odd to my ears, which still rang with the roar of the gunfire, the screams of the wounded. But for anyone not at the aquarium, I realized, this was just another news story, a story with a clear beginning and end. It would not live in their bodies, a part of them forever. It would not remain in the present while the rest of the world moved on.

The shooter, Joel Abathy, was a college senior who worked at the aquarium's help desk. He had smuggled in an assault rifle, emptied a clip from behind a food stand, and then vanished into hiding, perhaps with the help of a terror group, perhaps alone. His parents, stunned, said they'd had no clue that Joel was even political. This was the story of more and more families now: first the child's brutal crime, then the media circus, the lifetime of regrets.

Back then, no one worried as much about terror groups, no one kept their dresses ironed for the funerals every weekend. A few times a month you'd see an attack on your newsfeed, but you still felt shocked at a shooting in your own area. Few people back then understood—or wanted to understand—that these attacks were the start of a national conflict, a surge of guerrilla warfare throughout the country. We'd all heard of "The Conversation," an underground network begun in the war years, but we didn't know it was behind all these ecoterrorist cells, that it had chosen violence and chaos to achieve its aims. The next few years would open our eyes: the increase in guards and security checks, the fear in public spaces, the realization we were at war with a hidden enemy.

Minutes before the shooting, Joel Abathy had posted a statement to his social media. I read it several times before I went to sleep that night. The statement listed the "many crime" that had "justify" his shooting: the rising temperature, the ruin of nature, the risk of another nuclear war, wealth disparity, foreign labor practices, stolen Indigenous land. He demanded, above all else, an immediate shift to clean energy. *Wake up!* he wrote. *We ruin whole Earth! Earth our only home!*

This shooting, he said, was not an "attack," but a battle in a war: the war on industrial civilization itself. Our civilization was a "plague," a "cancer," a scourge that had poisoned the planet and built its strength through mass oppression, that had killed millions of innocent humans in a nuclear holocaust. The cure for this plague would never be a new form of mass government—all these, Joel said, had failed—but instead the forced collapse of the civilization itself. After this, the human species could return to a more organic existence, cleansed of our advanced technologies, our capacity to do such harm. A better future lay before us, but the way there was destruction.

I'd known about ecoterrorists before this, but I'd never read one of their statements, never understood the logic that compelled them. Joel Abathy wasn't "insane," as some articles were painting him: he had a clear motive for the shooting at the food court. He'd killed three people in protest, to spread chaos through a society he hated, to speed its downfall. One of them a senior in high school, a camp counselor named Patrick Yates.

My dreams of Patrick began the following night. I'd find myself back at the food court on that sun-dazed afternoon, the entire space now deserted except for the two of us. He gazed across the tables at me with his kind, curious eyes, very much alive despite the bullet holes in his T-shirt. Most nights we only stared at each other, his beautiful face becoming my world, my entire conscious awareness; in other dreams, less often, I'd walk up to him and touch his cheek, his skin oddly cold for a summer day. If the dream went on for long enough, if I sensed I had his permission, I'd run a finger along his shirt and down into a bullet hole, trace the texture of his torn skin, the ragged flesh, the maimed muscle. I could feel no pulse in his veins, no beating heart in his rib cage.

These dreams were the opposite of nightmares. I'd wake up to a sense of peace that lasted through the morning, that cast a spell on the rest of August and the start of my junior year. I talked far less to my friends now, but I was safe in my cell with Patrick, where I'd lived since the moment his spirit swept into my body. This felt, in a way, like what I owed him: if he hadn't been looking at me in the food court—distracted, about to wave—he might have noticed the shooter, might have taken cover in time.

His body was lost to him now, but he could still exist in mine, not drift off into oblivion forever. I loved how he filled my dreams, how the thought of him suppressed all other feelings. On dreamless nights, I woke up disappointed.

For weeks, I reread his obituary every morning. In the photo he stood on an outcrop with the vast ocean behind him, an amused, ironic smile on his lips. His family had posted dozens of videos in the days before the funeral: Patrick playing sports, blowing out candles, going on road trips with friends, exploring a butterfly garden as a little boy. In his Fav Pic section were mountain lookouts, churning rivers, the sea at sunset; he'd loved to take landscape photos, to capture the nature that still remained in the Pacific Northwest. At night I would lie on my bed, settle a pillow over my eyes, and picture him swimming through the twilight sea in his photos—his lithe body diving down to touch the ocean floor, then soaring with pulsing legs up to the surface—the scenes unfolding for me of their own accord, a gift of his breathing spirit. I too adored the ocean, its mystery, its sway, the willful water pushing against my strokes. Soon I swam beside him in these daydreams.

But I mentioned him to no one—not to my father, not to Fiona when she called from her overseas program, not to the trauma counselor Dad took me to see each week. I knew my feelings would worry them, that they would try to take Patrick away. They could see I wasn't coping well: more silent than ever before, dark circles under my eyes, hungry for only a few forkfuls at dinner. I had fallen in love, but I knew that they would call my love a sickness.

One evening in September I decided to draw him. I wanted a closer contact with Patrick, to take in his face through more than a photo or a video. My first attempts were awful—his head loose and wavy, his eyes blobby puddles—but I returned to the task the next night, and then the night that followed, and after a month I could pick up the pencil and sketch a face that was his, if still far too cartoonish for my liking. I'd save his lips for last, then smile back at my love. Soon I added his body to the page, sometimes in a tuxedo like his junior prom photos, sometimes in far less. I always drew his fingers curled, as if tensed with the same longing that tightened my grip on the pencil.

At the same time, I was watching more and more *Nuclear Family.* The show had always obsessed me, but a large part of this was the message boards and FamFics, the fun, creative fandom around the sitcom. But now I avoided the message boards and stuck to the show itself, discovered that I no longer needed to watch through the seasons in any order, that I could choose a single episode to focus on each week, watching it twenty or thirty times before I switched to a new one, internalizing every scene. By then I didn't need a screen; I could shut my eyes and the episode played in my mind. I could make up episodes of my own, shift around the world and characters, watch them on a screen inside my head. The dated language of the show became my own; I'd catch myself thinking in longer sentences, narrating my life to myself in that old-fashioned dialect. It was less a show than another world, a world more safe and familiar than the one outside my bedroom.

All the while, Patrick watched beside me. We could share the
show together, like my swimming, like my schoolwork, like every
thought that flitted through my mind. Over the months my sketches
improved, became more detailed and precise. Day by day, I noticed
a new stiffness to his limbs, a glossy sheen to his skin, hinges in the
nooks of his knees and elbows.

One night I set down my pencil and walked across the house to see
Dad. We used to hang out after dinner, watch old musicals together,
but now that I went back to my room instead, my door closed while
I drew and dreamed, he'd wash the dishes after we ate and go down
to his office in the basement. From the top of the stairs I could see
him on the basement sofa, his bald spot a little sunburnt from his daily
morning walks, some mellow Miles Davis song whispering from his
stereo. In his hand he cradled an old smartphone, one I'd never seen
before, a long crack slanting down its screen. The stairs were behind
the couch, so I saw the picture on the screen for an instant—
a laughing man in a crisp blue suit, some scarring on both his
cheeks—before Dad heard me on the stairs and tucked the phone
between the cushions. He turned and gave me a smile over his
shoulder.

Though I always felt Patrick with me, there were nights when
a stab of loneliness stirred me from this dream. In these moments
I'd miss my old closeness with Dad, how I'd felt like I could tell him
anything before the shooting. Perhaps this was still true: there was a
chance he'd understand about Patrick, a chance that he even carried
a ghost of his own, maybe one of his parents who'd died in the refugee
compound. He'd been a teenager at the start of the war, and I'd seen
the way his face changed on the rare occasions he talked about his
childhood, the distance that opened behind his eyes, the wistfulness
of his smile, staring into that vanished world before the bombs and the

millions dead, as if, even gone, it was far more real than the meager world we'd inherited. Perhaps both of his parents lived in his body, like Patrick lived with me.

"What up, little fish?" he said as I walked down the stairs. He looked startled, but pleased to see me out of my room.

I shrugged. "Not much."

"How homework coming?"

"It fine. I done soon."

I crossed the area rug and sat down on his desk chair. Years ago, he'd made our unfinished basement his makeshift office: a desk and a tackboard, a few old bookcases, some scuffed filing cabinets that he'd hauled around since college. Dad liked to print things out, liked to hold what he read in his hands—Fiona, more eco-conscious than us, would chide him about this sometimes—and stacks of paper stood everywhere in tidy heaps. The space was a snapshot of his busy mind, a profusion of thoughts and projects wrangled into a precarious order.

He said, "Well. Good you take break. Want watch something?"

"Nah. That okay."

"It still early. You want go out? Mini-golf? Bowling?"

I shook my head. "Need do calculus later."

I used homework as the excuse for all the time I now spent alone; in truth, I usually finished this work in study hall at school. It felt new and strange, lying to Dad so often. The awkwardness between us was also new.

"Well . . . okay," he said. "Let know if want help."

"Def. Will."

"I such nerd, no think I ever say this. But maybe you work *too* hard?"

"I fine, Dad. Really."

I sensed he wanted to say more: that I'd always had good grades without all this isolation; that I should leave the house more often, not just for school and swimming; that he knew why I was hiding—he'd been at the aquarium, too—and would I please, please open up to him, not push him away when he only wanted to help?

But he knew better than to do this. One night at dinner, in mid-September, he had handed me an envelope across the table, in which I found two tickets for the *Nuclear Family* convention. I stared at them for a second, then closed the flap and muttered, "Hope you get refund. I no want go." "No prob, no prob at all," he said gently, as if to a skittish animal. He asked me if I could explain my reasons, tell him what I was feeling. I surprised us both by standing up, by shouting, "How you think I feel? I feel *insane,* okay? Insane! Now stop bother me! Get fuck off my case!" I ran down the hall, slammed my door. Before I put on my headphones, I heard him crying quietly at the table. Since then he'd been more cautious in reaching out to me.

But tonight I almost hoped he'd ask those questions. I felt so lonely I might tell him anything. Nervous, I changed the subject.

"I see you hide that phone," I said, gesturing at the couch.

Dad sat up straighter, as if about to deny this. Then he laughed. "Guilty. You caught me."

"That Owen picture, right?"

He looked surprised. "You recognized him?"

"No. Just guess."

This was another lie. A few years back, Fiona had tracked down Owen's profile online. He wore a flannel shirt and jeans in every photo—laughing in an apple orchard, carving an oversized pumpkin—a middle-aged man who worked at a garden center, handsome despite his facial scars, the maimed ear his thinning hair tried to hide. There were only a few pictures, and one was with his boyfriend, Sam, the owner of the garden center, which was located in the Southwest, a good thousand miles from us. Fiona was four when Owen left, I not even one; we both knew little about him.

"Got nostalgic," Dad told me with a weary smile. "Silly. It happen sometime."

"You ever hear from Owen?"

"No. Think he in new relationship. Well, it sixteen year. No big surprise."

"That phone," I said. "Never see it before."

"It not hooked up or anything. Just few old photo on it."

"Can I look?"

"Sure. But . . . but not tonight. Little tired."

I nodded. We both knew this meant I'd never see the photos.

But Dad did look tired, his expression warm but distant, retreated into its own secret spaces. Like me, he'd also seemed different since the shooting: anxious, pacing the house at all hours, not going out much either. He never mentioned finding a new job now, or plans to travel this fall. Maybe that violence had brought back his own violent past, of which I knew so little. Maybe his own dead were more alive inside him.

"Dad," I said, "can I ask you question? It weird weird maybe. But just need ask."

There was a vulnerability in my voice, absent since the day of the attack. His face became more present. "Def, sweetie. Anything."

"It—well. It nothing. Never mind."

Dad sighed and leaned forward, his hands clasped between the knees of his pajamas. I could see him thinking, choosing carefully what to say. "It break my heart, little fish, that you go through this. Trauma, I mean. I prayed and prayed it never happen you."

"You pray?" I asked.

"Yeah. Sometime."

I was looking past him, at a bookcase near the sofa, where an old stuffed seal sat on an upper shelf. He'd had this seal since childhood, since before the war. "Your mom and dad," I said. "When you pray, you think they listen?"

His expression clouded at these words, but he kept his composure. "Maybe. I hope so. I hope they in better place."

"I no mean heaven. What I mean is . . . not sure how say it. When they listen, you think they listen *here?*"

"Here?"

"Like, in the room. Or . . . or in your body."

His eyebrows drew together. "I little confused, sweetie. You mean in my mind? My memories?"

I realized my mistake at once. Dad missed his parents, missed the past—but this didn't mean a spirit had taken residence inside him. Or that, like me, he lived in fear the spirit would leave him. I felt a flare of anger at Dad, irrational but strong.

"Anyway, need start calculus," I said, standing from the chair. "Prob take few hour."

"I say something wrong? Stay little longer. Please. I feel like we—"

"Just *so* much homework, Dad. You no idea. Talk later."

Before he could respond, I stood from the desk chair and strode across to the staircase. I hurried up the steps, the hinges rustling in my knees.

That December, my sister returned from her study abroad program. I'd just come home from swim practice, just boiled up some YumTum, when I heard a churn of tires in the driveway. I rushed to the window with my bowl of chicken.

Outside the snow had started again, a windy snow that swirled like pollen in the station wagon's headlights. Behind the lunging wipers I could see my father and sister, neither speaking. Dad sat behind the wheel, looking hurt, a bit confused; Fiona, half reclined in her seat, stared down at her phone with a blank, closed-off expression. She was skinnier than before, all the softness gone from her face, her shapely nose out of place among the angles. Fiona had always been thin, but there was something strange about this leanness, something severe, disciplined, almost ascetic. It felt odd to see them so quiet, my usually chatty father and sister, who'd talked about the evils of hydrofracking the entire ride to the airport back in July. Now Fiona sat silent beside him, not glancing up once as the car pulled into the garage.

We both sensed her distance that night. There was a chilliness in her voice as she greeted me in the kitchen, "Hey little fish," followed by the briefest of hugs. There was a quiet coldness at dinner, Fiona aloof about her time abroad, never going into details, never working in funny stories like she would have before. I felt disappointed, resentful: for the last month she'd skipped our calls, texted excuses about final exams—and now, after half a year apart, after I'd nearly died in a shooting, she was talking to me like a stranger? Did Fiona think she was better than us? Had she become a snob overseas? The old Fiona would have led this conversation, cracked jokes and told stories, asked Dad about his research, me about my swim meets, found ways to get us all laughing with family lore: the time Dad forgot to zip his fly when he gave a toast at a wedding; the time I stole her glitter lipstick for my fifth-grade photos, my mouth a sparkly mess in every shot. Now Fiona kept to herself, only spoke when asked a direct question, like she was fulfilling some work obligation with this meal. I asked about her new friend Janice, whom she'd talked about often at the start of her program, then not at all. "Janice nice. We might stay touch," Fiona said evasively. Dad furrowed his brow as he cut a slice of his chicken.

When dinner ended she said she was "beat," then strode off to her room for the night. The reunion was over. "Well, she travel all day," Dad said to the question that hung in the air. I could tell he was disappointed, that he'd hoped for more from Fiona's return, maybe to see me come out of my shell for the first time in months. I'd hoped for the same, in my own way.

"She seem normal to me," I muttered, annoyed at the hurt I heard in my voice.

Dad gave me a hug before I could leave; I stood frozen in his arms. *She prob just worn out, sweetie,* the hug seemed to say. Tomorrow, after a good night's rest, the girl we loved would return to us.

But she didn't. Two weeks passed. The house was no longer loud with her phone calls, with the comings and goings of friends, or the rapid, resonant pops of her Ping-Pong games with Dad in the basement. She spent most days alone in her room, or gone for hours on aimless strides, her hinges creaky with cold when she came back home. To my surprise, I felt even more isolated with Fiona here, more cut off from everyone but Patrick.

Dad seemed sadder as well. In just five months, a shadow had fallen on his once happy family, beyond his understanding or control.

We expected Adam, her longtime boyfriend, to make an appearance at some point, but this proved a surprise as well: when Dad asked about him one night at dinner, she said, "Adam, oh yeah, we break up," with no more emotion than if she'd canceled a streaming service. "Why no mention?" Dad said, startled. We'd known Adam since her junior year of high school, when Fiona had fallen dizzily in love with her fellow debate team member, written passionate love poems about him, asked our advice on presents. They'd been together for over four years, and we thought they might even get married, one of those unicorn high school couples that could make it into adulthood. Fiona shrugged at Dad's question, said, "Eh, we grow apart." She changed the subject and excused herself a few minutes later.

It was as if she'd never returned from abroad, as if another, colder young woman had boarded the flight in my sister's body. For as long as I could remember, Fiona had been my friend and ally, never too busy for hangs with her shy little sister, always there to guide me as I fumbled through puberty and adolescence. She cheered for me at swim meets, wrote FamFics with me in her bedroom, helped me through my halting attempts at a social life. To her friends, depending on their mood, I could be an equal or a surrogate child, taught makeup one day, cooed over the next, or shooed away, unready for adult mysteries. I loved to watch Fiona talk, loved the vivacious flight of her hands, how the other girls waited for her thoughts and reactions before they'd chance their own. I could enfold myself in her identity, feel seen and heard as I sat silent in the background. After they left she'd take me aside, tell me her real opinions, the latest gossip. She even brought me on outings with Adam sometimes, gave me the seat between them at the movies.

But I was invisible to this new Fiona. She had no interest in my school life, or in watching *Nuclear Family,* or in driving us out to the Waterfall Café, the seaside hangout where we went to bond as sisters, chatting by the huge koi tank over mugs of cinnamon tea. On her third day back, I asked when we could go to the café. She said, "Not sure. I let you know," then never mentioned it again.

Nor did Fiona mention the shooting at the aquarium. If I caught her in the kitchen, she might hang out for a few minutes, making small talk like I was a coworker in a break room. Then she'd give some excuse—reading ahead for a course this spring, applying for an internship—to stride back to her bedroom and shut the door. If I brought up anything personal, the hang would end even sooner. She seemed distracted whenever we talked, never looked me in the eye, as if I was some dark shape she could barely see for the light that glared behind me.

One night just before Christmas, I sat at my desk at two a.m., drawing Patrick's face in clean, confident lines. I had no bedtime over winter break, no fear of Dad knocking, and would linger hours later in the lamplight. I was sketching Patrick's chin, getting the cleft in his plastic just right, when I heard the crunch of footsteps in the snow outside.

Even back then I kept my curtains closed, always guarded my privacy. I crept to the window and teased back the fabric, looked out at our backyard in the smoggy moonlight. It was just like old times: Fiona stood beside our pine tree in her parka and winter boots, smoking a zing-stick covered with foggy mountains. She lowered the stick, a Misty Mood Boost, and the cloud of her exhale rose in the cold, a shaggy mass that drifted up over the hedges.

I'd caught her hundreds of times like this, getting zinged behind the house, and I made sure she never saw me, never suspected I knew her secret, that my straight-A sister had a nightly habit. She'd started long before she was twenty-one, then had hidden her use from Dad even after it was legal. Since his bedroom faced the street, this glimpse of her private life was all my own. I'd often caught Fiona with her friends as well, a circle of girls at the pine tree, whispering, giggling, passing the stick between their pinched fingers.

I felt kinder toward Fiona as I watched her in the snow, less angry about her distance the past few weeks. Yes, she'd blown off our café trip, but was it fair what *I'd* expected of her—to return our lives to normal, to heal all the trauma in our troubled home? Maybe she'd sensed our need for her, maybe it had overwhelmed her, both her father and sister so jittery, on edge. Dad checked his news app every few minutes, woke up at five a.m. and paced the kitchen, turned off shows and movies whenever a character pulled a gun. He talked for the first time about installing bars on the windows, which he'd once mocked as a neurosis of our conservative neighbors. Some days he even had our groceries delivered rather than leave the house. When he put on his coat for work each morning, pulling the sleeves slowly over his stiff plastic arms, I could see in his face the grieved young man who'd moved to this region as a refugee, who'd lost his home to nuclear war, his parents to a refugee compound. Before the shooting at the food court, I could never picture my well-dressed father in a labor compound, wearing the factory jumpsuits I'd seen in history books at school; but now at last I could imagine him there, not a tenure-track professor but a scrawny teen on a factory floor, standing at a conveyor belt, breathing the toxic fumes.

Fiona was only twenty-one, barely an adult. To come home to these changes—it must have been difficult for her, hard to process. I stepped back from the window, released the curtain.

Back when she lived at home, Fiona had often knocked on my door after she zinged. I liked her high, how she roared at my jokes, how her mind leapt from topic to topic, how she'd pause the show and double over laughing when, inevitably, we put on some *Nuclear Family*. I didn't expect her to visit tonight, of course, not with how she'd avoided me lately. I was back at my desk, pencil in hand, when her playful knock surprised me. I stuffed the picture in a drawer, called out, "Come in!" as calmly as possible.

Fiona stepped into the room, still zippered up in her parka. This confused me: she usually changed on the porch, kept any smell of the drug from the house. Her eyes were a mess, glazed, glinting, and I could smell her from my chair, not just the reedy tang of the zing but the lower, bass-clef odor of liquor as well. In one hand she held her favorite snack, a tin of Morning Bell Chicken Bites, bell-shaped nuggets packed in a viscous fluid.

She shut the door behind her, unzipped her parka and tossed it on the bed. When she spoke, it was in the rapid robot voice of Anita, our favorite *Nuclear Family* impression:

"Good evening Erin my dear sweet sister. I hope this moonlit night finds you nifty."

I replied without hesitation: "And a gracious good evening to you my exquisite sibling. To what wondrous cause do I owe your visit?"

"I come to say a warm hello and converse in a general manner. It is splendid to have a sister to occasion such exchanges."

"I also feel this way my older sibling. Please make yourself at home in my bedroom unit."

We'd often talked this way through the years, especially on long car rides (Dad rolled his eyes and turned up the music when we wouldn't break character). Our Anita impressions had reached their height two seasons prior, when the metal cylinder starts to date a robot pop star, Sebastian Surge, and becomes a famous influencer on BotTok. Her half brother, John, quits his job at Luggage Shack to work as her assistant—until he serves her the wrong oil right before a talk show appearance. Anita goes on a wild rant in the interview; Sebastian Surge breaks up with her the next day. For a while, Fiona and I could recite her entire talk show rant, sometimes performed the whole interview in the car.

"Sister hang initiating. Set motors for maximum fun," Fiona said in a tinny voice as she crossed the carpet. She flopped down on my beanbag chair, a hollow thud of plastic on vinyl. The stuffing bulged up around her. She was very drunk and zinged, not herself at all; in another way, this was the most herself I'd seen her since she returned.

"You watching show lately?" she asked me.

"Def. Never stop." I didn't tell her the way I'd been watching *Nuclear Family:* often not turning the show on at all, just shutting my eyes in my bedroom at night. Episodes with new characters and settings played on the screen in my mind.

"I love these new fur-cube character," Fiona went on. "They bonker. It so funny John go casino with them. I like, *John, no bet your time machine! You need that!*"

I laughed. "He get it back by end of episode."

"Course. How else he steal more dinosaur egg?"

She took out her phone and put on a LAS song: lighters flicking and sand pouring over a mellow funk beat, one of the best Rhythm & Noise genres she'd shown me over the years. Fiona had shaped my taste in music, steered me away from mainstream sounds and toward more nuanced noises: roller skates and snow shovels, trampolines and crumpled paper, sounds with shifting textures. She even played me my first BAMM song, the hypnotic marriage of beats and marine mammals. Without her, I'd probably just listen to Top 40 R&N.

She plucked a gooey nugget from the tin, chewed with a lopsided smile.

"You up late, little fish," she said, her normal voice more slurred. "What doing?"

"Oh, no much. Just some homework."

"Two a.m. on break. You do homework?"

"Yeah. It . . . long-term assignment. Research paper."

She looked past me at my desktop, completely bare. I wondered if she'd heard me hide the drawing.

"I just finish," I added too quickly.

Fiona raised her eyebrows: even drunk, she knew when I was lying. But she let this pass, finished chewing her chicken bite. As the lump slid down her throat, she glanced at the swimming trophies on my bureau.

"You get some new one," she said.

"Three. Win lot at regional."

"Dad tell me. Sound like real good season."

"Best yet, Coach Greely say."

"Damn. That wow wow, sis. Never know how you do it."

I shrugged. "Just love the water."

Fiona looked down at her lap, squeezed a nugget in the tin. The fluid pooled around her fingers.

"I see them all, you know. Your swim meet. I stream every one."

This confused me even more. At college, Fiona had always watched my meets on our team's website, but at her abroad program she'd said that the streams wouldn't load for some reason—maybe an issue with foreign sites, she wasn't sure. But even without her to cheer me, I'd won more races this last season than ever before, the water more intimate to me now, the clear conductor of Patrick's spirit, my love around me and within me as I kicked with the strength of two. If I kept up these lap times, Coach Greely said, I could expect at least half tuition, maybe a full ride to college.

"You watch my meet this fall?" I asked her. "Why no say?"

"Your coach right. Best season yet. It not just speed, but way you swim. Free. Forceful."

"And you watch live?"

She nodded.

"Then why no text? That like best part. Ever check my phone right after race."

"No be silly, little fish. You great athlete now. No need text from stupid sister."

"Not true. Miss you, Fiona. Dad and me, we both do."

She laughed to herself, a soft chortle through her nose. Then she responded as Anita:

"I appreciate your words of thoughtful kindness. Alas, the stressful semester hindered my normal texting habits. I now feel much regret."

"Eh, don't sweat it, kid," I said as Morris.

She laughed again.

Later, for years, I'd relive this talk, our last real conversation before she vanished. If I was keeping secrets that night, my sister was keeping many more.

Fiona was looking at the trophies again. A tiny swimmer perched on each pedestal, their arms outstretched in diving positions, their hands fused together palm to palm. She said:

"You and Dad, you both so dif since I get home. And you the most, sis. No offense, but you super weird now."

"Me? What mean?"

"You just *dif*. Way you talk, look—you real far off. Here, but not here."

I drew my toe along the carpet, etched a *P* that faded from the fibers. So Fiona had been aware of me after all. Watching me, like I was watching her.

"School hard this year," I said. "Ton test."

She wasn't buying that. "It attack? You still think it lot?"

"Guess so. Now then."

She and I had discussed the shooting just once on her calls from abroad. Like now, I'd been vague, evasive. Part of me wanted to tell her the truth—my months of obsession, my lonely flight from reality—but I was nervous as always to speak about Patrick. I worried I'd break the enchantment, that he'd leave me just as swiftly as he'd arrived. Fiona went on:

"But it more than that. Way you act, it like . . . secret. Like you hide big secret."

"You away long time. Six month. I prob just change little."

Fiona looked at me directly. "You pregnant?"

I let out a giggle, pressed a hand to my mouth, dissolved into hysterics.

"Pregnant!" I cried through my fingers. "From who?"

"How I know? I not here."

"Pregnant!" I cried again.

Fiona wasn't amused. "I know two girl get pregnant," she said. "They seventeen eighteen. Both act just like you. Weird. Distant."

I was wiping tears from my eyes, my laughter subsiding. The idea of me with child, of having enough of a social life to get into that predicament—it was the funniest thing I'd heard in months.

"You no need worry," I said. "Promise."

"Lot people freak out after terror attack. Act strange new way."

"Not me. Not that much."

"Then what go on with you?" she asked.

"You know, it not like you so normal lately. You much distant, too."

Fiona smiled. "We not talking me."

I crossed my legs beneath me, more relaxed after laughing. For a second I felt like my old self again, the girl from before the attack, who'd talked and joked with my sister for hours on nights like this. The girl who'd lived out in the open, not in a windowless cell with her love.

"You know what bug me?" I said. "These terror group. I get they have cause, big big cause, important. And it true: we def need less pollution, cleaner planet. But these group, they reckless, they go kill random people. *Innocent* people. And what if one those people— what if he, I dunno . . . Like, what if he your soulmate? Love of life, future husband. But now he gone. And when he die, it not like—"

Fiona was smirking, as if she found some dark amusement in my words. Self-conscious, I cut myself off.

"What funny?" I asked.

I sensed her coldness returning, a tension in the room.

"Think fifty year from now," she said. "Think hundred. More ocean rise, more animal extinct. More heat, storm, flooding, drought. If smart, we make change now, use clean energy. But people no want listen. Change cost too much money."

"But no need violence. Can protest peaceful—def much better."

Fiona shook her head. "People . . . they need feel this message *close*. We so obsessed our own world, we forget we part of nature, that we die if destroy planet. So message need cut deep, feel life death. Then we listen. No choice but listen then."

Her voice was firm and didactic, even with its drunken slur. I grew quiet for a moment. Finally I said: "So what happen to me at aquarium. You think that right?"

"Not glad it happen you, sis. But thing like that need happen."

"That scary. You sound scary, Fiona."

"You think that scary? What scary is world *without* ecoterrorist. What scary is us, right now, our civilization: the temp rising, the forest burning, so many species gone. The terrorist, they fight for better future. Someone need to. If not, we just dig grave. We digging long time now."

"But killing wrong," I said.

Fiona shrugged. "People kill in war. Not wrong if war good cause."

"We not at war, though. The war over."

She laughed, tossed a chicken bite into her mouth. "Oh, little fish. The war just starting."

# NUCLEAR FAMILY

## "The Fallout"

After school one day, Max sits in the bedroom set of his friend Liam. The boys lounge in leather armchairs, staring at a stream of photos on the opposite wall: a social media feed beamed from a ceiling projector. The faces of classmates and celebrities glide past them, breathtaking views and adorable pets, the occasional political ad of President Wafflin saluting the flag, an assault rifle slung across his bready grid.

Liam, a spiky-haired boy of fourteen, controls the feed with a rapid thumb on his phone screen. The bedroom around him is luxurious but messy—designer clothing strewn on the floor, empty soda cans on the window seat, some snack bags tossed beside the balcony door—the room of a rich kid left to his own devices. The set lights shine through the broad windows, bathing the boys in a fake winter sunlight.

With a moan of pain, Liam stops the feed at a girl from their high school.

"*Damn.* Just look at Amy," he says, ogling a female robot. The metal cylinder is propped in a Prada charging station, her light bulb nose glowing a soft violet. The caption reads: *I am acquiring the energy required for a diverting night on the town.*

"God . . . what a mouth slot," Liam goes on. "Wouldn't you love to stick your tongue in there? Get a spark?"

Max, seated beside him, makes an awkward noise of assent. The laugh track titters.

Liam scrolls to a picture of the Zane sisters, a pair of waffle twins, standing rim to rim with some whipped cream in their cheek squares. "Check out these two," he says, "they're a total snack. So what if they're ultraconservatives. Some guys aren't into waffles—but me? I'm a regular dough boy." The laugh track loudens. "What about you, Max? You like waffles?"

"I, uh . . . yeah. I liked a waffle once."

"Really? Who?"

Max takes a deep breath, as if on the verge of sharing a major secret. Then he glances down at a Burberry sweater on the floor.

"No one you know. It was at camp."

"Speaking of waffles," Liam says, "where's O these days? You haven't brought him over the past few weeks."

Max shrugs. "Not sure. He must be busy."

"He get a girlfriend or something? He wasn't at Todd's birthday either."

"Could be a girlfriend. Or hanging with other people."

"Don't you know?" Liam asks. "You live in the same cul-de-sac."

Before Max can answer, Liam glances back at the social media feed. There's a new post from Amber Zane, the more political of the waffle sisters, the disk-shaped girl holding a flag, making kissy lips at the camera. *God bless President Wafflin,* reads her caption. *He finally showed the world who boss. So proud 2 be citizen 2day.*

Below this is a link to a news article:

*President Wafflin Launches Nuclear Strike. Says "Justice Served" by Surprise Attack. Full Declaration of War Expected Soon.*

"What the . . ." Liam mumbles. "That's a joke, right?"

"Open it," Max says.

The boys lean forward in their chairs and read the wall-sized article, both silent in the simulated sunlight. They see the numbers killed in the missile strikes—estimated in the millions—then the larger number predicted to die from radioactive fallout. Below this is satellite footage of a missile strike: an aerial view of a seaside city, hundreds of boats in its harbor, its roads and bridges crowded with rush-hour traffic—until, in less than a second, the entire coastline vanishes in a vast swell of light, a geyser of cloud. Max and Liam watch the cloud surge skyward, billowing up to fill the camera frame.

The boys say nothing for a long moment.

"I don't get it," Liam murmurs. "Nuclear bombs . . . they're so unpopular. My mom said Wafflin would never use them."

"My mom, too," Max agrees. "She said he doesn't have the starch."

The laugh track gives a nervous giggle.

"He just killed, like—like five million people?"

"Well, it only just happened," Max says. "Those numbers might be wrong."

Liam nods. "Yeah. Maybe there's more survivors than they think."

On the laugh track a man chuckles, but the other audience members shush him.

Hours after dinner, Max and his parents sit in the living room set, watching footage of a fallout shelter on the news. Hundreds of people huddle in the warehouse-like bunker, robots and waffles and figurines, some pacing the aisles between the cots, some seated in worried silence, their suitcases stacked around them in messy heaps. A headline reads: *East Coast Prepares for Possible Nuclear Attack.*

"I'm surprised those waffles *went* to shelters," his father says bitterly. "Most of them, they're calling this a 'media conspiracy.' The stupid Batter Heads."

"Gary," Jess says in a warning tone. She tilts her head toward Max.

"Not O, of course," his father adds. "O's a great kid. But the rest of them? Don't get me started."

Gary's phone begins to ring on the coffee table. A photo of the caller, *Iris,* appears on the screen: a female robot propped on a sand dune, her googly eyes revolved off-center, a flower lei wrapped around her middle. The laugh track burbles in expectation.

"You can call her back later," Jess says. "You just talked twenty minutes ago."

Gary reaches for the phone. "She's terrified. I'll be quick."

"She and Anita—they live out West. They're the safest of anyone we know."

"Iris, hey," he says, the call already answered. "How you holding up?"

A metallic voice booms from the earpiece, audible to all in the room. "Hello Gary my dear ex-husband. We are still the same thank goodness, but alas we grow more anxious with each hour. My processors are spinning like a windmill in a tempest."

"We'll get through this, hon. We will. We'll all get through it together."

"The horror of this, ex-husband. So many millions melted at the altar of one man's pride."

"Well . . . let's just be glad we're not on the coast. That's where the danger is right now. If the missile defense fails—"

"I do not mean to scare you, former spouse. But my data scans reveal a greater danger. A danger the news has hidden from the masses."

"Oh, Iris. Don't go on those websites where—"

"I ask you this, my onetime groom. If our enemies assail us, why will their warheads not strike farther inland? Alas, I fear they may with deadly speed. For now we all must watch the sky for portents."

Gary glances at his son. Then he stands and strides down the hallway to his study.

"Is that true?" Max asks his mother. "The bombs . . . they could fall anywhere?"

Jess shrugs. "Iris is a robot, sweetie. She's online way too much."

The laugh track roars.

The news now plays a press conference from earlier today. President Wafflin stands at a wide podium, his circular body strobing with camera flashes. In an aggrieved voice he says:

"Weak. That's how they treated us—like we were weak. Like they could push us around, do whatever they wanted." He slams a rubber fist on the podium, stirring the cords of his bolo tie. "Well, now they see who we really are. Now they see we're strong. History, folks—it's full of moments like these. When you stand up to the bully, or just let the bully win. Because that's what they are, folks, these nations against us. Bullies. All of them, bullies."

"He's so . . ." Max begins. "What's the word for it, Mom? When you think everyone's against you?"

"Paranoid."

"Yeah. He's so paranoid."

Jess runs a shaky hand through her hair, staring at the vengeful breakfast food. Down the hall, Gary steps out from his study.

"Give my love to Anita," he says into his phone. "Make sure you both stock up on lots of oil."

The laugh track howls.

Later that night, Max lies awake in his bedroom, his dolphin blanket pulled up to his chin. Fake snow is falling past his window, streaming down in rippling trails; fake icicles are glued onto the frame. Outside he hears a car trunk slam, then a hurried churn of tires through the snow.

As the car grows fainter, Max sits up in bed and looks into the camera. He lifts his stuffed seal into his lap, then begins to narrate out loud:

I wonder what O is doing right now. Knowing him, he's probably arguing with his parents. Telling them the bombings were wrong, that their hero President Wafflin is a mass murderer. Will his parents listen to him? No, of course not. But he'll try—he always does.

I wish I could call him tonight, check that he's okay. But, well, things changed between us last month . . . *really* changed. We had this sleepover at his house, and we snuck some beers from the pantry, and we both got drunk so fast, I didn't expect it. Then all of a sudden we were kissing, kissing like crazy. O held me against his bread, told me he'd wanted to kiss me for years.

It felt like magic, like a fantasy come true. But the next morning, when I woke up in his arms? I was terrified. So I hurried home, ignored his calls, avoided him for weeks. And now—now I'm too embarrassed to even text him.

Well . . . I guess I'll go talk to Morris.

Max pulls back his blanket, shuffles across the dark bedroom set. Above the bureau, the little Christ snores softly on his cross. Max pokes his stomach and he murmurs in his sleep: "Oh . . . wow . . . that's awful. Goneril. She's the worst."

The laugh track rustles. Max pokes his stomach again.

"Whoa," Morris says groggily. "I was having the *dullest* dream. I was at this Christmas party with King Lear. He kept talking and talking."

"Who's King Lear?"

Morris shakes his head. "No one you'd want to get stuck with in the snack line."

The laugh track bellows.

"So, uh . . ." Max begins. He still holds his stuffed seal, gripped against his side. "Did you hear what happened today? The missile strikes?"

A look of grief settles on the Savior's face. Sadly he says, "I'm on a cross, kid. Not living in a cave."

Some men on the laugh track guffaw; others refrain.

"I just don't understand it," Max goes on. "These bombs shouldn't even *exist*. How can anyone be this cruel?"

Morris wiggles his fingers, showcasing the nails in his palms. "It's been this way for a minute."

"But why does God allow it? Can't God just make it stop?"

An urgent knocking comes at Max's door. An instant later his mother steps into the room, flipping the light switch on with a brisk hand. She is bundled up in winter clothes, a puffy magenta parka, a plaid scarf and snow pants. Her face looks alert, threatened, like a deer hearing hunters in the distance.

"Mom," Max says, "is everything . . ."

"Sweetie, I need you to listen, okay? I need you to really listen. We have to—we have to leave. We have to get out of here. In the next ten minutes."

"Leave?"

"Some missiles made it through. Quite a few missiles. There's lots of radiation."

"We were attacked?" Max asks, a step behind her.

"I've already packed you some clothes. Now get your suitcase from your closet, grab a few things to take. But be fast—and put on your snowsuit."

"How . . . how close did the bombs fall?"

"We'll talk in the car. Just pack now, sweetie. Quick."

His mother strides off down the hall. Max, stunned, stares at the empty doorway. Down the block, he hears another car fleeing through the snow.

"Uh, Max?" Morris asks from his cross.

Max glances over. The Savior gives him a nervous smile.

"Could you take out my nails for a minute?"

"You want to sing a song?" Max asks. *"Now?"*

"It's how I express myself best."

"Morris, there really isn't—"

"Fine, no dance number. I'll make this snappy. Hit it, boys!"

A jittery rock groove plays on the soundtrack, a jagged guitar riff above a jumpy bassline. The spotted light of a mirror ball sweeps across Morris, who sways his splayed body to the drumbeat. He sings:

> *Tonight begins a new world war,*
> *A global conflagration:*
> *Millions dead and millions more*
> *In flight from radiation.*

*So hurry now, no time to waste—*
*Put on your snowsuit, Max—*
*And when you grab your suitcase*
*There's one guy you ought to pack . . .*

A row of wooden icon paintings appears on the wall beside him, all showing scenes of Max and Morris together: cheering at a Shmuglin game, running from a haunted mansion, playing dodgeball with two floating cubes of fur, each with a giant eye and a whirring propeller on their top. "I *get* it," Max says impatiently, "you want me to bring—" But Morris is already launching into the chorus:

*Your loyal little Savior!*
*Your pal from Calvary!*
*From Pilate to the manger*
*There's no other friend like me.*

*Your loyal little Savior!*
*Your buddy on the cross!*
*What sidekick could be better*
*In a nuclear holocaust?*

*So don't forget old Morris*
*When you flee from your home:*
*It's no fun for a crucifix*
*In a fallout zone.*

"Okay! Enough!" Max cries. The rock track ends abruptly; the mirror ball stops spinning. "I was planning to pack you, Morris. You didn't need to sing a whole song."

"Really? *Phew*. That's such a relief. You know, Gethsemane and all . . . a guy like me gets ditched sometimes."

The laugh track wails.


Max comes stumbling down the stairs in his snowsuit, lugging his overstuffed suitcase with both hands. Below him, his parents make hectic preparations: Jess shoving chicken breasts into a cooler, Gary staggering to the garage with a huge rat cage in his arms, the bars adorned with an intricate roller skate pattern. Inside, her forepaws clasped in prayer, Daphne kneels before an altar with a tiny funeral urn. The base of the urn reads:

> *Blorko, Blorko, he did not die:*
> *He's bound for that roller rink in the sky.*

Across the set, the doorbell gives two sharp, sustained rings. Jess lifts her head from the cooler with a look of concern.

"I'll get it," she says to Max. She hurries to the foyer, presses an eye to the peephole.

"It's O. Just O," she says with relief. She pulls the door open.

Under the porch awning, the fake snow falling behind him, the waffle boy stands shivering in his jacket, his bread swelling and contracting with his heavy breathing. In his right mitten he grips a bulging duffel bag.

Jess notices the duffel; the relief leaves her face. "Hi, hon. Is there . . . Can we help you with something?"

The waffle is covered in damp spots from the snow; a sheen of tears rims his rubber eyes. In an unsteady voice he says:

"I'm so sorry to just . . . to show up like this. But my parents— they told me they're not leaving. They think it's all a hoax. A *liberal scam*," he adds with an angry quaver.

Jess looks amazed. "They think we weren't bombed?"

"No, they believe that part. But the radiation . . . they don't think it's spreading this far. All their message boards are saying it—that the media's just trying to make Wafflin look bad."

"They're staying here. Dear God."

"I told them we need to *go*. Right now," O continues. "But they're not budging. Neither is my brother."

Jess glances back at Max, who stands behind her in the doorway. O catches sight of his friend and raises an awkward mitten in greeting. Max raises a hand as well.

"So . . . what are you saying?" Jess asks the waffle.

Max exhales noisily. "Don't play dumb, Mom. His bag is right there."

"But honey, we need our supplies. And the minivan is—"
"*Mom.*"

"You're right, you're right," Jess says. Shamefaced, she turns to the shivering teen. "I'm sorry, this is all really . . . what a night, you know?"

"I can come with you?" O asks, his face brightening.

"Of course, dear. Of course you can. Now come in out of the snow. You'll get all soggy."


The final scene is filmed in an outdoor location. The opening shot shows a highway between two fields of melting snow, the road stretching for miles into the wintry distance. Hundreds of cars are packed bumper-to-bumper in the icy lanes, most of the engines silent to save their fuel. Many people have stepped from their cars, milling about in the morning sunlight, sitting on hoods, peeing over guardrails, munching on pre-boiled poultry. A game of Shmuglin is underway along the center median, ten figurines with muddy paddles sprinting across the slush.

Max, a blanket drawn around him, sits reading at the back of the family minivan. Now and then he looks up at O, who lies sleeping at the opposite end of the bench. A giant beanie covers his upper curve; his bread is slightly bent with the angle of the seatback. As the waffle shifts in his sleep, Max gazes tenderly at the indents of his face.

The two are alone in the minivan. After a moment, O stirs again and stretches his stubby legs, his snow pants crinkling. He looks bewildered at first, blinking awake on the frigid bench. Max lowers his eyes, pretends to be reading his book.

The waffle yawns and turns to the window. He stares out at the traffic with a faraway expression, the squares of his face tightened in a subtle play of emotion, as if the events of last night are returning to him slowly: the bombings, the flight from his home, the loss of his family. Then, with a startled laugh, he squints at the slushy figurines on the median.

"They're playing Shmuglin?" he says.

Max nods. "It was Dad's idea—no big surprise there. He went around knocking on windows. Turns out lots of guys brought their paddles."

"How long have we been here?"

"Three hours or so. The radio said it could be all day."

"And . . . we're safe?"

"For now. We got pretty far from the fallout last night."

O chuckles again. "Well, the world's ending. Guess they should Shmugle while they can."

"We can go out and watch if you want. Traffic's not moving anytime soon."

"No thanks. After what Wafflin did, I'll keep away from figurines with paddles. They'll probably try to chop off my crust."

The laugh track gives an uncertain chortle.

Max looks out at the highway. Figurines and robots are everywhere, but not a single waffle has stepped outside their car. A robot father and son play catch on the roadside, shooting a ball back and forth between their mouth slots.

"It's so unfair," Max says. "You *hate* President Wafflin."

O gives a weary shrug. Then he takes his phone from his parka and switches it on. "You getting service?"

"Not a bar since last night. Lots of towers got knocked out."

"It's so weird. My family . . . I'd always planned to leave them anyway. When I got old enough, went to college—that'd be it, I'd break off contact. But I didn't think it would be like this. Nothing like this."

"They might be okay, you know. This scientist was on the radio. She said the radiation isn't as bad for bread."

The laugh track stays silent.

O wipes a tear from his eye, but his expression remains the same, as if he's only brushing away a crumb. "You don't need to pretend, Max. I know they're goners. And . . . and it's okay. I mean, it's *not* okay. Of course it's not. But maybe—maybe I don't even love them."

"Sure you do. They're your family."

O wipes another tear away, then looks back out the window. "Wait a second," he says, "is your dad the *Shmugler?*"

Indeed he is. In one of the goal zones, Gary crawls on all fours with a purple bucket strapped to his head, trying to catch the ball when a paddle hits it his way. His face is slathered with slush, his snowsuit filthy. Jess, seated on a guardrail, one of thirty or so who watch the game, looks past her muddy husband toward the icy, glittering tree line in the distance. None of the spectators clap or call to the players, as if unaware a game is happening at all.

The boys grow quiet, watching Gary scrabble through the muck. Then, in a tentative voice, Max says:

"You know . . . we could be your family now. Me and my parents."

O rolls his eyes. "C'mon, Max. Cut the bullshit."

"What?"

"I'm your *family* now? You don't even want to be friends."

"Of course I do. How can you say that?"

"You didn't answer like fifteen texts. You avoided me at lunch. You changed your gym class."

"That was a scheduling thing. I needed a—a different science lab."

"Look," O says, "you didn't want me to die last night. Thanks for that. But short of a nuclear war, you were done with me."

Max raises a finger to the steamed window, squiggles a looping line. "I just felt . . . scared, I guess. Weren't you scared?"

"What's to be scared of?"

"You and me, we've been best friends for years. Then, out of nowhere, we start making out all night? Confessing our feelings? And all in—"

"It wasn't out of nowhere."

"No, I guess not," Max admits.

"I thought you'd be happy. *I* was happy."

Max turns from the squiggled steam. "You see, that's why I couldn't talk to you. You think everyone can be like you—brave, unique, different. But I didn't grow up like you, rejecting my family, getting all independent. I'm not used to being different. I don't like it."

"It's not about whether you like it, Max. It's just who you are."

"But I don't *like* who I am. I didn't ask for this. For any of it."

The waffle sighs. "Fine, you were scared. But did you have to be such an asshole? I shared so much with you—and then you just blew me off. Cut me out of your life."

Max looks down at his feet, where his suitcase lies tucked

beside the bench. There, jutting from a side pocket, Morris frowns at him from the cross. *You need to a-pol-o-gize,* he mouths in silence, shaking his thorn-crowned head.

The laugh track whoops in time to each syllable, pleased at the obvious humor.

Max opens his book, glares down at a random page. Then he huffs and slaps it closed.

"I *am* sorry, you know. It wasn't right, avoiding you. But dammit, O, don't tell me I was done being friends. That's just stupid. You're all I thought about. I missed you every day."

O is silent for a moment. Finally, in a cold, far-off voice, he says: "I'm fucking in love with you, okay? I have been forever. The world's ending, my family's dead, and I don't want to play these stupid high school games. High school's over anyway."

Max stares at the waffle in amazement. But before he can say a word, they hear an unexpected sound: a vast rumbling of vehicles in the distance.

The boys turn to the back window. A half mile down the median, they see a long column of army trucks approaching, their chain-wrapped tires whipping up the slush, so that the trucks look like they are driving through TV static. Each truck has a covered cargo bed, room for many passengers in their holds. Behind the windshields sit waffle soldiers, all dressed in violet hazmat suits, their rubber features blurred behind their face shields.

"Great. More fascist waffles," mutters O. "Just when I couldn't get any more popular."

A loudspeaker blares from each truck: *Attention! Please exit your cars and line up in an orderly manner! One piece of luggage per vehicle! Attention! Please exit your cars and line up in an orderly manner! One piece of luggage per vehicle!*

Not looking away, Max reaches down for O's hand. Their mitten and glove squeeze tightly.

"Uh . . . Max?" says an anxious voice from the suitcase. "Sounds like you're packing again. Don't forget your loyal little—"

"It's okay, Morris. I'll make sure you're with us."

Morris relaxes on the cross, as much as he can with nails in his palms and feet. "You know, this might not be all bad. I bet lots of people packed crucifixes like me. Maybe I could get a poker night going."

There are a few uneasy chuckles as the credits begin to roll.

## 11

The blanket lies disheveled on their bare plastic bodies, its satin border rumpled across their chests. Nestled together, Erin and Jacob loll on her pillows in happy fatigue. Their clothing is scattered on her carpet, jeans and bra and boxers, his gray hoodie, her Klacky Klack T-shirt. A condom wrapper glistens below the bedside lamp, next to some index cards with NAT study questions.

Jacob chuckles to himself, the lamplight gleaming off his tired, sated face.

Well, he says. That one way get ready for test.

Erin smirks. We should do that in car tomorrow. Right before you go in. You ace your NAT no prob.

Sure. But Grandma there, too. Might be little awkward.

So we tell her stay home. *Your grandson need quickie in parking lot.* She def understand.

Jacob laughs again, turning on the pillow to face her. His

wide-set eyes, though not focused on Erin, convey an intimate warmth.

God, I exhausted. That wow wow.

We study like seven hour. We earn it.

I love we get *loud* at your place. In my Body, so nervous Grandma hear me. Like I hear her and Dave.

Erin giggles. You poor thing. Need buy you some earplug.

I put on headphone, trust me. Just wish I get more warning.

Maybe she text you first? *Hey Jacob, me Dave about get busy. Turn up music next ten minute.*

It last longer than that, he mutters.

Erin slips a hand inside his hair, watching the strands of nylon sift through her fingers. Well, you stay here anytime. Next booty call with Dave? Just text and I come rescue.

Thank. You my hero.

It come with price, she says and gives his neck a nibble, her plastic teeth tapping against his surface.

The figurines snuggle closer, Erin resting her cheek on his chest, their glossy legs exposed among the tangles of the blanket. After a moment, Jacob says gently:

Hey. I want ask you something.

Sure.

So . . . listen. If you no want talk it, I understand. But last time I ask, you just change subject.

Ask me what? she says.

If you have boyfriend before me. Or girlfriend. I much in dark.

Erin stares across the room at her bureau, where her row of trophies once stood. She doesn't respond.

No presh, he adds. You just never talk your past much.

That true. It . . . it kinda painful.

Def, he says, a shade of unease in his voice. Forget I mention.

But maybe—maybe it time now. You tell me all your stuff. Only fair I tell mine.

Jacob smiles. Not gonna lie, I wonder for while.

Thing is, sweetie . . . it real embarrass. I worry you judge me.

How *I* judge? I tell you my first time sex. That hookup when first get Body.

Erin laughs. When that girl become giant caterpillar?

It most embarrass ever. I so new there, no check her Kink List—no know that a thing. All sudden I in bed with horny insect. She saying, *Make me butterfly! Make me butterfly!*

But my stuff, Jacob . . . it not like that. It not funny. It, well—it sorta strange.

Sex with caterpillar not strange?

This strange in dif way. In high school, I real bad shape.

In a quiet voice, Erin begins to tell him her history with Patrick. She describes the day of the aquarium shooting: how a handsome boy had smiled at her an instant before the gunfire, how she'd felt his spirit rush inside her when he crumpled to the pavement. She describes how Patrick remained with her, the years of dreams and drawings, the world she built for them in EZ Pal—how, for a long time, this world had seemed more real than the one outside her Body, a predictable world, a world she could control.

Jacob rubs her back as she talks, his palm stroking her surface with a soft friction. An edge of his lip twitches whenever she mentions the aquarium shooting. After she describes her life in EZ Pal, he puts his arm around her and says:

Oh, Erin. Me you, so much in common—ever hide away from world. That program, you still go there?

No, no. Not for over year.

How it end? What make you leave?

Erin hesitates. I just come to senses one day. He not real, none of it real. So I log out. Never go back.

I sorry you lose him. The real Patrick, I mean. How old he?

Eighteen. About be senior.

Jacob shakes his head. Fucking terrorist. So unfair.

She sighs. Truth is, Patrick—he total stranger. Never really know him. Just get obsessed.

Well, it make sense. You right there when he die. When that fucker kill him.

First time I see someone die. First terror attack, too.

Jacob's upper lip twitches again. She takes his hand, drifts a nervous thumb along his knuckles.

And . . . you no think it weird weird? she asks.

What mean?

That I live with dead boy? Build house for him?

You go through trauma. Bad bad trauma. This world, there nothing "weird weird" anymore.

Guess that true, she says with a muted laugh.

It sound lonely, though. Hate think you so alone.

Yeah. Wish I tell my dad more. That my big regret.

Jacob holds her closer against him. One day, the government catch them—all these terrorist. Lock them up, strap them in meltdown chair. When younger, I hate death penalty. But now, for *them?* Not sure what think.

Erin rests her head against his chest, wraps her arms around his hollow torso. A look of worry clouds her sunken eyes.

Bent forward at the steering wheel, the windshield lashed with rain, Erin eases her sedan into the parking lot. At the far end stands a long brick building, its roof battered by the downpour,

its front sidewalk lined with flinching puddles. NATIONAL APTI-
TUDE TESTING CENTER, reads the sign above the awning.

In the passenger seat, Katherine stares through the rain at
the bland, squarish building, three stories of gray brick with no
windows on the first two floors. A car in the lot comes splashing
toward them; the driver, a teenage boy in a sweater vest, weeps
openly at the wheel.

Just love it here, she mumbles.

Erin swashes through a pothole and parks a few rows from
the entrance, in sight of the metal sliding door where Jacob will
soon emerge. An armed guard stands under the awning, blurred
behind a curtain of water that shimmers down and shatters on
the sidewalk.

It such bullshit, Katherine says. They should let us go in get
him. What they think we do? Start smashing up computer?

Erin checks the time on her phone. Only five more min. God.
He prob do exit counseling now.

I wish could smash computer. Smash their face, too.

He seem much ready, though, Erin says. He pass PNAT few
day back. And he say good sleep last night.

The old woman opens her purse, takes a quick nip from
her flask. She offers it to Erin, who takes a gulp as well. Their
worried faces sour as they swallow.

On the front wall of the building glows an LED screen, playing a cheerful cartoon for the parking lot to view. In it the mascot of the test—a peppy kangaroo named NATalie—hops up to
a testing center on a bright summer morning, a Study Guide
peeping from her pouch. The guard, a jolly panda, high-fives
the kangaroo as she approaches. *You got this, NATalie!* reads the
caption.

Katherine gives a bitter snort of laughter, then sips again from
her flask. In a thickened voice she says:

I need keep perspective here. Even if Jacob fail test . . . not end of world. It sad, very sad, but life—*life*—it not about dumb test. It about family, friend, community. People you love.

Erin nods at the flask. Great point. I have some more that?

The old woman chuckles. Her face is serene for a moment, until, as she passes the flask, the cartoon kangaroo catches her eye once more. NATalie is now on a tour of the center, hopping down a hallway of glass-fronted offices, each with a well-dressed animal at a computer: a tiger in tweed, a bespectacled badger, a pigeon pecking a keyboard. *This where it all happen,* says the tour guide, an ostrich in a pantsuit. *Each day top expert improve our test—that way we best society possible.* NATalie shakes her head in wonder. *Craze amaze!* she cries.

Want strangle that kangaroo, Katherine says.

This video new. When I take test, they play army recruitment video.

Erin's phone chimes in her pocket. She pulls it from her jeans and reads: *Just get done. Coming out now.*

It him? Katherine asks. What he say?

He finish. Here in sec.

Nothing else?

No . . .

Oh. Well. Okay.

Erin gropes below her seat, grasps a tiny travel umbrella. I go get him. Be right back.

Katherine gives her a dim smile. I too old for this. Dear Lord.

The storm is louder outside the sedan; Erin's sneakers are soaked in seconds. The frail umbrella quakes above her as she hurries toward the entrance, her rigid legs barely bending in her haste. Rainfall rushes off the roof, angles down the awning, roils the puddles along the sidewalk, a seething sound like water at full boil. She whispers under her breath: *Let peace be my whole thing. Let peace be my whole thing.*

As she nears the entrance, the metal door slides open. Jacob stands in the lobby with his cane extended, his finger hinges tight around the handle. His mouth is set in a firm line, his sunglasses silvered in the storm-light. He takes a few steps and then comes to a stop, his face bare of emotion, like some stoic wax sculpture of himself.

He grips his cane tighter when he hears Erin approaching. She lowers her umbrella, rests a hand on his stiff forearm.

Oh, honey, she says. Least it over. Can forget now.

Jacob says nothing.

You hungry? she asks. Want get some Boil Barn?

He clears his throat. Erin. My test score . . . I no understand. I study so much.

It okay. You no need talk it.

Not sure how—how get that score. Just so confused.

You prob in shock little. But listen, we figure all out. This not end. Just beginning.

He inclines his head. Really?

Really.

Good! he says, lifting his face. Because I pass!

Erin takes a step away. Wait. *What?*

I in top ten percentile.

You *pass?*

Well, top ten for region.

You asshole! she cries in joy. You total asshole!

She drops her umbrella and hugs him, embracing Jacob so hard his plastic moans. Behind them the guard says: This not coffee shop, people—time you go now. But even the guard sounds pleased, reluctantly moved.

In the parking lot a car door wrenches open. A frantic voice foghorns through the rain:

*Pass? He pass?*

Katherine stands drenched beside the sedan, her purse knocked to the pavement, her argent hair plastered to her cheeks. Erin cups her mouth and shouts to her: He pass!

The old woman falls back against the car, shot dead with relief. Then she takes a tipsy step forward and raises both her middle fingers at the LED screen.

Go fuck self, *NATalie!* she yells at the kangaroo, who now whistles a happy tune as she hops to her testing computer. Go fuck self and die!

Erin, laughing, links an arm with Jacob. We better go. Your grandma gonna get us all arrested.


She drives from the lot a few minutes later, bopping her head to the BWAA track that bubbles from her stereo: brisk accordion chords over the whir of bicycle wheels. In the back seat, Jacob says excitedly:

And I just focus. Just *lock in.* No need my ChillDude even. It freakin' amaze.

See? Katherine says. You genius. Like I told you.

Genius—ha! Just glad that over.

Katherine leans back in her seat, her sodden raincoat squelching. God, can finally breathe. No breathe in month. In year.

Jacob laughs. First thing I do now? Delete my Study Guide. Never think that shit again.

Amen! Erin shouts.

Amen! he repeats. Oh, and I forget tell you. This guy from NAT class, Tyler Riggs? He there today, pass, too.

He funny one, right? Class clown?

Yeah, Tyler much hilar. He ask if we want celebrate tonight.

Sure. Sound fun.

Great, I message him. He in Smartworld many year. Got big mansion Shimmer Space.

Shimmer Space? Erin says, her voice more subdued. Whoa. Fancy fancy.

Guess his family rich. He say he send us guest pass.

Erin turns down the music. Shimmer Space . . . that ad-free area? No commercial there?

Not sure. That place so pricey, maybe no commercial.

Good you, honey, Katherine says drowsily. Her eyes are closed now, her dripping head rested on the window. Get know those rich kid. No stay poor like grandma.

Erin follows a ramp off the access road, joins the crawl of traffic on the gusting turnpike. High above the cars glows a heaven of advertisements, dozens of mascots posed with their products like gods who work on commission, the rain slashing sideways through the letters at their feet: SHAPEGREAT! PLASTIC SURGEON, WOWSA WALLY CAR LOT, EAGLEEYE DRONE SCHOOL. A pigeon flutters past the holograms, flitting through the storm like a flip-book animation.

So what think? Jacob says. Want see Tyler tonight?

Erin stares at the crowd of mascots, a pensive depth to her eyes.

Sure, sound great, she says at last. Def want celebrate big.

Jacob hears the strain in her tone. Everything good? he asks.

Yeah. Just lot traffic. So rainy today.


The mansions float together in the void of outer space, a neighborhood of dream homes that hover in the night, the streets arranged to form the shapes of zodiac constellations. Though the mansions have many different designs—some classical, some neo-modern, some soaring medieval castles—each structure is made of solid glass, their smooth exteriors shimmering in the starlight. Some owners have darkened their walls, shielding their rooms from sight, while others allow an open view of their amenities: the indoor ski slopes, the kayaking rapids, the dance clubs packed with AI clubbers, the roller coasters with screaming AI riders. In a sprawling Victorian mansion, two identical twins race each other on the backs of velociraptors, dodging through an obstacle course of knife-wielding clowns.

In the Gemini sector floats an immense pyramid, a towering triangle of glass, divided into fifteen luminous floors. Midway up, in a balcony garden, Erin and Jacob sit in the cradled arms of a Bigfoot, their legs dangling above a burbling stream. He is the hairy Sasquatch from legend, ten feet tall or higher, his hirsute feet spread wide in the wavelets. Their host, Tyler, sits across from them in a silver tuxedo and sneakers, lounging on the lowered head of a dragon. He talks at his guests in a fast, caffeinated voice:

Last party at my beach house . . . shit, it get much creaky. This six year back—I freshman high school—make lot rookie mistake. Well, you know how go: fun fun fun, drink drink drink, then, one drink too many, kid drop like fly all over. Need call ambulance, get stomach pump, police show up—bad trouble. My dad so mad, he make big rule: no party beach house *ever.*

Tyler shakes his head at his youthful follies, absently plucks a hair from the dragon's mane. Its nostrils breathe a brief snort of fire. He goes on:

I throw lot party elsewhere, course. But then today, when I pass NAT, I get thinking: *Hmm, it long time now, ask Dad again why not.* So I find him living room, I talk all nice—*How yacht? How Porsche? How work?*—and then, real cas, I bring it up,

"Hey Dad, end this month, you need beach house?" And he look at me suspicious. "Why?" he ask. "Oh," I say, "if you no need, maybe I throw qunky party?" And Dad, he shock, his eye go wide, he like, "Party? Beach house? Joke me now? Last party beach house, eighteen stomach pump! Lucky no kid sue!" And I look down, I say all quiet: "Dad . . . I feel so blummo. Since you leave Mom, I much depress. Need party, Dad. Need party cheer up better." And Dad he sigh, he sip his scotch, he like, "Fine, Tyler, fine. But I no liable! Your friend, they need sign waiver." So craze fun bash real soon—it be way way. I even rent party clown from Jolly Jester. But yeah, uh, you need sign inherent risk form. That okay you two?

Erin and Jacob exchange a dubious look. Guess it no prob, Jacob says at last.

Then flippy fun big soon! shouts Tyler, his sneakers bouncing off the dragon's jaw. You def need come, both you. Just try no stomach pump, 'kay? If no stomach pump, Dad say maybe—

Tyler cuts himself off, staring out beyond the balcony. The starlight gleams on his gelled hair, swept into a sharp faux hawk.

Look look! he announces. Monica and Olivia coming!

Off in the distance, two chic young women soar above the rooftops, their stilettos shooting jets of flame behind them. One woman wears a midriff blouse, bedazzled bell-bottom jeans; the other a studded halter top and a leather miniskirt. Around them many figurines fly above the mansions, bursts of fire flaring from their footwear.

Tyler leaps off the dragon, clearing the stream, landing beside a bed of Venus flytraps. See you down there! he says as the fly-traps snap behind him. He rushes from the garden.

He Monica big crush, Jacob says to Erin.

You know those girl?

They both in my NAT class. Fail test in high school, like me. But no clue they so rich.

Jacob taps the Bigfoot to lower them; the mythic creature kneels and sets them softly on the grass. They stroll through a gem-studded doorway into the vast interior of the pyramid, passing entertainment options on all sides: a stage for concerts, a ring for rodeos, a dance floor where AI Kandi Kids thrash in an endless rave. Beyond the rave is a glass escalator, which carries them down past a fitness center set in a Roman throne room, past a recording studio at the mouth of a volcano, past a bowling alley with a leprechaun at each lane, hurling the balls hard in their buckled hats and britches.

What think about Tyler party? Jacob asks her.

Geez. Really not sure.

Same here. It sound kinda . . .

Messy.

Still, maybe fun.

There def be stomach pump, Erin says. Tell you that right now.

They descend into the entrance atrium of the pyramid. The floor is a huge glass eye, its colossal cornea reflecting the stars through the skylights. Tyler stands in the dilated pupil, chatting with Monica.

Oh, glad like my tux! Your outfit wow wow, too, he says, gesturing at her necklace of serrated teeth. Those shark tooth?

Monica nods. Yeah! Rip them out myself.

Shiny. I need play *Sea Brawl* sometime. You like?

Good exercise, that for sure. Though little violent. My leg get torn off lot.

Her friend Olivia also stands in the pupil, her plastic abs glinting below her crop top. Hey, look who here! she cries, seeing Erin and Jacob stride across the iris.

Congrat on test! she says to Jacob. Hear you do amaze.

Thank! How it go you?

Olivia tucks a curly forelock behind her ear. I pass, thank *God.* I worry that thing forever—now *finally* get go college. Oh! You hear what happen Bruce?

He not pass?

Olivia giggles. Really, bad I laugh. Bruce pass fine—but then he go jail.

Jail?

It classic Bruce. Right after test, he think: *Hey, I know how celebrate! I take some wuppo, then drive home!* It plenty safe, he think: wuppo start slow, he no trip hard till later. Then, halfway home, Bruce get new thought: *This not real. This video game.*

Oh shit. He okay?

He all fine, but car not. He drive sidewalk, he drive lawn— think get high score maybe. Then, almost home, car go smash big tree. You hear about this, Tyler?

Hear? Tyler says. I bail him out.

Jacob laughs. God. Wuppo sound bonker.

Much bad for driving! Olivia says. But most time it flippy as hell—just need guide keep safe. You never trip?

Not even close. Only get zinged once.

Hmm, Olivia muses. You go Tyler party? At beach house?

Prob, yeah. Just need sign waiver.

Amaze! Maybe I get us some. Know dealer.

Erin, struggling to smile, glances between Olivia and Jacob. She looks uneasy at this line of talk, this woman with a bare midriff—who has not even said hello to her—proposing a private drug trip with her boyfriend. Beside them, Monica lets out a sudden yelp of surprise.

What the *what?* she says, pointing at the open doors of the pyramid, which give a view of the glass Guggenheim down the block. An antique bicycle flies above the museum, a smirking boy seated in the saddle. Is that . . . *Gordy Glue?*

The group all turn to look—and yes, it is Gordy. The little boy pedals through the void in a silver cycling cap, escaped from an ad in which he tours about on a tandem bike. A walrus, smoking a bubble pipe, pumps the pedals behind him. Gordy glitches every few seconds, flickering in and out of sight, but this does not disrupt his course through the darkness, flying in a straight line toward the pyramid doors.

Weird weird, Tyler says. Since when Shimmer Space have ad?

Maybe Gordy buy mansion here, Olivia says with a giggle.

Gordy rings the bell on his handlebars and swoops down for a landing; the walrus blows out a long stream of bubbles. Far below, Erin watches the mascots from inside the glass pupil, her starlit face alert with indecision. Then she grips the top of her head and pulls upward.

The simulation disappears, the glowing pyramid gone. Erin, in her Smartroom, drops her rubber helmet to the padding. It rolls over to her pile of clothes in the corner.

In her jeans pocket, her phone begins to ring. After a pause she asks: Carla, who calling?

Jacob calling, replies the chirpy voice.

Erin shuts her eyes. Carla, ignore call.

## 12

That night, just after eleven, Erin gets in her car and drives to the edge of her suburb. She turns off a street of scruffy strip malls, waits at a weathered stop sign, then pulls into the paved sprawl of Owen's apartment complex. It is a jumble of concrete buildings spread across an asphalt lot, their doors grilled with metal bars, their roofs lined with dated satellite dishes. At the center is a wan courtyard, a few patches of grass among the picnic tables.

Erin parks in a space with faded lines, then locks her car and strides into the complex. Owen's apartment is a distance past the courtyard, down an uneven sidewalk still puddled from the afternoon rain. She stops at the door of his first-floor unit, standing on a doormat that reads: SOLICITORS WELCOME—IF BRING WINE!

Before she rings the bell, she opens PrayZone on her phone. She scrolls through the categories in the Creaky section— Confusion, Frustration, Guilt, Worry—until, with a sigh, she closes the application. She bows her head and whispers into the silence:

Oh God. If you there. If you . . . listening. Never pray this way before—never speak to you direct. I need help, God, so much help. Please guide me. Please be near.

The silence grows around her, encircling her as she prays. It is intimate in its absence, a presence too encompassing for sight or sound to capture, enfolding her in an invisible embrace. She keeps her head bowed a moment longer, then presses the doorbell.

The bell echoes inside the apartment, but no other sounds emerge from within. She rings a second time to the same result. She is about to send a text when a soft thumping approaches the door.

Hang on! Owen calls from behind the peephole. He begins unlocking the dead bolts.

The door opens on his small apartment, most of the unit visible at first sight. There is a compact kitchen off in the shadows, a living room with a well-worn loveseat, a floor lamp lighting a poster of Van Gogh's *Wheatfield with Crows.* Houseplants dangle from the low ceiling—aloe vera and peace lilies, bromeliads and lucky bamboo—filling the dim rooms with their leafy abundance. In the doorway Owen stands on crutches, giving his guest a look of groggy concern. His right ankle is raised at an angle, the cuff of his sweatpants empty.

Hey sweetie, he says. What up?

I wake you. Shit. Sorry bother you so late.

No worry that. You okay?

Yeah, I . . . I fine. Just need talk.

Sure, he says. He unbolts the door grille. Come on in.

Erin shakes her head. Not inside. Better talk courtyard.

Courtyard? It middle night.

She doesn't reply, only gestures her chin toward the far-off picnic tables.

He furrows his brow. You sure you okay, sweetie? Nothing wrong?

We talk out there. I explain.

Okay . . . he says in a worried voice. I just need put on foot. Not good on crutch that far.

You no have wheelchair?

Not here—I loan it James. I put foot on, no worry.

Sorry this, Owen. Really. You want help?

No, no. Need get better at it anyway. Make some tea, I back soon.

He turns on his crutches and swings slowly down the hall, the rubber crutch-tips denting the carpet, water-stained here and there from leaky planters. His apartment teeters on the brink of messiness: some dishes stacked in the sink, some laundry draped on an old recliner, some mugs loitering on the coffee table. He swings into the bedroom and shuts the door.

Soon Erin stands in the kitchen, filling a kettle under the sputtery faucet. As she sets the kettle on the stovetop, the apartment turns abruptly dark around her. A spotlight shines down from the ceiling; strings play on the soundtrack in a nervous, edgy staccato. But this time Erin ignores the spotlight, resists the lure of launching into song. The music fades as she opens a box of tea bags and sets one inside a mug.

Erin waits for the water to boil, staring down at the burner, the cupped palm of fire below the kettle. Quietly she says:

Sometimes I feel like I'm done with the past, like those bleak years are behind me. On the nights when Jacob stays over, when I fall asleep beside him, when I wake up early and see his face on the pillow, I can feel like a different woman than the one I've been since high school: normal, calm, contented, not haunted by my losses. I can believe that I've healed from my father's death, forgiven my sister's betrayals—that I'm ready to forget Fiona ever existed. But the past . . . it doesn't seem done with *me* yet. Every time a mascot visits, I feel like I'm right back in junior year, living again through the winter my sister vanished.

After our late-night talk in my bedroom, Fiona went back to her distant behavior for the rest of winter break. She seemed even more remote now, like I'd offended her that night, and didn't return my hug when we said goodbye a few weeks later, her skinny arms at her sides as I embraced her. I shut myself in my bedroom, shed a few angry, confused tears—but I didn't see anything dangerous in her behavior. Neither did Dad: the night after she left for school, he asked if I'd noticed how much weight she'd lost. "She might have eating disorder," he said. "So much pressure on girl be thin." That was our concern back then.

Two months went by. Fiona rarely called or texted us, always claimed she was "busy busy." Then, late one night, Dad received a call from his old friend Sean, a grad school buddy who now taught at Fiona's college. Sean could barely talk through his tears: there had just been a bombing on campus, he said, three floors of a residence hall destroyed, an unknown number of students killed or wounded. "It Sanders Hall," Sean added, "wanted tell you right away." This was Fiona's residence hall, the mazy dorm at the edge of campus where we'd dropped her off as a freshman, the corridors bustling with students who might be buried under wreckage right now, killed while they slept or chatted in a common room.

Dad and I stayed awake the entire night, fearing she was dead, planning to drive the seven hours first thing in the morning. Fiona didn't answer her phone, didn't post she was "safe" on her profile, didn't appear among the names on the college's updates. Then, around six a.m., the police knocked hard on our front door.

Dad steadied himself in the doorway, put an arm around my shoulder, expecting to hear the worst from these uniformed men. But no, they told us, Fiona had not been killed. It was just the opposite: she was the killer.

"That no possible," Dad said. "Must be mistake."

I nodded beside him, numb with fear.

But the surveillance footage left no doubt. It showed her outside her dorm, standing alone in the parking lot, holding a slim remote beside her leg, a cover flipped open on its top. It showed her press the button with a hesitant thumb, showed her glossy face reflect a glaring light. A painter's van with an open door drove up behind Fiona; a woman in a ski mask called out to her from within. But my sister just stood there, staring at the building, her blank face shimmering with the flames. Finally the ski-masked woman leapt out of the van and hurried her into a seat. The vehicle sped off into the night.

As the police played us the footage, a different type of van drove down our block: a van from the Terrorism Bureau. The agents stepped out in their dark suits and relieved the officers on duty, then escorted my father and me to separate rooms. They spent the rest of the day questioning us, searching through our home, ransacking my sister's bedroom in particular. Whenever I glanced out the living room window—they kept me there past midnight—I saw neighbors watching our house through parted curtains.

So the ground cracked open beneath us; our lives began their free fall into the strange abyss of scandal. Dad and I huddled inside, avoiding the press, burying ourselves in distractions. I devoted more hours to Patrick, to my personal versions of *Nuclear Family;* Dad worked in the basement on "research," which, when I listened at the top of the stairs, just sounded like he was watching nature videos and old Sondheim musicals on his laptop. Though we were stranded there together, cut off from the outside world, I rarely even ate dinner with him in those days. Dad would knock on my door, tell me the chicken was boiled; I'd say, "Okay, thank," and then eat it cold at my desk later that night. There was no mention of seeing a counselor now, no talk of us "growing through trauma."

After a leave of absence, Dad resigned his job at the college and found some teaching work online. By then we had changed our last name from Reynolds to James. We didn't love our new name, but it gave no hint of our past, called no attention to itself. One night someone threw a brick through our window; Dad had bars installed the next day.

We felt uneasy inside our house, no longer trusted its rooms and hallways, and not only because some vigilante might find us here. So much pain and death had erupted from the home we thought we knew, had lain dormant for years while we lived in its rooms and performed our harmless rituals, brushing our hair and tying our shoes and tossing our clothes in the dryer, hanging fake cobwebs for Halloween, carrying the Christmas tree down from the attic, playing Rock Paper Scissors to see who'd do the dishes. Nothing that could have predicted the scorched remains of Fiona's dorm, the melted bodies in the common room where she'd introduced me to Leah, a friend she'd killed in the bombing—and so how well could we have ever known our home? The doors and curtains, the carpets and cabinets all seemed ominous now, as if they might have warned us had we thought to listen. Sometimes Dad would give me an uncertain glance, a look both worried and suspicious, as if, for all he knew, he might have raised two killers in this house. Then he'd smile weakly at me, try to comport himself like my father, not a man so grieved he barely had an identity at all.

I stayed home from school for a week after the bombing. On the morning I tried to return, I sat in Dad's station wagon and watched the streets slide past my window, the first time I'd left the house since my sister's crime was broadcast across the nation. Most articles had used a photo of her at a debate event last year, looking fervent and combative as she argued at a podium, one hand gripping the edge, the other gesturing emphatically. The talking heads discussed our family, wondered what kind of home life had formed this monster. The entire ride to school, I watched a news drone fly above Dad's car, pausing when we stopped at intersections, swooping down low as we pulled into the high school parking lot. To my horror, I saw two camera crews assembling on the sidewalk. A slick-haired reporter rushed up to our car, a dark lens bobbing just behind him.

*"Drive us back,"* I snapped, fumbling for the pill bottle in my backpack. That morning I quit the swim team, made Dad switch me to a homeschool curriculum.

Inside our house, the curtains closed, I was safe from the news cameras. But now, more each day, I could feel a different camera filming me. This camera zoomed in for close-ups as I drew Patrick at my desk, tracked along beside me as I left the room for my chicken, framed me in a full shot as I stood at the basement stairs, listening to the old musicals on Dad's laptop. The camera captured me like a character from *Nuclear Family,* turned my vacant days into episodes of their own. I gave these episodes titles: "Bye Bye Bedtime," "Missing the Pool," "Staying Home from Prom," "The Pace of Dad Pacing." Sometimes the camera even filmed the musical numbers in my mind.

Throughout this time, I earned good grades in all my online classes. I was grateful for the numbing routine of schoolwork, even for the tedium of my NAT study guides. I drew more, watched more, spent more time in bed, in dreams of dreams. I didn't grieve: I burrowed.

The water begins to boil in Owen's kitchen, a curl of steam wheezing from the kettle. The tea bag swells inside the mug as

she pours. On the side of the mug is an illustration, a garden center ringed in blooming flowers. Erin sits down at the kitchen
table, absently stirs the tea bag on its string. She continues:

The following spring, I was accepted to a college across the country.
Dad had steered me toward colleges far from home, where there'd
been less coverage of our family, where no one would remember my
face from the local news. I would have preferred to stay in the house,
earn an online degree in my bedroom, but Dad insisted that I should
"make clean break" with our suburb, our whole region. The thought
of sharing a dorm room, of using a common bathroom, of sitting in
packed lecture halls—it kept me up at night, seemed like a nightmare
worse than reporters at my high school. I told all this to Dad, but he
continued to make his case, saying I'd thank him once I'd moved and
started over. One night at dinner I lost my temper, accused him of
wanting me gone, of hating me because I reminded him of Fiona. I
ended up crying and hugging him tightly, saying I was sorry again and
again into his shoulder. "It okay, little fish," he told me, stroking my
hair. "It okay."

    If I had to leave for college, I asked him, maybe he could move
with me? Maybe we could live together near my new school? This
wasn't just about me: I worried about him alone in the house, lost
inside his memories. "That nice you, sweetie," he said. "But you need
get away, make life for self. Just try one semester, okay? If you hate it,
can come home." I was too tired to argue more. Doubtful, I agreed.

    In the end it didn't matter. By the summer, Dad had started to
notice dark patches on his plastic, first on his feet, then on his legs
and stomach. He hid this from me for a few days, but then sat me
down after he spoke with his doctor. There was no real treatment for
Brad Pitt Disease, just the body's slow dissolution, the rotting of his
plastic to ash. The rot would move gradually up his body, until the

final stage when it overtook his torso; the prognosis was six months to a year. He said I should still leave for college, that he would hire a nurse to help him. Instead, I emailed the school that night.

Three months into his illness, when his feet began to crumble, Dad needed a cocktail of pain pills every few hours. In this haze of medication, he became less guarded about his past, even started to tell me stories, as if the pills also treated the pain of reminiscence. He told me about his childhood, which seemed like a paradise to him now, those fourteen years of peace before the war: he had lived in a quiet cul-de-sac, a spoiled only child, his room wallpapered with penguins, his shelves lined with books on the sea, his life happy in ways that he took for granted, that felt less than happy at the time, because his parents could never stop fighting, often seemed on the verge of divorce. "It funny," he said, "how your perspective change. After they refugee, Mom Dad talked all time about past. Made it sound perfect, like never fought at all."

As he spoke I sometimes thought, *Oh, I need tell Fiona this*. We had wondered so long and often about his life. Then, with a pang in my stomach, I remembered she was gone.

Though Dad was more open about his past, I still never asked about his marriage, afraid this might shut down our conversations. Our talks were warm and chatty, we'd laugh some days until our eyes teared, but there was always a depth of grief below this laughter. We knew these were our last months, our last conversations, and I worried the wrong topic would be too much for him, make him draw back inside himself. I never brought up Fiona, a subject neither of us could handle. I let Dad decide the topic, how much he wanted to say.

Then, one afternoon, he began telling me all about Owen. My whole life, I thought they'd met in his thirties, a hasty marriage which quickly fell apart. I thought Dad had decided on kids while single, had hired the surrogate years before his marriage. He'd never told me this outright, of course, just implied it by breezing past the entire topic. But no: it turned out Dad had **grown up** with Owen. That Owen had been a close childhood friend.

"Wait, you serious?" I said on the afternoon he revealed this. "You knew him when *kid?*"

Dad laughed in bed, his tray table stirring on its stand. Now that he'd begun to unveil his past, he liked how he could startle me, how I hung on his words like the students in his advanced classes. As he told me the story—how he and Owen confessed their feelings at a sleepover in high school, admitting to years of secret infatuation— he opened the drawer of his nightstand and started to rummage. Next month he would lack the strength for this, patches of rot on his hands and arms, his motor function limited. But right now he could still feed himself, still work the TV remote, still have me wheel him outside to see the sunset. This always left a trail of ashes on the floor, which I'd sweep up while he slept.

From under some papers, Dad slipped out his old smartphone. He tapped at the screen and showed me a dated picture: two teenage boys at a basement table, bent seriously over a board game with tokens everywhere. This was the first picture I'd seen of my father as a boy, and it jarred me how many features he'd shared with Fiona: the serious lips, the prominent nose, the precocious, wide-set eyes. Across from him sat Owen, young, unscarred, frowning down at the dice that he'd just rolled.

He told me childhood stories for close to an hour. Then, exhausted, he gazed out the window, watching a pine branch stir in the breeze.

"I make lot mistake," he said. "I def make lot. But . . . we talk this more later, okay? Think I need nap." He napped four or five times a day now, his energy always erratic. I kissed his forehead, trying to ignore the faint patches on its surface.

The next afternoon, when he seemed in better spirits, I asked him another question about his past. I'd debated whether to ask at all, but it had kept me up worrying the night before, well past three a.m.

"So, about Owen," I began when he'd finished with lunch, most of the boiled chicken left on his tray. "After war, when you decide have kid—Owen, he there with you?"

Dad hesitated. "Yes. He there."

"Because, well, I ever think you single back then. That you hire surrogate alone. But yesterday, when you talk about past . . ." I trailed off.

Dad smiled sadly. "No worry, fish. He not your father like that. I wanted Owen give specimen, asked him many time. It normal, you know, for couple like us: they mix it together for surrogate. But he ever said no."

"Why?"

"Oh, he lot lot reason. Said his family bad genes, history illness, thing like that. Me, I think he just hated that family—no wanted his kid look like them, be like them even little. They homophobe, much conservative. *Loved* President Walton."

I thought about all this. "Maybe Owen never want child? He leave when we so young."

"No, that not it." Dad glanced down at his tray, ran a finger along the edge. "He loved you two so much, more than anything. I knew him before war, but when you two born? That happiest I ever saw him."

I could tell he was getting tired again, reaching the limit of what his pills could soothe. But he went on:

"You see, I wanted fresh start for us. I wanted forget the war, all that pain, not pass it on to kid. I think I made Owen feel . . . made him feel toxic. Like it problem he had trauma. He went through lot in war—lot more than me—no able just move on. When he left? He said it to protect you and Fiona. That what he told me."

Tears glistened in his eyes. I said, "We no need talk this, Dad. I sorry upset you."

"And the joke is," he continued, as if he hadn't heard me, "I so wrong. So wrong about everything. You can try be perfect parent. You can say right thing, pretend you fine, keep your pain secret. But who you are—the *person* you are? You pass that on to kid, no matter what. They still get your pain. Your anger."

I felt a pressure behind my eyes, blinked back my own tears. I was afraid to upset him more, wished I hadn't asked these questions in the first place. "Oh Dad. You amaze father. Best ever."

He laughed to himself. "Right. Father of Year. That not what news said about me."

"Fiona . . . she make her own choice. It not your fault."

"All those year, I told myself: *If I never talk about past, then it not their prob. They make new life, no worry that.* But deep down, under surface—I angry, Erin, so angry. You no idea. Angry for my parent, for all those people die in war. Angry for nature: how corporation poison planet, kill species after species, ruin our future. All for what? Money? It disgusting."

"Sure, everyone have those thought. But you never seem angry, Dad. You kind. Caring."

His voice was becoming sharper, losing the placid remove of his pain meds. "In my head, you know how many people I murder? How often I kill politician, judge, billionaire? Thousand and thousand of murder. Brutal murder. She got that from me."

I didn't know how to respond. I'd longed to know more about Dad forever, but now that I'd glimpsed his regret, his grief, I wasn't sure I could bear it. I said, "But Fiona . . . what she do. That dif. Way way dif."

"If I honest with you both? If I not hide my anger? Then in college, when *she* got angry—then maybe she talk me about it. I could have prepared her for world. *Prepared* her."

Dad covered his face with his hands and started to weep. I'd seen his eyes tear up before, heard him crying in other rooms, but never once had he broken down like this in front of me. I stood up from my chair and wrapped my arms around him as softly as possible. The doctors had told him to limit his physical contact: the pressure could weaken his plastic, speed the effects of the rotting.

"I selfish. Ever so selfish," he said when his crying subsided. He stared down at his hands, the dark spotting on his palms, a sign of ashes to come. "*I* no wanted talk about past. *I* no wanted think about war. *I* no wanted face my guilt—that I left my parent at refugee compound, left them to die. So I drove Owen away. Made my children feel alone."

"That not true. Not true at all."

Dad let out a long breath and closed his eyes. He remained quiet for several minutes, so that I thought he might have fallen asleep in my arms. Every day I felt more like a parent to him—in charge of his physical needs, anxious about his emotions—our roles reversed by the sad alchemy of terminal illness. Another minute passed, then he cleared his throat and looked up at me with a tired smile.

"I okay, little fish," he said. "You no need worry. I just miss them, you know? Fiona. Owen. My mom dad. Just miss them."

To my surprise, Dad continued to share his past after that day. Our talks, however, now stayed in the sunny boundaries of his childhood, never strayed into the war years, about which he told me only sparing details. His stories stopped on the day after the bombs fell, when soldiers began to round up refugees fleeing the radiation, ordering them from their cars on the backed-up highways. Dad had watched the convoy of military trucks churn down the snowy median, had heard their loudspeakers cut through the winter air. He had been crowded into a cargo bed, where, on a freezing bench, he'd stared out the canvas flap as the trucks drove to a "Rest Facility," as his childhood shrank into the distance.

I thought he might not talk about Owen again, but it was just the opposite: Dad loved to discuss their friendship as children, loved to describe his early memories—sneaking out at night to roam their neighborhood, gathering friends to film wacky home movies, creating fake social media accounts to troll the bullies at school—memories he must have treasured in silence for decades.

As the weeks went on, as the ashes spread up his ankles, I began to see that Owen was more to Dad than an old love, a former flame. He was the love of Dad's life, always with him despite their many years apart.

I remembered the name of Owen's garden center—Bloom Shakalaka—so it wasn't hard to find his profile again. I wrote him a brief message, telling him Dad's diagnosis, asking if they might have a phone call before the end. I wondered if Owen would reply; like Dad, he'd have his own complex relationship to the past. But a few hours later, as I boiled dinner, my phone chimed with his response.

*It so good hear from you, Erin,* he wrote. *No believe it when saw your name. But my God, this worst news. Just worst.* Was there any chance I could talk tonight—or, if not tonight, then as soon as possible? *So sorry be intense, but this shook me to core.*

After Dad went to sleep, I stepped outside and called Owen, cupping my hand around the phone as the wind rose. He answered on the first ring.

"Erin . . . wow," he said. "Last time I saw you, you were baby. Asleep in crib."

"Wish I go back there. Life lot better in crib."

He laughed. "You got your dad sense humor."

I'd expected not to like Owen, this man who'd abandoned my family, but something about his voice set me at ease, something gentle and attentive in his tone. I said, "Yeah, he still crack joke all time. We laugh lot these day, believe or not."

"And Fiona, she home, too? She do okay?"

I leaned back against the screen door. It had all been so public—Fiona's murders, our family's downfall—that I assumed everyone knew by now.

"You no watch news?" I said at last.

"Uh, not much. I kinda out loop down here. Fiona in news?"

"You need go online. Search her name."

"Right now?" he asked.

"Yes. I wait."

I strode behind the house as he tapped his phone, sat down against the pine tree in the windy night. I wasn't about to explain the bombing to Owen, to state those details out loud: more than a year later, I'd only spoken of this with Dad, and then sparingly, elliptically, like the other day in his bedroom. "Twenty-two student . . ." Owen murmured in disbelief, his voice far from the mic. Then, closer: "Erin, okay if call you back? Just need . . . need minute. Maybe few minute."

I looked out at the yard, the jagged shadows of the hedges. "Sure. Take time."

*Well, that's that,* I thought after he thanked me and ended the call. Whatever his grief for my father, whatever his interest in me, he'd want no contact with people who were under such a curse, whose home had produced a mass murderer still in hiding. I'd experienced the same with my friends, that unsettled drawing back, and I'd cut off contact with them rather than face their rejection. I felt furious at Owen, at all these people who lacked a shred of empathy, who understood only blame. Owen would keep himself far from our chaos, safe with his boyfriend, Sam, hidden from the news cycle in their lovely garden center.

My phone lay beside me in the deep unmowed grass. It startled me when it started ringing, when I saw Owen's number appear on the screen. His voice was unsteady, thickened from crying. "What you gone through . . . I no imagine. I so sorry, Erin. So sorry." He said he'd like to come visit, to book a flight for this week. "If that work for you two. I no want intrude."

I said a visit was fine with me; I could ask Dad about it tomorrow. My tone was reserved, matter-of-fact: it was the only way to keep myself from sobbing.

The next morning, when I told all this to Dad, he laughed to himself and gazed up at the ceiling. "And he really want visit?" he said.

"He want come this week. If it okay you."

"Well, I in my fifties. I dying. Guess I can try be mature adult."

"Dad. If this too much . . ."

"No, no. I glad you do this. It good we say goodbye."

Later that week, Owen entered my life. He and Dad spent hours in the bedroom on the afternoon he arrived, their voices hushed and subdued, so that I'd have needed my ear at the door to hear their words. I managed to restrain myself. Owen had a room at a nearby motel, and I thought he might stay for a few days, but, with Dad's permission, he rented a small apartment on a month-to-month basis, started sitting with Dad every afternoon, helping out with the cooking and cleaning, all the care. When Dad went into hospice a few months later, Owen and I took shifts at his bedside day and night: we never knew when Dad would wake up, when we could offer him a comforting word as he slipped in and out of troubled dreams. In the last year, Dad had become obsessed with female jazz singers, and their songs of love and longing played from a speaker on the windowsill: Nina Simone and Billie Holiday, Ella Fitzgerald, Lena Horne. Owen put a vase of gardenias on the sill.

On the whole, Dad's passing was peaceful. Near the end, when they upped his pain meds, he became disoriented much of the time, but I think he always knew that we were there. Once, in a lucid moment, he put an ashy hand on mine, smiled at the rolling lawn outside his window. "You know," he told me, "I glad I get chance live.

That the main thing—that you get chance. Love a few good people, see this gorgeous planet. Or maybe," he added with a laugh, "maybe this the meds talking."

As for me, I felt little of this peace. The morning he died, I left his room and stormed out of the hospice, punched a tree on the lawn so hard I chipped a knuckle. I felt more anger than sadness, a deep, vicious disgust at the injustice of what he'd suffered. Some people led easy lives, lots of them total assholes—people who'd supported the war, who'd cheered for President Walton—but my father, a loving, generous man, a man who'd wanted nothing more than to raise his children and share his knowledge, *he'd* somehow received a life of loneliness and loss: his parents dead young, his daughter a killer, his nights spent pining for the husband who'd left him, his body rotted to ashes in a narrow hospice bed, his dear, familiar face half crumbled to dust.

I turned around and saw Owen, who'd followed me out to the lawn. I could see that he was grieving—his cheeks damp, his breathing pained—but the look of concern on his face enraged me. This man had no right, no right at all, to pretend he cared about me. When he tried to hug me, I stepped away.

"You abandon him, you fuck. You leave him. With two little kid," I said, my voice quiet with cruelty. We'd become good friends the past few months, but that seemed over now. "You know how much that mess him up? Ruin his fucking life?"

Owen stood silent in his wrinkled T-shirt, staring down at the manicured grass. It was his shift at the bedside today when the end had finally come, when Dad, after gazing for hours at the dark TV across the room—any program seemed to upset him, but the TV engrossed him when it was off, as if he could fill the blank frame with his own imaginings—had gone into a coughing fit and slipped away after a dose of his pain meds. Owen had woken me up with the call and I'd driven over at once, then felt the rage sweep through me when I stepped into the room, seeing the husk of ash and plastic that remained of my father.

Owen nodded at my harsh words. "That true. That all true."

"So just go now. Go back your fucking garden center. Leave. That what you good at."

He looked up at me. "But I not leaving."

It annoyed me that I was crying now, that my voice kept breaking. "Fine. You can go his funeral. But stay out my fucking way. I done pretending you decent person. That you not complete piece shit."

"Erin . . . can we sit down minute? I few thing tell you."

Still furious, I followed him to the hospice's dining area. There, over mugs of coffee, he told me he'd made a decision: he would be moving to this suburb permanently, finding a job, renting a new apartment.

"What about your boyfriend?" I muttered. "Sam. He moving, too?"

"Nah. That prob ending. Maybe for best." Owen sipped from his mug; I sensed there was a great deal he wasn't telling me. "If you no want see me, I understand. But I be here. I want live near your dad grave."

I couldn't meet his gaze. "I not here ease your conscience. You asshole in past. Total bastard. Moving here no change that."

"You right, sweetie. Nothing change past. I live that every day."

He leaned forward and took my coffee from me. My hands were shaking badly.

Owen helped me plan the funeral, helped me pick out the coffin and headstone, stood beside me in the receiving line while Dad's old colleagues at the college—the people who'd deserted him in his time of need—arrived to utter platitudes and pay their last respects. Owen took me out for air whenever he sensed my temper rising, that any second I'd start shouting at those hypocrites. He gave the eulogy as well, praising Dad's "amaze strength" in the face of "many challenge" (Owen kept away from specifics), while I stared at the carpet in a fog of SettleSelf.

In the months that followed, we settled into a weekly routine. We attended CODA on Sunday mornings, met up on Thursday nights to binge some *MERcenary* episodes, the adventures of merman-for-hire, Vlad Vigorshark. I'd laugh at all the silliness—Vlad outswimming submarines, falling for sexy electric eels (his "Achilles' eel," as he called it)—while I held my father's old stuffed seal in my lap. I always kept it near me now.

During this time, I learned that Owen had "Suspected Status," that he'd spent seven years in prison during the war. The status restricted his life severely: he could never attend college, never vote in an election, never know if the Terrorism Bureau was bugging his phone or apartment. He had to disclose his status to employers, which kept him from jobs with much pay or room for advancement. It took him two months of applications before he found the sales job at Tablet Town, an entry-level position for a man in his fifties.

"I wasn't terrorist or anything," he told me. "Hell, there not even terror group yet. The war . . . world very dif back then."

I never asked him more about this, nor about his time with Dad during the war. Whenever Owen mentioned those years, tried to share an anecdote with me, I'd go quiet or change the subject to some *MERcenary* subplot, so curtly that he would laugh, letting me know he got the message.

I wanted the past behind me. I wanted less pain.

Erin finishes her tea, sets the mug on the table. She stares out through the kitchen window, looking at the vacant courtyard at the far end of the path, the scumbled moon shining through the smog. After a moment, she hears Owen come creaking from his bedroom, the rustle of his cane on the hallway carpet. He shuffles into the kitchen, his right sneaker larger than his left.

This new foot no like me much, he says. It do anything stay off. But tenth try a charm.

Erin stands up from the table, attempts to smile.

f you want worry me, you do good job, Owen says with a nervous laugh as they reach the courtyard. He hobbles along next to Erin, not confident on his cane yet, a little out of breath. The concrete buildings loom above them, their long walkways lined with windows, the blinds and curtains closed as if to hide all signs of life. The faint sound of a DOT song, drums over tractor noises, drifts from a far-off corner of the complex.

Three stories up, on an empty walkway, a figurine in a nightgown sits painting at an easel. A nude of the god Poseidon covers her canvas: the brawny deity standing tall among the crashing waves, his trident raised above him, his beard coursing water, his pectorals slick with spray. No detail of him is spared, least of all his genitalia, the waves parted to frame their mammoth heft. In the next apartment over, a little boy holds open the window blinds, watching the sea god emerge with a mesmerized face.

Erin sits down at the nearest picnic table, patting the bench so Owen will sit close beside her. She chooses the side that faces the building, her eyes fixed on the woman at the easel.

Wish that lady no there, Erin says.

He chuckles fondly at the painter. Her nightgown is printed with astrology symbols; a headlamp, strapped to her forehead, illumines the well-endowed Olympian on the canvas.

That just Mandy, he says. She harmless.

Still, keep voice down.

What going on, honey? You scaring me little.

I serious. Talk soft.

Fine, fine. I whisper.

Prob no bug out here, right? she asks. No one listening?

Doubt it.

Erin sighs. Okay. This not easy, so—so I best just say it. This . . . it about Fiona.

Fiona, he repeats. I worry it that. Something happen?

Yeah. For while now.

For the first time, Erin begins to tell him about the Smartworld mascots. Their visits, she explains, had started the autumn after her father died, back when she spent her evenings online with Patrick. One night in *Jungle Jam,* while they took a break on a branch, she had noticed a snazzy gorilla swinging toward her on a vine, a primate dressed in horn-rimmed glasses and a tailored suit. This was a mascot for Simian Tax App, the main sponsor of *Jungle Jam,* one of many dapper gorillas in the game zone. The apes sat on branches with tiny laptops, their faces switching between two expressions: the first a sullen frown as they typed in their fiscal details, the second a stunned elation when they saw the size of their refund. At this they beat their chests, filled the forest with joyful shrieking. SIMIAN TAX APP, read the banner above them. SO EASY, YOU GO APE!

Before this night, she had never seen a Tax Ape leave its

perch. Now the primate thudded down on her branch, lumbered toward her and Patrick with its little computer. Erin was about to pull off her Smarthead when the gorilla shrieked and thrust the laptop at her, as if she should read the screen. The screen was blank, of course, but the laptop did have a full keypad. This the gorilla pointed at insistently.

"You . . . you want type something?" Erin asked it as she stood. She felt a little crazy to be talking to a mascot.

The gorilla burst into its smile, nodded vigorously. Slowly, one key at a time, it typed: *E-R-I-N. I H-A-V-E M-E-S-S-A-G-E Y-O-U.*

She took a few steps backward, almost toppled off the branch; the gorilla shot out a hairy hand and caught her arm. Then its massive finger resumed typing.

After a few words, Erin began to grasp the message: there might be a terror attack soon at the MegaGrub near her work; she should avoid this supermarket at all costs. *Just no go near,* the gorilla typed, *keep safe.* The message concluded: *If you want tell Terrorism Bureau, that no prob. We see their surveillance, go plan attack somewhere else.*

Erin stared down at the laptop, startled, baffled. After the final word of the message, the gorilla leapt off the branch and clambered up a nearby tree, joining some other stylish apes immersed in their taxes. All intelligence left its movements: it typed with random keystrokes, screeched at the empty screen.

A few years earlier, she would have logged off right then and called the Terrorist Hotline. She would have done it at once, without thinking; she couldn't have lived with herself otherwise. But that night she sat down with Patrick, their legs dangling off the branch, and considered her options. If she called the hotline tonight—if she, the sister of a well-known terrorist, told them about this warning—then she'd be put under twenty-four-hour surveillance, forced to choose between helping the bureau or a charge of "passive assistance," one of the harshest laws in the Silence Is Violence Act. They might want her to work undercover, might use her as bait to find the source of the message, which, of course, could easily get her killed. Or they might confiscate her Smartbody, lock her out of Smartworld, banishing her from her new life with Patrick.

The more she considered her situation, the more it seemed pointless to call the bureau. The gorilla itself had told her this: the terrorists would see the bureau's surveillance, would simply move their murders elsewhere. No lives would be saved in the end, and her own might be destroyed. It didn't sit well with her conscience—the thought of innocent figurines shot dead in the MegaGrub aisles, killed in an attack she could have prevented—but she couldn't risk her entire future on the word of a Tax Ape. Who controlled that mascot, anyway? Someone sent by Fiona?

For the next month, Erin checked her news app every half hour. At midnight she'd drive past the MegaGrub, watching the last of the workers leaving, assuring herself that no one had died there that day. There were no retail attacks in town that month, and the next one was miles away, at a Rad Dad clothing outlet. She had no clue what it all meant—just hoped no other mascots would give her an ethical crisis.

But a few months later a new one arrived: a six-foot smartphone with giant sneakers and undulating arms. It wobbled toward her across a grassy knoll, interrupting a round of *Conspiracy Clues* as she waited for the president's motorcade. Words scrolled across the phone screen, warning her of an attack at a BigSeat Cineplex.

In the years that followed, many mascots would visit her: a banjo-playing peacock, an umbrella on antidepressants, a weight-lifting length of razor wire. Of all the attacks they forecast, not a single one took place. Erin asked the mascots questions, even lost her temper at them, but they always just gave their warnings and departed. One night she pleaded with a floating spray-paint can, "Do you know Fiona? Are *you* Fiona?"—but it just went on tagging its warning on a prison wall of *Alcatraz Escape!*

And there was another reason she never called the hotline. She didn't exactly want these visits to stop. Most likely her sister was behind these warnings, hiring hackers to contact her this way: it felt like the last trace of Fiona's love, of her lost family. Erin worried about the Terrorism Bureau—a knock on her front door, officers cuffing her at work, a multi-year sentence through Silence Is Violence—but these sentient slushies and ice-skating zebras were her only real link to the past. After they left, she'd be filled with memories, the good ones she'd almost forgotten: Fiona and her father cheering at swim meets; Dad showing them his favorite musicals, *Sweeney Todd* and *A Little Night Music;* Fiona driving her out to the Waterfall Café, blasting Bass and Bird Call songs the entire ride—moments so ordinary at the time, so precious and painful in retrospect. How could Erin cut her last thread to that world, when calling the hotline would help no one?

So when a new mascot arrived, she felt as much anger and guilt as affection. In the meantime, she paid to boost her security firewall, hoping to conceal these visits from the Terrorism Bureau. It must have worked, because she'd never heard a word from them in those years.

Then, after she buried Patrick, after she deleted their unborn daughter, everywhere in Smartworld just reminded her of her loss. She left that virtual paradise, save for the yard where she kept his grave, a commercial-free Domain. There, alone with her grief, no Destiny Diaper Duck came honking at her from the horizon, no Hank the Waltzing Hammer twirled to greet her from his toolbox. She missed the mascots at times, but overall, she felt much calmer—until, that is, she met Jacob and returned to Smartworld. A Fat Cat was soon bounding her way, a Gordy Glue cycling through outer space.

I so sorry, Owen, she whispers to him in the courtyard. It wrong involve you, I know that. Feel blummo this.

Owen looks lost in thought, staring at a scuffed plank of the picnic table. No, sweetie—glad I know. Wish told me sooner.

I no want cause you prob, not with your status. I just . . . I so alone this. For so long.

He wraps an arm around her, drawing her close in the cooling night. At last he says:

So you think Fiona behind this?

Maybe. No way be sure.

I not here judge you. But Erin, after first mascot? You should have left Smartworld. Never gone back.

I know. But Patrick there. That my whole life back then.

Owen gives a troubled nod. That real hard time. Your dad just pass.

She falls silent at the mention of her father. Above her, on the walkway, the painter brushes a tattoo on Poseidon's ankle, an image of a rearing horse. The little boy seems to have lost interest, his curtains closed.

Jacob and me . . . it go so amaze right now, Erin says. But how long it last? I need lie all time, pretend I no sister, pretend I normal past. Now what I tell him? That my Smartbody broken? That I never fix it? Me him, we in Smartworld every day.

What if tell him truth? He know you, care about you. Might understand.

Or might leave me. If terrorist in your family? Most people think whole family bad.

Is Jacob "most people"?

With this? Not sure. He just lose mom in attack. He *hate* terror group.

Owen shrugs. You like him, though. Like him lot. How long you keep lying?

She rests her elbows on the table, her chin on her knuckle hinges. God. This all so dif from Patrick. Crazy how dif.

Oh, sweetie. It good it dif. Much better for you.

But I no *want* tell Jacob this. It so messy. All such mess.

A ripple of wind crosses the courtyard, Owen's sparse hair shifting in the breeze.

You lot like your dad, know that? he says. Max ever kept lot secret. Hid so much inside.

They lapse back into silence at the sound of Max's name, as if hearing an echo of his voice on the cold night air.

You right, Erin murmurs, as if to herself. I much like him. Full of secret.

He not like that when boy. Only after refugee compound.

Erin slips her pill bottle from her purse, swallows down a capsule. She looks out at the strip malls beyond the parking lot.

When people die, what you think happen? Think they just gone? Nothing?

Owen smiles sadly. CODA say they join Great Unknown. Become part of Holy Mystery.

I no mean that. CODA just . . . I dunno. It never ask big question. It all self-help.

Nothing wrong self-help. I need it lot.

Sure. But what I mean is . . . you think we have soul? That we more than body?

Oh. Wow. Well, I def hope so.

Erin turns her head and looks at him in the muted glow of the streetlamps, dimmer on this ailing edge of town. A trace of tears gleams on her lower eyelids. She says:

Maybe you could tell me little? About you and Dad, during war?

You sure?

Yes. Yes, need know.

Owen lets out a soft exhale. Then he zips his jacket to the collar and starts to tell the story.

## NUCLEAR FAMILY

### "The Brochure"

One night in spring, Max and O sit cuddling on a sand dune, the figurine leaning back against his boyfriend's dimpled bread. From their perch, the young men gaze out at a partial view of the ocean, visible through the chain links of a tall security fence. Watchtowers rise at intervals above the razor wire, their roofs recurring down the dark coast of the refugee compound.

"We could be watching classic films," Max is saying with annoyance. "Or great TV from any era. Or *news* programs— what a thought! But what do they play at Relax Time? Every single night? *Galaxy Gossip.* I ready to burn down the Rest Hall."

O laughs. "It not so awful. Jenlithia kind of a bad ass."

"She a strong protagonist, sure. But every stupid episode is the same. First, Jenlithia finds out someone is talking trash. Then she digs up dirt on them and takes them down. And there not that many people in the spaceship! I mean, how many times can she blackmail poor Stephtooni? Fine, Steph had sex with her second cousin, that not great. But Steph has a sex addiction, and she been on that ship *four years*. Jenlithia needs to get over it."

"You just mad they killed Benredrick."

"You gotta admit—when Lizlorko shot him from the air lock? The show went downhill fast. And that not even my point here. Shouldn't it be democratic, what we watch? Shouldn't we vote on it?"

"You should talk to the soldiers about it. I sure they thrilled to hear about voting."

"God I miss the internet," Max says glumly.

Now seventeen years old, Max is almost adult in appearance, his forehead wider, his eyes set deeper, his chin more pronounced. O has aged as well, with a crisper crust around his perimeter, fuller lips inside his widened mouth square. Both boys wear dark green jumpsuits, the words *Wound Glue Worker* stitched into the chest. They stare past the razor wire, past the soldiers on the watchtowers, to the restless waves that break on the island's shore, the foam shuffling up the beach and then back down to the shallows, crossing the same stretch of sand like pacing feet.

"So," O says, reaching into his pocket, "I have something to show you."

"You got the tattoo?"

"No, not yet. It—well, here. Look."

The waffle pulls out a metal bottle cap, the top to a jar of Gordon Rubber Cement. Over the image of Gordy Glue—the boy riding an enormous parrot—someone has stamped the letter *C* in a curve of precise punctures.

"Is that . . . ?" Max begins.

"Yeah. An invite to The Conversation. Tomorrow night."

"Holy shit. Who gave it to you?"

"I promised not to say. They could get in so much trouble."

Max frowns down at the cap, the pierced metal glazed with moonlight. Finally he says, "You know, I not against them in principle. People *should* be talking, thinking of ways to fight back. But, O—if a soldier caught you? You could forget about college when the war ends. You be Suspected Status. That it."

"Yeah, I know. But maybe this is more important than college."

"More important than your *future*?" Max says. "The Conversation . . . what is it really? Some people who meet in a basement?"

"I just so curious about them. If, you know—if the rumors are true. If they talk about revolution there. Overthrowing the government."

"It not worth the risk. Sure, maybe they talk about important stuff. But do they *do* anything?"

"They meet all over the country. In lots of compounds."

"That another rumor," Max says.

The waffle looks away from the ocean, turning his gaze to their island prison. Before him, for miles and miles, sprawls the bland expanse of the compound, a dreary grid of streets that covers the island like a miniature city. There is a sector of apartment buildings, blocks of identical towers that soar high above the smog line; a sector of cafeterias, a boiled drumstick painted on each roof; a sector of Wound Glue factories, each brick behemoth several blocks in length, their chimneys pumping fists of smoke into the starless sky. A wartime logo is on the factory doors: Gordy, dressed in combat fatigues, skateboarding to a fallen soldier with his glue tube.

"But aren't you angry, Max?" O says. "After what happened to your parents? After what happened to mine?"

"Of course I angry. But when the war ends, I want to leave this place."

"If they *let* us leave," O mutters.

"No way they keep us after the war. And then we can go to college. Then we can get political. We can vote, organize, protest."

O turns the bottle cap over, pondering the exactitude of the punctures. "You ever hear that quote? 'The only thing necessary for the triumph of evil is for good men to do nothing.'"

Max rests his head on O's shoulder. "Skip the meeting, okay? Promise me. Don't risk this."

"Fine, I make you a deal. I won't tear down the government—for now. But you need to watch *Galaxy Gossip* with me."

"Wow," Max says with a laugh. "You *very* committed to revolution."

"All nineteen season."

Max groans. "This is extortion."

"Do we have a deal?"

"Yes, yes. Just don't get arrested, you beautiful piece of dough."

"We better get a move on then. It starts in fifteen minutes."

They rise to their feet and step to the edge of the dune, where they opt for a faster mode of transport: O lies down on his back and Max takes a seat on his fluffy squares, tucking his legs like a rider in a toboggan. The young men squeal as they go zipping down the incline, sand spraying behind the speeding disc of bread. At the bottom O sticks out his rubber hands and skids them to a stop.

Soon they are strolling through the Residential Sector, both panting a bit as they pass the apartment towers. Max slings an arm around the waffle, nestling his hand in a back square. The towers are crammed close together; hundreds of factory jumpsuits dry on lines between the windows. Here and there a waffle soldier looks out from a watchtower, scanning the streets below for signs of unrest.

Farther down the block, a small crowd of refugees stands around a crime scene, some crying as they stare at a taped-off section of sidewalk. There a dead figurine lies facedown on the pavement, splayed out below a fifteen-story building. Both his arms have popped out of his torso; holes gape open in his shattered head. His thinning hair lies over the hollows, sprinkled with shards of his skull.

Without a word, Max and O turn down a side street. After a silence, O says numbly:

"How many does that make this month?"

"That would be, um . . . eleven suicides."

"They need to put up some nets. Cheap bastards."

Headlights flash across the boys, a military jeep headed toward the crime scene. Several waffle soldiers sit inside, the two in back passing a whiskey bottle.

The boys drop their arms from each other. They skitter off down another side street.

The next afternoon, Max sits at a desk in the Education Sector, one of thirty students in a classroom with sheet metal walls. A video plays at the front of the room, showing a cheerful waffle in a cowboy hat and spurs. He stands at the center of an industrial chicken coop, row after row of wire cages stacked up to the ceiling.

"As we learned today," the waffle says in a folksy, laid-back voice, "the jury's still out on whether the 'HeatLeap' is even real. The temperature of our planet has changed many times, long before we burned Ground-Up-Bone. But know what nobody can debate? That burning chicken bone is 'wow wow,' as you kids like to say. It powers our whole world."

The waffle starts to stroll past the cages, waving at a smiling worker who pushes a cart of feed bags. "And because we never run out of chicken bones, we never run out of power," he goes on. "Wind, solar, hydro—sure, they *work*. But can they power a strong nation? A nation that never backs down, that always stands up to the enemy? Sorry, folks. For that you need GUB. You need GUB and grit."

The school bell rings in the classroom, chiming from a speaker on the corrugated wall. The students, most dressed in factory jumpsuits, stand groggily from their desks and drift to the door. They pass a poster of teenage workers at an assembly line, all giving each other high fives behind the conveyor belt; in front of them poses President Wafflin, holding a globe in his palm. *We in this together!* the poster proclaims.

Max wears a well-worn sweatsuit, today his afternoon off from the factory. As he shuffles toward the exit, his teacher calls out to stop him:

"Fluga wug! Max blin!"

His teacher is an odd-looking creature, her furry body floating in the air above her desk. She is shaped like a shipping box, a square of shaggy hair, kept airborne by a whirring propeller that juts out from her top. On her front is a massive eyeball, a smile half hidden in fur; two stubby arms stick out from her sides.

Max turns as other students file past him. "Yes, Mrs. Glorber?" he says.

"Glonk glonk," replies the cube of fur. She reaches down to her desk, picking up a glossy brochure from among her papers.

Then she glides across the room to Max, his hair rippling in the wind off her propeller.

"Zugga da gor?" she asks him.

Max shrugs. "I doing okay, I guess. Not bad."

"Shuu da splum. Flink."

"Wow wow. That nice of you to say. But . . . I not sure what you mean?"

"Wob. Ackin. Traggle."

Max takes a small step back. He looks startled, awestruck.

"You not serious. Really?"

"Raggle roggle."

"Thank you, Mrs. Glorber," he says with growing wonder. "I—I kinda in shock."

The teacher chuckles and gives Max the slim brochure. On the cover sits a boy in a college classroom, raising his hand with an eager smile, his classmates turned in their chairs to hear him speak. A robot perches at the desk beside him, its light bulb nose glowing an affable green. *From Compound to College,* reads the title, *Scholarships for Top-Notch Refugees!*

Max stares at the words, speechless. At last he says, "I just curious. Any chance my family can come with me?"

The fur-cube frowns sympathetically. "Prap dap. Toogy."

"Right. Right, of course." The elation wanes on his face. "I so grateful. Really. Can I take a few days to decide?"

"Ooogin, Max. Blug da borg."

"Okay. Thank you again. I let you know soon."


The brochure tucked in his pocket, Max steps into the court-yard of the Education Sector. A circle of sheet-metal buildings surrounds the yard, linked together like storage units across the pavement. Students of every age swarm the area: a jungle gym of shrieking children; a sandbox where toddlers crawl under the eyes of hovering fur-cubes; some picnic tables where older students huddle among themselves, immersed in their adolescent intrigues.

O, dressed in his jumpsuit, sits alone on a metal bench, paging through a beat-up algebra textbook. He wears a sour, fatigued expression, but his bready features brighten at the sight of his boyfriend approaching. Max lowers himself to the bench; they share a quick but intimate kiss. Two girls on the jungle gym see this, then look at each other and giggle.

Max notices the waffle's tired eyes, his slumped upper rim. "How it going?" he says.

O sighs. "You didn't hear? Another accident at the factory. It so stupid that fur-cubes work there. Way too dangerous."

"Shit. Who get hurt?"

"Ginny."

"Oh God. She okay?"

"I heard it from Tim. She was flying over a glue vat, and a tiny gob—that all it took—spat up into her propeller. And down she went," O adds with a shudder along his bread.

"And she . . ."

"They didn't get her in time."

Max shakes his head. "Poor Ginny."

"Her boyfriend, Alan, he was in the break room when it happened. He heard the alarm bell, but he came too late. They had to stop him from flying in after her."

Both grow quiet as they picture this: the grieving fur-cube fighting to join his girlfriend in the glue, his fellow cubes restraining him in midair.

O sighs again. "Anyway. Let's change the subject. How was your day?"

Max glances back at his classroom, his face even more conflicted than before. A whisper of waves carries to him from the
island shore.

"Boring. Same old same old," he says. He reaches down and
takes the waffle's hand.

"Hey, lover boys!" cries a senior at a picnic table, a figurine
with a glue-scorched nose and a hostile grin. "Get a room!"

"Don't forget the syrup!" chimes in another. The table erupts
in raucous laughter.

O swings his circle around to face them. "You shut the fuck
up!" he yells.

The table is hushed for a second, then bursts into an even
louder laughter.


Later that day, while O works his shift, Max heads back home
to the Residential Sector. The elevator is out of service, so he
struggles up the steep stairwell, his breathing ragged, his right
hand gripping a damp sack of chicken. At the eleventh floor he
leaves the stairs and strides down a narrow passage, its walls pale
and water-streaked, its carpet pocked with stains. On each door
are two dead bolts; the slitted keyholes watch him pass like cat
eyes. Scraps of conversation can be heard behind the doors, loud
or soft, kind or harsh depending on the mood, a broth of voices
burbling on all sides.

Max unlocks his own dead bolts, steps inside his family's
apartment. The main room is dim and cramped, only space
enough for a couch and a kitchen table. His father sits hunched
at the table, reading a sheet of paper clutched tight in his hands.

Gary turns in his chair when he hears the door open. He is a
thinner, frailer man after years inside the compound, his portly
face now gaunt and webbed with crackles. The top of his head

is half melted by glue, the plastic bubbled among his patches of hair. His legs are two short nubs, amputated at the thigh, hidden inside the tied-off legs of his sweatpants.

He raises the sheet of paper in trembling fingers. "A letter from your sister today."

Max is still catching his breath. "Oh. Amaze. What does Anita say?"

"Some great news. They're expanding her role on *Lovelorn.* Turns out Sheila Greenthrob has a twin sister."

On the wall beside him hang photos of Anita, taped between the spreading water stains. In most, the robot stars in stage productions: the cylinder set upright at the body of Polynices, or carried in the arms of a weeping King Lear, or rolling her googly eyes at Henry Higgins. But the largest picture is from her soap opera, *Lovelorn,* the robot in bed with a square-jawed hunk, while a woman with streaked mascara aims a gun at the metal seductress.

Max sets down the sack of chicken. "Mom still asleep?" he asks.

"Those pills, they just knock her out. Her back was acting up last night."

"She needs to do her stretches more. I know they hurt, but she needs to."

Gary gives a gloomy nod. Then, rousing himself, he rolls back his chair and gestures with a flourish at the table. "And look what else Anita sent me."

On the table sits a board game, its colored cardboard the splotched green of a muddy field. Metal athlete tokens cover the field, each holding a minuscule paddle. *Shmuglin: The Home Game!* reads the title.

"Can you believe it?" Gary marvels. "You do the whole thing with a spinner wheel. And the detail!" He picks up a player from a goal zone, a miniature bucket on its head. "Just look at this Shmugler. He even has kneepads."

"Great. That really great, Dad."

"Come sit down. I'll show you how it works."

"Actually, right now . . . it not the best time. I need to get started on homework."

"Oh. Okay," Gary says, trying to hide his disappointment. He forces a smile. "School good today?"

"It fine. Mrs. Glorber played *Our Good Friend GUB* again."

"*Again?* God. So much propaganda."

Max reaches into his pocket, as if about to remove the college brochure, tell his father the news. Outside the window, plumes of smoke ascend above a factory chimney, the billows bending sideways, shredded to pieces in the ocean wind.

"Well, see you a bit later," Max says, taking his hand from his pocket. "I left some chicken for you on the counter."

"Thanks!" Gary responds, a false singsong in his voice. "If you want to play Shmuglin later, you know how to find me!"

As he leaves the room, Max passes a rusty rat cage. There are no rodents in the cage, only a framed photo on the altar, set beside two tiny pewter urns. The photo shows Blorko and Daphne in their sequined jumpsuits, gazing at each other as they go soaring above a ramp, Blorko kneeling in midair with a ring box in his hand, Daphne holding a stunned forepaw to her chest. On the left urn are the words: *Daphne. She grieves no more.*

Max shuts the door of his bedroom, little larger than a walk-in closet. On the bed lies his stuffed seal, holding out its flippers with blank-eyed affection. "You in for it now, Team 2!" his father cries from the other room. The spinner wheel gives an enthusiastic *whoosh.*

While his father moves the tokens, Max sits on his bed and leafs through the brochure. He stares down at the centerfold: an aerial photo of a college campus, stately buildings and tree-shaded lanes, students strolling the quad in morning sunshine. He turns to the final page: a group of joyful refugees in graduation robes, throwing their caps high in the air, the tassels fluttering like flute notes as they soar.

"What you got there, kid?" asks a gruff voice above him.

On the wall hangs his old friend Morris. The miniature Christ is no older, still in his early thirties, with the same loincloth and painted beard, the same thorny crown.

Max gazes at the graduates a moment longer, then slips the brochure in his pocket. "Oh, Morris," he says at last. "I so confused."

"Well. Better tell me then."

Max explains the scholarship offer: the chance to attend college this fall, to leave the refugee compound, to resume the life stolen from him by this merciless war. It hurts how much he wants this, but it would mean abandoning his parents, who've needed his help so much the past two years, ever since that glue vat exploded on their shift. It would mean abandoning O, the waffle he loves.

"Whoa. That's a tough one," Morris says. Then, tentatively, he adds, "So, uh, in college—you're in a dorm room, right? With a window?"

"I not sure. Probably."

"That would be pretty great, huh? A view of the quad. Some trees outside."

Max frowns. "Is that really your response? That you'd hang on a better wall?"

"Gosh, remember the bedroom at your old house? The

penguin wallpaper? The jellyfish curtains? I dream about it sometimes."

The laugh track chuckles weakly.

"This is completely beside the point . . ." Max says.

"I guess I should still be grateful. I could hang in a bathroom or something."

"Can we focus for a minute? I need to make a huge decision."

Morris nods. "I hear ya, kid. Why don't you take my nails out? I'll explain it all to you."

A breezy banjo starts to play on the soundtrack, a shuffle beat with brushes—but Max shakes his head and the music stops at once. He goes on:

"Maybe I need to stay here. Go to college later. I supposed to *help* the people I love. Not ditch them."

"I think you're forgetting something," Morris says.

"What?"

"You'd be helping *me*."

Max raises his eyebrows. "Morris, you live on a cross. Would your life be all that different?"

"I don't know. Maybe I'd join a frat."

With a gasp of relief, the laugh track roars.

The wind blows stronger off the sea as night descends on the island, rattling the miles of razor wire around the compound. Curls of sand whip down the sidewalks; the jumpsuits, strung between the buildings, lurch about like troupes of modern dancers. A waffle soldier wobbles at the railing of his watchtower, his green fatigues flapping against his bread.

Max strides against the gusting wind, his breathing strained and shallow. The sunset fades above him like a memory from childhood, its vivid blush softening into mottled stripes of color. He strides beyond the buildings, beyond a low brick wall, then across the sand to a vacant stretch of fencing. There, between the chain links, he sees the vast rim of the shoreline, the churning depths of the ocean. The sun sinks below the horizon like a waffle on fire.

Max leans his forehead against the fence, grips the chain links on either side of his face. He looks out at the waves, glistening emerald in the sunset; he listens to the many-hued murmurs of the tide.

On the soundtrack plays a wistful piano, a legato violin, matching the musing rhythms of the waves. He sips the wind with pursed lips, and then, in a quiet tenor, begins to sing:

> *Some guys dream of engagement rings,*
> *Their boyfriend on one knee.*
> *But I don't crave romantic things,*
> *Just knowledge of the sea.*
>
> *To study oceanography,*
> *To get my PhD,*
> *To learn from brilliant faculty*
> *Who see themselves in me—*
>
> *Could I leave Mom and Dad to go*
> *Pursue this lifelong dream?*
> *Could I spend years away from O*
> *To study the marine?*
>
> *A voice says yes, a voice says no;*
> *I watch the ocean gleam.*

*What choice is best? It's hard to know*
*When you're just seventeen.*

The music fades to silence, lost in the susurrant sea. From the distance a seagull wings into sight, calling out as it soars; he watches the bird fly higher and higher and disappear among the clouds, its liquid shadow slipping from the waves.

Then, not far behind him, he hears the crunch of sneakers on the sand. He looks over and sees two men in jumpsuits striding through the dunes, a waffle and a figurine in their twenties. Between them floats a male fur-cube, his right hand gripping a liter bottle of vodka. The fur-cube flies at a halting pace, tilted to one side, his propeller slowing and speeding with fitful sputters. His friends exchange a worried glance as he stops and drinks deeply from the bottle.

"Flor googa," the fur-cube says in a muddled, drunken voice. "Grun buk."

The waffle puts a gentle hand on the cube. "No, Alan, that just not true. You couldn't help her."

"He right," the figurine says. "It was too late when you got there. Ginny was already under the glue."

Alan stares straight ahead with his bloodshot eye. Then, with a violent sweep of his arm, he throws the vodka bottle to the sand. His propeller buzzes louder as he soars swiftly upward, ascending above the fence in a tipsy, zigzag line.

"You okay, buddy?" the waffle calls. "Come on back down, okay?"

But Alan seems to have made up his mind. "Morka *gor!*" he cries, his eye glinting with tears, and then zooms away from his friends with a sudden, reckless speed. He flies like a wraith over the fence, then over the windy beach, then over the surging waves along the shore. He leaves the land behind him, hurtles out to the open sea.

His friends shout the entire time: *"Alan, come back!"* *"It too far! You won't make it!"* *"Don't do this, please! There lot to live for!"*

Their shouting draws the attention of a waffle soldier squinting at a crossword puzzle on a beachside tower. He looks up from the difficult word, spots the suicidal square of fur. "That makes twelve," he mutters.

Max watches the doomed fur-cube, buffeted back and forth as he fights against the wind. Alan shrinks from a square to a pinpoint in the upper curve of the sun, he and the ball of fire sinking together toward the horizon, drawn into oblivion by the same indifferent gravity.

Before the speck of Alan vanishes, Max turns from the fence and runs like a frightened child from the sight. He hurries through the dunes, not stopping to catch his breath, not slowed by his pained gasping. He pulls the brochure from his pocket, clutches it tightly as he flees.

# 15

The streets flow past in shadow as Erin drives home from the grocery store, the lawns and houses steeped in twilight, dimming in the slow dissolve of dusk. The fenced backyards slide past her windshield, the loops of razor wire, the dozens of security signs (GUN IN HOUSE or ARMED+READY) zip-tied to the grilles of window bars.

On her back seat sits a bag of chicken breasts, stirring like a restless sleeper as she drives. *MegaGrub: MEAT You There!* reads the logo on the bag. As she passes a grim lawn sign—a drawing of a beheaded terrorist, his eyes wide in his ski mask— her phone chimes with a text notification.

Carla, play text in car, Erin says.

Playing text from JACOB, the phone responds. *Hey there! 8:30 tonight still good? No wait see you, it way too long! If want, we def leave Tyler party early. Just need give Olivia zing-stick back. See soon!*

Erin grips the grooves of the steering wheel as she listens. In an uneasy voice she says:

Carla, reply Jacob.

Ready for reply.

She clears her throat and says:

Yay. I no wait see you, too. Much sorry I get so busy. I put on party clothes, then pick you up.

Carla reads back the message. Approve?

Add exclamation point. All sentence.

Exclamation point add.

Send text, Carla.

Erin flips on her turn signal, steers the car down another dusky street.

*It's killing me,* she narrates, *all the lies I'm telling Jacob. He thinks I'm working again at Tablet Town, that I've been going in every day to help with reopening. He thinks my Smartbody's broken, that I shipped it off to corporate for repairs. I feel guilty, lonely, nervous, but I just can't find the strength for this—to tell him the truth, to see the judgment on his face.*

She stops at an intersection, then turns onto her own street. A second later she slams her foot on the brake, the grocery bag toppling to the floor.

Three vans are parked outside her house, the long panel vans of the Terrorism Bureau. Their back doors are swung open, revealing stacks of items from her home: her television on its side, her floor lamps heaped together, her Smartlegs jutting above a box flap—one of the many boxes in the vans. Her house is also open, the front door propped with a chair, through which a dark-suited agent now comes striding onto the lawn, holding a box in his rubber prosthetic hands. Behind her bay window, she glimpses the outlines of other agents moving behind the curtains.

Erin reaches down and puts her car in reverse—as if she will roll back around the corner, abandon her home to these well-dressed intruders. But she stays halted in the road, her sneaker pressing the brake, her face perplexed.

Behind her an engine growls; a new bureau van drives fast around the corner. It squeals its siren twice, then a voice booms from its loudspeaker: *MS. JAMES. PLEASE PARK AT HOUSE. STAY IN CAR TILL TOLD.*

*TAKE SLOW NOW, NICE EASY,* the loudspeaker adds as she crawls down the road to her driveway. The agent on the lawn stops to watch her; in his box, piled high, sit some of her father's old binders and notebooks.

Soon she stands on her front lawn, her hands clasped on her head, her elbows clenched so tight their hinges creak. A female agent gives her a thorough frisk; an agent with a crack in his cheek reads Erin her rights. She is now in "indefinite custody" under Article 189 of the Silence Is Violence Act: she has no right to an attorney, no right to petition for release, no right to a trial without the bureau's approval. The act permits torture if needed, though only "non-melt" methods of interrogation. In a house across the street, a sliver of face peers out from behind a curtain.

The agents do not cuff her, do not lock her in a van. Instead they lead her inside through the propped front door, where a half dozen agents pick apart the rooms with a practiced finesse, sifting through drawers, taking down paintings, shooting their scanner guns at the walls and ceiling. The whole house rustles with the efficient hiss of their hinges. One older agent, a short man with a chunk gone from his nose, tells his partner about a recent scuba vacation. Those dolphin, they swim right with ya, he says, lifting a box crowded with Erin's swimming trophies. The pedestals jostle from side to side, the diving figures poised at the edge, as if preparing to leap.

In the living room, the agent with the cracked cheek leads

Erin to her sofa. Agent Fuller here soon, he says, please take seat. She lowers herself to a cushion, her face struggling to keep its composure.

From the next room comes the hum of a wheelchair motor. *Give it up, Al! You too old scuba!* cries a buoyant female voice. As the agents laugh, an electric wheelchair glides into the living room, steered by a middle-aged woman with a notch across her forehead.

Erin James! Such pleasure meet you! she says, flashing a smile as she rolls up to the sofa. The woman helms the chair with perfect posture, her polished face glossed with sunset, her short hair parted sharply to one side.

All this mess here—I need apologize, she goes on. It standard procedure, I afraid. You just never know where terror group plant bug.

I not with . . . I not terrorist, Erin stammers. She brushes a tear from her eye.

The agent chuckles kindly. Ah, Erin. Ever so anxious. Of *course* you not terrorist, dear.

I never collaborate, either. No help them.

Yes, hon, we know. If you help them, think we chat like this? You be out in van right now, bag over head. By way, we get you some water? Juice?

Uh, no. I fine.

Well then. Let introduce myself. My name Agent Barbara Fuller. Feel free call me Barb.

Erin nods, tries to smile. The woman continues:

Now. I know this all big shock. Terrorism Bureau at house! Super scary. But we not here punish you, dear—trust me. We just need talk. Get on same page.

Erin tucks a hand under her knee, stops its jouncing. But

outside . . . they say I violate Silence Is Violence. They say I indefinite custody.

Well sure. You hide those mascot from us. Much illegal.

But I never—I never know what they mean. I think they glitch in program.

The agent chuckles again. You no need lie, hon. We watch you in Smartworld. Those mascot tell you about attack, you never call us—much prison time. But we give you way out. If want it.

You mean, like . . . go undercover?

A louder laugh bursts from Barb. *You?* Oh my. Oh, Erin. You barely survive first date with Jacob—how you infiltrate terrorist cell? There not enough SettleSelf in world for that.

Erin falls silent. I take some water now. If that okay.

Def. Hey, Dennis, will you . . . Barb says to the agent with the fractured cheek. He strides off to the kitchen.

Across the room, an agent removes some wooden crates from a closet. The crates are filled with framed photos, the family photos that no longer hang in her hallway. As if to herself, Erin mumbles:

So . . . how long you watch me?

Barb shrugs. You sis of famous terrorist. Half terrorist we catch, it family contact. All these middle-class kid, they get real mad, they kill bunch people—but then, once in hiding? They bad homesick. Want talk their mommy.

Dennis returns with the glass of water. Erin takes a slow sip with her eyes closed.

I like you, hon, Barb goes on. Really, I do. You nurse dying father, you answer Good Samaritan Alert—you not bad person. But you also criminal, no forget that. This shiny favor we do you.

Erin exhales. This get me killed, this favor?

Def not. It simple simple. Just need have chat with someone.

Chat? With who?

Barb forces down a grin. Want guess?

No . . .

I give hint. You no see her in five year. You same dad.

Erin stiffens on the sofa, her face blank with disbelief. The water quivers at the midpoint of her glass.

This big surprise us, too, Barb says. We search your sis long time, but Fiona gone gone. We just one clue—those mascot—but hacker too good to trace. Then not long ago, out nowhere, we get phone call.

Fiona call you?

We no believe it either. She tell us we need meet soon: she have important info, want cut deal with bureau. And not just deal for her. Deal for you, too.

For me, Erin murmurs, staring at the crates beside the closet.

You should thank her. If deal go through, you both immunity. You need it, hon.

Erin shakes her head. This whole thing, it—it make no sense.

It exciting, I say that much. We get terrorist flip now then, but Fiona Reynolds? That big fish.

I no understand. She want betray her group?

Sure seem that way. We plan meeting for tonight. She want see her sister, talk for bit. After that, she get new name, leave country.

Excuse me, but this *terrible* idea. What if—

Listen, Barb interrupts. She bends forward in her wheel-chair, rests a hand on Erin's arm. You want stay out prison?

Of course. But—

Then you need come with us now. Need talk your sis.

Erin keeps her eyes on the crates. In the nearest one she sees a photo of her and Fiona as children, the little girls playing a clapping game on the grass beside a hot spring, steam curling up from the crater of water behind them. The steam and the dust on the picture frame are of a similar hue, so that it looks like the mist has escaped the photo and clouded the glass as well, obscuring the sisters' faces, two blurry ovals beneath their nylon bangs. Erin watches the play of light on the glass, bleaching their summer dresses from sight, restoring them with a shift of an agent's shadow. At last she says:

But what Fiona want tell me? I nothing say to her.

Wish I knew, dear. But she not in custody yet. She say she meet us there.

Where? Erin asks.

She say it place you know.


Dennis, now dressed in a Hawaiian shirt, steers a bulky station wagon around the bends of a beach road. He keeps pace with an old sedan that curves through the mist ahead of him, their close formation the only sign they carry law enforcement.

Barb also wears a loud Hawaiian shirt. She turns to the back seat and says to Erin:

Listen, I know you nervous. But look bright side. You get skip that party tonight.

Erin remains silent, gazing out at the fog along the coast. The ocean glints with shards of moonlight, strewn like broken glass on the dark expanse. Barb continues:

That kid Tyler. He much annoying, huh?

Yeah. Sorta.

Oh, c'mon. I see you at his "pyramid" last week. You ready scream, that kid so spoiled. And listen, hon: you need watch out that Olivia girl. She all flirty after you leave—I no like it. I rooting for you and Jacob. You real cute couple.

I dunno, Dennis says. I kinda miss her AI boyfriend.

Barb scoffs. *Patrick?* He computer software.

No bother me. I married eleven year—wish my wife like that. Never get moody. Never complain. No, *Dennis, why you work late?* No, *Bethany husband take her cruise. Where my cruise?* Just TV, sex, sleep. Keep it simple.

Barb pats his shoulder. Very enlightened, Dennis. Great stuff there.

She reaches into her fanny pack and pulls out Erin's phone.

Hey, hon, she says over her shoulder. I send text for you. We no want Jacob worry.

She taps in the passcode and thumbs a message, speaking the words as she types: *I need go work tonight. No make it to party. See you later.*

Erin leans forward in her seat. Maybe that not—

There, Barb says, sending the text. Now he know you safe.

The phone chimes with his response a minute later. Barb reads aloud: *Work tonight? That so last minute. Weird weird. Anyway, look like Olivia Monica drive me. Hope we hang soon, much creaky not see you.*

Barb tilts her head. Huh. He sound upset. Well, you make it up to him.

Erin does not reply. She turns back to the window.

The beach road is empty of buildings, to the left the spectral shore and to the right a plain of grass, the pine trees dark in the misty depths of the meadow. The road curves in a wide arc, bending slowly beachward, and then, far down the shoreline, a lone structure swivels into sight above the fog, lighthouse-like on a rise over the ocean. The building is a metal column, a cylinder of steel; water gushes down its sides, splashing into a moon-shaped pool that circles the building like a moat. On the rooftop burns a neon sign: WATERFALL CAFÉ.

The fog rises higher as they pull into the parking lot, its feathery hands fraying against the windshield. They park in a space near the beachfront, ghostly and deserted with its drifting rags of mist.

Okay, hon, Barb says to Erin. Now try relax. Just go inside, sit in booth—Fiona say she find you. Eezy peezy, right?

If I no punch her, Erin mutters to the window.

Barb smirks. Yeah. Try avoid that.

And this clear my record? I done after this?

Yes. *If* you cooperate. *If* we make deal with Fiona. So it best you act nice. Best for everyone.

Erin closes her eyes. Fine. Okay.

This meeting, Barb says, it good bad both. On good side, Fiona want talk you—maybe say thing she never tell bureau. We have mic in every booth, record it all. On bad side, we out in open here, not exactly safe. So listen, hon: get her talking, have nice chat, but no dillydally, 'kay? We want know big stuff—her group, what she do past five year. I let you know when time wrap up.

You sure all this? It seem real—

You not alone in there, no worry. Lot undercover agent. Me and Dennis, we pretend we newlywed. This our honeymoon.

I wish, Dennis says drolly.

Barb, guffawing, elbows his arm. Careful there. I call HR.


Erin strides alone across the lot, stepping into the long column of the café's shadow. A glass revolving door glistens at the entrance; the waterfall rages on either side, piquing the pool into a tantrum of froth. She draws her windbreaker tight around her, her knuckles creaking in the pockets.

*I've never managed to hate my sister, hard as I've tried,* she narrates. *Resent her? Every day. Dream about yelling at her, screaming into her face? For years that dream woke me up most nights. But I could never simply despise her, or wish she was gone from my life. No, there was always this irrational hope: that the gulf between us would heal, that the old Fiona, my hero, would come back to me somehow, that our days as loving sisters would resume. Crazy, I know, to want this with a murderer like her. But maybe that's how betrayal always feels—like the person you love has doubled, like their former self might still return, might erase this stranger who's stolen their face and name.*

Erin stops at the revolving door, the glass panels misted with waterfall spray. She whispers under the roar:

Oh God, please be with me. This so much. Too much. Need help.

She presses the damp glass; the door spins her into the lobby. Inside she looks about at the many familiar attractions: a holographic rock band that performs on a small wooden stage, an alcove of pinball machines and ancient arcade games, an eight-foot-high aquarium tank where koi and guppies swim through a sunken city. Booths with tufted cushions run along the curved walls, most of them empty.

Erin slides into a booth with a view of the sunken city. The miniature buildings are dark and abandoned, the sidewalks cracked with seagrass, the cars along the curbs caked with coral. Dunes have gathered against the storefronts, their shredded awnings stirring in the current. At the center stands a grand hotel with all its windows shattered, the curtains waving back and forth like truce flags.

She looks around uneasily at the others in the café: the servers in their pinstripe vests, the singles at the bar, the figurines who sway in front of the holographic rock band, whose pale, stubbled singer, strumming an acoustic guitar, lilts an eerie ballad about catching and eating a mouse. Her sister is nowhere in sight.

A bar with a mirrored counter runs behind the dance floor, reflecting the paper lanterns strung from the ceiling. An old man in a shaggy sweater sits among the velvet barstools, chewing a bite of chicken from a crushed tin box. *Morning Bell,* reads the brand name on the tin.

After a sidelong glance at Erin, the old man struggles up from his barstool. He grasps his cane and dodders across the dance floor. He is a scrawny octogenarian, his rigid torso inclined with age, a maze of crackles across his mustached face. Erin watches him approach, a question in her gaze, until he lowers himself to the opposite bench and says in a female voice:

Hey, little fish.

## 16

Fiona laughs through her fake nose, ruffling the threads of her mustache. She folds her hands on the table, a paste-on crackle loosening along her knuckle.

Sorry I startle you, fish. I much paranoid right now.

Erin stares at her. This real fucked up, Fiona. Even for you.

God. Just need look at you for sec. It so good see you, sis. You no idea.

There are tears in the old man's eyes, gleaming below his wooly brows. Erin looks down at her place mat.

I sorry all this drama, Fiona says. If I think you read it, I send you letter through bureau. But you prob ignore letter. This too important.

People keep say that to me: *Listen, listen. Important, important.* Wish just leave me alone.

Fiona dips two fingers in her chicken tin, plucks out a dripping morsel. She holds it up to her eyes like a precious gemstone.

These ever my fav. Remember?

Sure, Erin murmurs.

I eat them lunch, all high school. Eat them when study, when zinged. But no eat long time now. No able get.

Fiona swallows the moist morsel, sucks her fingertips dull. She goes on:

I ever hope this happen, fish. Chance you me talk again. You think me evil, cruel—but it not like that. I hate that I lose family. Hate I hurt you.

Not just *hurt,* Erin says. You destroy our family.

Hate that, too.

And now? You run from terror group. Try send them prison. Those people you kill—all for nothing.

Fiona shakes her old man's head. I no want them go prison. Just want stop this attack.

Erin looks across the café, where Barb and Dennis now share a booth beside the fish tank, both munching from a bowl of boiled wings. All gaiety is gone from Barb's expression—glancing discreetly at patrons, meeting the gaze of undercovers, alert to any new arrivals through the revolving doors—a far less relaxed woman in this unprotected setting. She keeps a finger casually pressed to her ear, listening to the siblings on an earpiece.

Erin looks back at her sister with a weary resolve.

I just never understand it, she says. Why all this happen. You such normal girl in high school. Straight A. So close to Dad.

A shadow of grief crosses the ancient face. I *seem* normal in high school. But that when it all start. That when I wake up.

Bullshit. In high school, you good person. You in love with Adam. You best on debate team.

You know what wake me up? It weird weird think it now. Owen Foley. Dad ex-husband.

Erin pauses. Owen? You no see him since little kid.

But remember in junior year? When I find his profile?

Sure . . .

Well, I find other stuff, too—much disturbing. You in middle school then, real young. I decide not tell you.

Fiona explains. Back in high school, her search for Owen had brought her to a "protest website," Suspected-No-More.com. The site was a platform for citizens who had received Suspected Status, a place to share their stories of government persecution. Many of these people had committed no crimes, faced no formal charges, but at some point they'd gained the attention of the Domestic Security Office—attending one too many rallies, posting too often on certain topics—after which, with their name on the list, they lived under far more restrictions than other citizens. They could never vote, never seek higher education, never know when they were under state surveillance.

Fiona found herself in the website's Refugee section, watching a video where Owen told his story to an interviewer off camera. He described his flight from nuclear fallout, then his years of labor in a refugee compound, where, at the age of twenty, he'd attended two secret meetings of The Conversation. He had attended not to "betray" his country, but from a sense that his nation had lost its way, that serious thought was needed about its future. No one had mentioned violence in these meetings; mostly they'd talked about planning a labor strike. The day after the second meeting, soldiers had detained him on his way to work, then shipped him to a black site prison for "disruptive" refugees. There, without a trial, without an official charge to appeal, he'd suffered like a convict for seven years.

These prisons were notorious, a threat that kept other refugees in line. Here there were cramped cells instead of apartments, longer shifts in the factories, the most hardened soldiers for guards. Suicides were more common, sexual violence and unexplained deaths, extremes of heat and cold. The Conversation was also more active here, more violent and ambitious in outlook. Though Owen kept to himself, steered clear of The Conversation, young refugees like him were always vulnerable to the guards. He was raped several times when he first arrived, after he refused the advances of a senior guard; later he was trapped in a stairwell and beaten—a beating that almost killed him, that left his face with permanent scars.

After his release, Owen tried his hardest to lead a normal life. He reunited with his longtime boyfriend, Max, settling in a Northwestern suburb, starting a family together. For years he had dreamed of this postwar future—but now, in their cozy house, with a beautiful child and plans for a second, he spent most of his days feeling distant and numb, or riddled with an anxiety he couldn't control. The core of him was still in captivity, his jailers his own memories and traumas. He tried therapy and medication, but they did nothing for his flashbacks; when he managed to sleep, he had nightmares that made insomnia feel like a blessing. Often he struggled with anger, picked fights with Max for no reason, jealous that Max had suffered less in the war years, escaped their compound early on a college scholarship. Max had a PhD now, taught classes at a university; Owen struggled to even get hired as a busboy.

In the end he longed for an escape, something stronger than medication or the zing-sticks he smoked most nights. Soon he found a dealer in town who could sell him harder drugs, drugs that released him from his inner prison, let him vanish into a sofa cushion while his hollow body sang with surging bliss. Owen hated his need for escape, longed to be a good parent, but his lust for these pills and powders consumed him, made his entire life revolve around his next high. His marriage collapsed a few months after their second daughter was born, and he decided that his family would be better off without him, that a man like him could only bring pain to the people he loved. Though he'd found sobriety in the years that followed, 12-step and a new relationship, his life remained a daily struggle.

At the end of the video, he said to the interviewer: "If I go back, do all again? Maybe, at start of war, I stay with my parent. Not run from radiation, not try escape. Maybe that my big mistake: I not meant to live. But no . . . I no mean that. It just been hard, you know? Not easy."

Fiona, sixteen, unaware of such horrors, sat in her comfy bedroom—her walls covered in band posters, pictures with her boyfriend—as Owen described his years of abuse, his lonely battle with addiction. As she would realize in the weeks to come, watching all the videos on the website, this suffering was not uncommon for refugees. Hearing their stories, she understood her father's silence about the war years, why he always evaded her questions. Who would want to give those images to their child's imagination: the battlefields and burning cities, the melted bodies in scorched sedans, the forsaken millions breathing the toxins in refugee factories? Who would want to tell their child the truth, that this nightmare-ridden nation was their home? No wonder The Conversation had spread from the compounds after the war; no wonder its message had focused on revolution.

That website, it open my eye, Fiona says in the café booth. Owen video—it play in my mind, over over.

Erin stares at the aquarium tank, the dark traffic lights above the streets, the tattered newsstands. Softly she says:

I search Owen online, too. Few year later. But never see that video.

Course not. Bureau take website down. They call it "recruitment tool" for terror group.

I know he go prison. But I no idea he addiction. No idea he . . .

Lot refugee suffer that way, Fiona says. This country—we only remember what want remember.

Fiona turns in her seat and flags down a server, a man in his twenties with a glass nose ring, spiky jet-black hair. In a hoarse male voice, she orders a pitcher of Tipsy Trappist Ale.

You want frosted mug, sir? the server asks respectfully.

Oh *yes*. That sound lovely. Me and my granddaughter here, we *love* our ale.

Across the café, Barb catches Erin's eye. She taps an invisible watch on her wrist, as if to say, *This family stuff great, hon—but that not why we here.*

Fiona sits with her back to the agent, unaware of these silent commands. When the server is gone, Erin says:

So those video, that why you leave us? That why you turn into killer?

I not killer, sis. I soldier.

Fine. *Soldier.* If soldier, guess killing not murder.

Fiona sighs. Those video, they only beginning. But I start see world new way. No able stop.

By the time she left for college, Fiona had given herself a secret education. She'd read countless articles on their corrupt system, on the ticking clock of the ecological crisis. The articles discussed inequity, the continued stockpiling of nuclear weapons, the brutal lives of the billions of chickens who powered their civilization, the dire future promised by the HeatLeap. This last issue upset her the most, the sheer outrage of the temperature rise, that the greed of a few generations would haunt her species for millennia: rising oceans, mass migration, hurricanes, drought, starvation. The problem grew worse with each new day of excessive GUB emissions, but did the people in power stop burning chicken bones? No: the burning increased. Her civilization— though it touted itself as history's greatest achievement—soon seemed unhinged to Fiona, not only violent and oppressive, but setting fire to the very ground on which they stood.

Most nights, unable to sleep, Fiona snuck out to the yard with a Sweet Serenity zing-stick. She needed to get very high to settle down her rage.

That my other big secret back then, Fiona says. All high school, I zing lot night. But much much after that website, when I so angry.

Secret? You smoke right outside my window.

Not right outside. At pine tree.

My light even on half time, Erin says. You out there coughing.

Ha! So you know? Think I so slick.

Fiona takes a sip from her frosted mug, delivered to the table during her story. She goes on:

I feel guilty in high school, keep so many secret. But, look back, that how we raised. Dad keep everything secret.

True, Erin agrees.

He change when he sick? Open up more?

Erin gazes at the holographic band, the front man now seated at an electric piano, bent close to the mic as he sings over jittery drums.

So you hear about it, she says. That he die.

Yes, I hear. Dad . . . he way too young.

A mug sits before Erin as well, condensation slipping down its sides. She grips the frigid handle, drinks the ale.

It—it best we not talk him. Not good for me.

Sure. No worry, fish.

Go on with story, though. I want hear rest.

Fiona continues. In her sophomore year of college, the terror groups had unleashed their first attacks on the public, dominating the news with their murders and manifestos. It was different from the usual violence in the streets: not an angry employee or a disturbed loner, but a focused movement aimed at revolution. While this tumult swept her nation, Fiona boarded a plane for her study abroad program. There she roomed down the hall from Janice Brooks, a quiet girl from a northern suburb who kept to herself outside of class, who never attended the weekend parties and bar crawls. She rarely combed her curly black hair, rarely washed her thrift store T-shirts, but Janice was brilliant and hilarious once she got talking, especially after some hits on her zing hookah. It turned out they had lots in common—favorite books, movies, Rhythm & Noise, and politics most of all, both enraged at the systems that kept down the poor, that thickened the ash in the sky. She and Fiona formed a clique of two, spent every free minute together.

One night, high in her dorm room, Janice lowered the hose of the hookah. With a shy smile, she asked if she could tell Fiona a secret. "Def, anything," Fiona said, intrigued. Janice cupped Fiona's ear, then whispered that she was "rooting" for the terror groups. She didn't just like them—she *loved* them. She'd read everything about them. "These terror attack, it sad sad so much death. But they fighting for our future. They trying save our species."

Fiona let out a squeal and gave her a huge hug. Before that moment, she hadn't known how profoundly she agreed.

After that night, their talks took on new horizons. Together they dreamed about the future, a world where the terror groups had succeeded, where figurines lived close to nature without the burdens of "nation" or "property." They talked about the news media, which the terror groups used to disrupt the society, creating the chaos needed for their government's collapse. The media—God bless them—would always boost the *most* chaotic message, always spread fear to gain more viewers. They talked about The Conversation, which had founded and funded the terror groups, their genius in creating mass panic as the first step in tearing down the system. Even the title "terror group" struck Fiona and Janice as brilliant, a name their nation had used for fearful enemies in the past. "The Conversation" sounded peaceful, thoughtful—but the *terror groups* could stalk your dreams, become angels of vengeance, ghosts of history, omens of a new era.

During this time, Fiona broke up with Adam. Whatever her choices for the future, she could never pursue the life they'd once desired: children, careers, vacations, a lush retirement. She cut back on her phone calls home, sickened by the voice of her former self, that middle-class girl obsessed with grades, blind to systems of power. Late that summer, when her father and sister survived a terror attack—huddling below the bullets at the aquarium—she felt shaken at their brush with death, but also a strange excitement. These attacks were everywhere now, affecting her own family. The violence of the groups unnerved Fiona—but, she reasoned, maybe that was a good thing.

On the last night of the abroad program, Fiona and Janice met up for a final hang. Janice seemed tense that night, changing the music midsong, pacing the room when she usually sat on her bed. Fiona assumed this was emotion—she would miss her new friend, too—but then, at three a.m., when it was almost time to part, Janice reached in her pocket and handed Fiona a slip of paper. On the slip was a phone number, ten bare digits. "What this?" Fiona asked.

Janice explained. Last spring, the son of a family friend had posted a manifesto online, then driven downtown and shot up a Boil Barn during the dinner rush. Derek was twenty-one, an honors student, an editor at his college newspaper; he'd abandoned a bright future when he disappeared into his terror group. A few nights after the shooting, a tapping came at Janice's window, loud but not enough to wake her parents. And there he was, the terrorist, the hero, in a hoodie with its hood up, breathing heavily. Derek knew Janice well—they'd gone to some protests together, made out a few times in his car—and he handed her this number before he vanished back into the night. It was the number for an all-female group (his group took only men), and she should text it a single word, *service,* if she wanted to make a difference.

Janice apologized for not telling Fiona sooner. She felt like a coward, a "total wimp," but she'd never come close to texting the number, just carried it in her wallet since that night. She lacked the courage to be a fighter like Derek, to leave behind the entire world she'd known. But now, with their time abroad over, with them heading back to their separate colleges, she wanted Fiona to have this number as well, her own chance to make this impossible decision.

Except that, for Fiona, it wasn't impossible. By the time she boarded the plane that morning, she knew she would text the number. The cause was just too urgent, too important. How many millions would die from the HeatLeap if chicken bones kept burning at this rate? Or if another nuclear war engulfed the planet? People called the terrorists "crazy," but it was just the opposite: it was crazy to sit and do nothing while there was still time.

Midway through Christmas break, Fiona waited alone in the food court of the SmileMile Mall. The middle-aged woman who strode to her table, who introduced herself as Niko, could have been one of her cooler college professors, relaxed in her jeans and corduroy jacket, her hair cut short and paling at the roots. In a placid, intelligent voice, she told Fiona her own story—how she had trained for years as a therapist, how she had come to see that The Conversation was the best way to help figurines: not trying to heal the neuroses of a dying civilization, but fighting for a new and healthier one. Niko said she saw herself in Fiona, the woman she'd been when she first joined the movement, eager to fight, to make a difference, but scared what this might ask of her. In the years since then, she'd risen from a soldier to a cell leader in Artemis, a group with a national reputation, an impressive combat record. Even if she died tomorrow, she would know her life had mattered, that she'd given all of herself to create a better world. Fiona sat in awe of this woman, her confidence, her air of total fulfillment.

Niko took a sip of her bubble tea. "And that bring us to matter at hand," she said, a harder look settling behind her smile. Her group was excited about Fiona—she'd been a topic at their meeting this morning—but, before she could join their cell, she would need to perform a "solo attack" to demonstrate her commitment to the cause. They made this step simple for new recruits and had a plan in mind for her already. One afternoon next semester, when Fiona was back at college, an Artemis member would trip and bump into her, pressing the code of a gym locker into her hand. There Fiona would find a backpack with a bomb in the main compartment, the detonator remote in the outer pocket. Later that night, at ten p.m., she should leave the backpack in her dorm room, then go outside and push the detonator button. An Artemis van would be waiting in the parking lot.

Fiona's mind reeled at the plan, but her first distinct emotion was relief. She wouldn't need to feel guilty anymore, complicit with her vile civilization. She would be part of the change, part of the solution.

In the days before the bombing, chatting with friends in her dorm; at the locker on the day itself, seeing the backpack there as promised; in the minutes before she left her room, getting a text from her friend Leah across the hall (*Want quick study break?*); in the elevator going down, nothing on her person now but some cash and the remote; in the shadows of the parking lot, her thumb on the small black button—all this time the violence had remained abstract to Fiona, a door she needed to pass through, a necessary evil, not a concrete act that would shatter her classmates, leaving twenty-two dead, fifty-seven wounded, hundreds traumatized for life. She didn't know the strength of the bomb, hadn't even unzipped that part of the backpack; she secretly hoped it was a fake bomb, that the group had planned a test just to see if she'd follow orders.

Then she pressed the button. From behind her top-floor window came a sharp crack of thunder, a sound she would never escape in the years ahead. Every window on the floor shattered outward; a mist of glass shimmered down to the sidewalk. She felt disoriented at once, an odd exhilaration, wondered that this massive noise, this storm of glass and fire, had coincided with the pressure of her thumb. A vehicle pulled up behind her— she'd forgotten all about the van—then a woman in a ski mask clutched her arm and rushed her into a seat. "Welcome," "Good job," "You brave," said other ski-masked women around her as the van sped away. As if in a dream, she struggled to grasp why these women praised her, then remembered she had just committed a massacre.

She felt exhilarated on the van ride, exhilarated when they parked the van outside a modest farmhouse, exhilarated as they led her to a false wall in the kitchen, then down a steep staircase to the network of rooms where the women resided, four underground floors of living quarters with a gym, an office, a training center. She felt exhilarated when she reached her bedroom, a narrow and windowless cell. A banner—WELCOME FIONA! YOU ROCK!—hung over the bed. On the nightstand stood a porcelain figure of a goddess in a tunic, her face turned in profile as she pulled a slender arrow from her quiver. It was the mascot of the group: Artemis.

Niko gave her two sleeping pills, left the new recruit to rest. Alone now, Fiona lay on the hard mattress and stared at the ceiling. She felt both wide-awake and exhausted, both inside and outside of her body, like she was looking down at herself in this spartan cell. There were two Fionas in this room: the Fiona who'd never planted the bomb, never pressed the remote, and the Fiona who'd watched the glass rain down to the sidewalk, who still felt the explosion reverberate through her hollows. She worried she'd stay awake for hours, might be up for days. Then she fell asleep at once.

It was normal enough for a new recruit to enter a state of shock, for this shock to wear off slowly. Niko understood this, sat and talked with Fiona most nights. In a few weeks Fiona regained her strength and started to train with the others, but her focus never returned to her, not with the scenes that played on an endless loop in her mind: her dormmates chatting in the common room, or studying at their desks, or scrolling their phones in bed—then a heat blast ripping through the wall, splitting off limbs, melting bodies beyond recognition. She imagined her father and Erin receiving the news, the bureau showing them photos of her disfigured classmates. She'd anticipated some guilt, known it was necessary for the cause, but she'd had no clue how it would actually *feel*.

Nor was her training going well, the nightly drills in the shooting range and obstacle course. Six months after the bombing, Fiona still tripped on her feet and dropped her gun, couldn't hit targets even at close range. Her whole life she'd excelled at whatever she tried—but now, when it truly mattered, when she was fighting for her species' survival, her body refused to obey her will, to slip into the kinetic rhythm of combat. The women in her cell were supportive; they'd also suffered from "attack fatigue," also scheduled times with Niko to discuss their traumas. After major attacks, they even held group therapy meetings in the briefing room. But they could see it was different with Fiona, that this kid wasn't built for combat.

Niko tried her out on two missions: a shooting at a public park, the bombing of a veterans parade. In the first, Fiona had a panic attack before she could shoot her rifle; in the second, she passed out after the blast and was carried to the van unconscious. Niko knocked on her door the next morning with a carafe of blackberry tea, and, with her usual warmth and tact, said they should "have quick chat" as she poured two glasses. She explained that every army needed "many type of soldier," not just fighters in the field. In fact, she could use Fiona's help with a different project entirely. Their cell was about to receive a generous gift from Artemis headquarters, one that might greatly boost morale in the bunker. But Niko herself had no time to spearhead the project; she needed a soldier to volunteer for the good of the group. The gift was a virtual reality suit, known as a "Smartbody."

This got be joke, Erin interrupts at the table. You work with Smartbody?

Just like you, sis. I run session in bunker.

You have Smartroom there?

State of art, Fiona says. It tough in bunker, all cooped up together. Sex, nature, adventure—Smartbody help us lot.

But terror group, they hate technology. They want destroy all that.

They practical, when need be. Smartbody good for now. They destroy in long run.

Fiona lifts their beer pitcher with a geriatric arm, pours a foamy arc of ale in their glasses. The pitcher is almost empty, their voices looser, more relaxed.

All these year, I picture you in combat, Erin says. Shooting machine gun, setting off bomb. But no? You cleaning Lady Insert?

Fiona sips her mug. It not so bad. Smartbody . . . it kinda amaze.

Despite her failures as a fighter, the suit made Fiona popular in the bunker. The women arrived for their sessions cheerful, emerged smiling and refreshed, usually back from a liaison with some sexy AI. Fiona soaped and sprayed the Body, dried it quickly for the next user. Though she never returned to the field, never suffered one chip in her plastic, the women remained her friends and colleagues, her rivals at the card table, her acting partners in the plays they often put on in the gym, throwing Fiona roses at curtain call whenever she acted the lead. And at night, while the others drilled, Fiona had hours for her own Smartworld sessions. In time she befriended some hackers, learned to hide her movements, to travel wherever she wanted in the World. She needed money for the better-built paywalls, so in secret she invented a fake persona, Rita, a single mother who worked data-entry jobs on the side, whose paychecks Fiona could spend however she pleased.

She'd never forgotten her family, not for a single day, and soon Rita had sent a retainer to a PI firm, hiring them to look into her father and Erin. The news was terrible: her father had died a few months ago, a victim of Brad Pitt Disease, an illness that had rotted much of his body to ashes. Fiona, like many terrorists, still harbored some magical thinking—Niko discussed this topic often in group therapy—the hope that she'd reconnect with her family in the years to come. But Dad was gone now, buried in a graveyard she couldn't even visit. They'd never go for another long car ride together, never watch old musicals in their pajamas, never tell each other weird dreams from the night before. She would never explain to him why she left, never know if he could forgive her for her crime. Fiona covered her mouth, careful no one could hear her, and wept bitterly for the parent she'd abandoned.

Now, more than anything, she feared she might lose her sister as well. She knew from the PI firm that Erin had recently bought a Smartbody, that she seemed to spend her evenings in the suit. So Fiona paid a hacker for lessons and began to track her sister online, speaking to her only through mascots, the least traceable form of Smartworld contact. She never revealed her identity, afraid that Erin would leave Smartworld altogether if she knew.

I ever suspect it you, Erin says in the booth.

Fiona laughs. That why you act so bitchy?

Well . . . it super stressful. No know what think.

My group, we live in your region. Sometime plan attack right near you.

But those attack never happen, Erin says.

Course not. After I warn you, the bureau start watch that place. My group plan somewhere else.

Erin sets down her mug. Wait sec. You *know* that bureau watch me?

Figure they must. You tip them off, right? Call hotline?

No. I never call.

Never? Fiona says. But I tell you to.

I too scared.

Wow wow, sis. It good I get you immunity. I think to self, *Maybe she need it.* Guess I right.

Fiona opens her tin of chicken bites, tilts it over to Erin. They both pluck out a bell and chew slowly. Next to the aquarium, Barb widens her eyes and spins her finger in a fast circle.

If honest? Fiona goes on. After Dad die, I not do too well . . . I find any excuse see you. And I *worry* about you, fish. It good you have Owen—but that EZ Pal guy? Not healthy. So glad you date real person now.

Erin bows her head. God. What my life, some TV show everyone watch? How many people spy on me?

I not spying, sis. There message I need tell you—I try for last few month. But you just log off.

Look, it nice you want me safe. But I been in couple attack now. There lot terror group out there.

This attack, little fish—it whole other scale. You need understand: It why I leave my group. It why I make you come here.

It bombing? Erin asks.

Fiona nods. They get sick of small attack. Change their strategy.

A few months back, Niko had called an unscheduled meeting in the briefing room. She looked self-conscious, almost flustered at the podium—the first time Fiona had ever seen her that way. "God. What a day," she said with an exhale. "Girls, we just get some big big news." Early that morning, in a rare visit, a leader from The Conversation had come to their bunker, telling Niko in detail about a new initiative: Project Sable. Only the highest leadership had known of Project Sable until this week, along with the scientists and engineers at its helm. Now the time had come to plan for its implementation.

After much cost and effort, The Conversation had acquired six nuclear devices, each compact enough to fit inside a car trunk. On a single day, not long from now, six mushroom clouds would surge above the landscape, destroying strategic locations across the country. Chaos would sweep the nation; the global economy would plummet; their government would be brought to its knees, closer to collapse than she, Niko, had ever dreamed of seeing in her lifetime. "And we, we in this room today," she said to her soldiers, "we part to play in this historic moment." Their cell—unlike many others—had been chosen to scout the bomb site for their region.

The soldiers sat in a charged silence when Niko finished her speech, then all at once they started to applaud. Many had tears in their eyes; a few gave festive war hoots; some older women stood from their seats and struck an archer pose, reserved for the height of Artemis celebrations. In their faces shone a new awareness, a sense of historical destiny, of books being written about them long after their deaths. Niko gave them a grateful smile, then struck an archer pose as well.

Fiona forced herself to clap, her hollow hands resounding. For her the key word in the speech had been *nuclear:* a vision of forests burned to cinders, birds blazing into flame midflight, the sun blackened behind a thicker crust of ash. She wanted to shatter the government as much as anyone in her group—set a torch to the whole system—but what of the Earth, their home? Before this meeting, she'd thought their movement was in league with nature, a defender of what remained, unwilling to maim the planet like industrial nations. But now that had changed: The Conversation felt that *any* means justified its ends. They would start a widescale nuclear war; they would drive more animals to extinction; they would jeopardize the survival of their own species.

After that, I feel like stranger there, Fiona says to Erin. I start realize . . . deep down, I not like them. Even if they right—even if nuclear only way—this just madness. If we do this, we no better than President Walton. At first I think: I go talk Niko, tell her my opinion. Maybe she pass it to The Conversation; maybe other feel like me, too. But then I think: My God, they prob just kill me. Plan of this scale, this cost? They no take risk I betray them.

A few nights ago, Fiona had snuck upstairs from the bunker and knocked out the soldier on guard at the farmhouse porch. She met a taxi a mile down the highway and rode to a posh hotel in the city, the last place that her Artemis sisters would look for her. They didn't know about Rita, didn't know Fiona could afford to hide in style. She stripped off her humble Artemis clothes, her overalls and work shirt, and relaxed into the steam of her suite's jacuzzi. She listened to the rumble of cars in the street, to the drunk figurines laughing and flirting outside the nightclubs below. Was it for *them* that she was doing this, giving up on her dreams, on her fight to destroy industrial civilization?

Well, those drunks outside were a part of her species, too. She had always wanted to help them somehow, these misguided plastic people. Now everyone in this city might soon owe their lives to her.

Soon as I get immunity, I tell bureau even more, Fiona says, gesturing a hand at the unseen microphones around them. Last few month, I learn lot about Project Sable. But listen, sis: you need leave country. Get Jacob, get Owen, get far. Terrorism Bureau—they clumsy, they mess up lot. This def could happen.

Erin drinks the last of her mug, sets it pensively on the place mat. Across the café, Barb no longer watches their booth: she types rapidly on her phone, her face drawn tight in a look of controlled alarm.

With a tired laugh, Erin glances back at Fiona in her old-man disguise.

Few hour ago, I scared go party. Now need flee country.

Best you leave soon, Fiona says. They have bomb already. Only planning left now.

Just seem impossible, you know. Something like this.

It happen in Dad generation. Bet they think it impossible, too.

The sisters grow quiet at the table. Fiona stares off at the band stage, her eyes distant as she watches the stubbled singer, now playing a piano ballad with a chorus of haunting jazz horns. At last she says:

Can I ask you stupid question? It real dumb dumb. But I curious.

Sure, Erin says. Why not.

If it work out . . . if me and bureau stop attack. You think Dad proud me?

Dad?

I mean, if he not gone. Because then I save so many life. Much more than kill in college.

Erin runs a finger along her mug rim. Dad ever love you, if that what asking. Those people you kill . . . he blame himself, not you.

Fiona gives a startled laugh. Blame himself? Why?

When he sick, Dad tell me lot. He think he give you his anger: at government, at injustice. Think you get from him.

He angry? Huh. Never seem that way.

Erin smiles sadly. Poor Dad. So much guilt. He ground us when we young? Even once?

One time, yeah. You little then. But only for hour or so—he no keep it up. He take us out for chicken pop instead.

Erin wipes at her eyes. Shit. I crying now.

Last five year, in bunker? It Dad haunt me most. Even before I know he gone. Because, most my life, I make him proud. That best feeling. And he ever—

Before Fiona finishes her sentence, a blaze of light sweeps across their booth. With the light comes a roar of explosion, a bomb erupting under the wooden stage, splitting apart the planks with a sundering fire. Shrapnel sprays in all directions, gusting through the bodies of the hologram band, knocking the patrons nearby to the floor, hitting the aquarium tank with such force that the glass instantly shatters, a flood of miniature cars and billboards spilling out from the city streets, streaming onto the dance floor among the panicked, thrashing koi.

The shrapnel misses Erin's booth, but now there comes a different roar—a burst from an assault rifle. Fiona spasms backward with a sudden, unnatural force, pressed against her seat as if by invisible hands that shake her, her body convulsing in time to the rattle of gunfire. Then the vicious hands release her and she sits there slumped and lifeless, her wig crooked, her mustache missing, her left eye cracked open in its socket. Three ragged bullet holes gape from her forehead; a dozen or more have shredded her shaggy sweater.

Erin turns and sees a slender woman sprinting through the smoke. Her black balaclava hides her face; her work boots splash between the fallen bodies. When she is out of sight, Erin huddles down in the booth and stares at her sister. She gazes at the holes in Fiona's forehead, the dark interior behind her punctured plastic.

Around her the café reels in a watery chaos. Patrons kneel beside their wounded friends, screaming into their phones for help, brushing away the fish that writhe about them. An agent with two broken arms struggles to his feet, then slips and falls to the floor with a wretched groan. Dennis lies unconscious on the ground beside his booth; Barb, also unconscious, sits flung forward on the table, the palm trees on her shirt coated with wood dust.

The camera zooms in on Erin as she sits up in the booth, as she looks out at the ruins of the café. Then, with a sharp inhale, she slides from her seat and rushes splashing across the dance floor. She reaches Barb and Dennis, who put up no resistance as she searches through their pockets, first finding her phone in Barb's fanny pack, then the fob to the station wagon in Dennis's jeans.

The camera follows her as she runs past the splintered glass of the bar top, past the smashed displays of arcade games, past the charred paper lanterns on the floor. She reaches the door and pushes a cracked panel, revolving out into the night. The fog has thickened above the ocean, only a faint glitter of moonlight on the waves.

Erin climbs into the station wagon and starts the engine.

## 17

# "SEND IN THE CLOWNS"

The episode opens on the misty beach road rushing past her windshield, its center lines a fluid blur unspooling from the fog. Erin watches the bends of the winding road, the traffic signs glimpsed and gone in the pallid glare of her headlights. To her left the ocean runs for miles in a long, unbroken view, clearer and cloudier at times as she curves along the shoreline.

Her phone sits in the cup holder, wobbling as she speeds around the bends. The screen displays a call with Owen, in progress just under four minutes. He speaks urgently over the road noise:

Sweetie, you not thinking straight. I get you want warn Jacob. But you driving from *crime scene* right now. You need go back.

I almost there, Erin says in a clipped, impassive voice. Only two mile more. Tyler house not far.

Just *call* Jacob. Pull over, call him.

I try already. No answer. Prob too loud at party.

God. This all . . . I no believe it. Fiona, you sure she . . .

She gone, Erin says numbly.

What you just saw happen, your sister? Honey, you def in shock. This not time to—

Fine, I in shock. It no change situation. This bombing happen anytime. You need promise me, okay? Promise me you leave country. Right away.

In the background Owen opens a cabinet, twists the top off a pill bottle.

Erin, please, I begging you. Pull over now. Just pull over and—

A service message interrupts him. *Phone service suspended,* says a neutral female voice. *Order of Terrorism Bureau. Phone service suspended. Order of Terrorism Bureau.*

Fuck, Erin mumbles. She stares out at the shore, the mist unfurling in sinuous threads across the sea. Then she rolls down the window and hurls her phone into the dune grass.

A mile later, she slows the station wagon and steers into a posh neighborhood, the sidewalks lined with wrought-iron streetlamps, the rooftops peeping above the privacy hedges. The camera cuts to an aerial shot, showing a street of beachfront mansions, each raised on stilts above the sand, each with a long private pier running down to the waves. A crowd of partyers revel in the yard of a stucco mansion, drinking, zinging, making out behind its security fence. The stereo blasts a Drum and Motorcycle song, many dancing with drunken abandon to the DAM track.

Their luxury cars congest the curbs, taking up most of the spaces near the mansion. Erin drives down the block and parks on a side street, tucking the wagon between a Porsche and a Hummer. She brushes some wood dust off her jeans, watches the pale particles drift to the floor. A glimpse of grief flits across her face.

The camera tracks beside her as she leaves the wagon and hurries to the party. Clowns in massive shoes and bow ties stand among the crowd, bending balloons into neon poodles and swan hats. A Bigfoot float hovers on a string above the pool, his upraised arms waggling in the sea breeze.

At the front gate stands a security guard in a party hat, no trace of the festivities in his matter-of-fact expression. He finds Erin's name on his tablet, checks that she signed her liability waiver. Then he hands her a string of Mardi Gras beads and admits her to the property.

As Erin strides up the flagstone path, the entire scene freezes around her. The hundred-plus partyers halt in place, motionless, unstirring, as if paused on a screen in their many exuberant postures. Some are frozen as they funnel a beer, some as they kiss on picnic blankets, some as they toss a Ping-Pong ball at beer cups. One figurine, paused with his arm stretched out, is snatching the nose off a clown with a half-tied balloon giraffe.

A spotlight shines down from the smog overhead, the beam following Erin as she strides toward the static crowd. On the soundtrack plays a vaporous synth, drums with a cavernous echo. She sings:

> *Isn't it cruel?*
> *Just so unfair?*
> *Happy at last in this town—*
> *Then nukes everywhere.*
> *Here come the clouds.*

Erin gazes at the partygoers, suspended in their carousing: a strand of tequila dangling in place as a boy pours a shot; a girl in a tin tiara smoking from three zing-sticks at once; a fully dressed boy paused in midair as he leaps into the pool.

*Look at these fools,*
*So unaware*
*That millions may melt to the ground*
*In the fiery glare.*
*Here come the clouds,*
*Those huge mushroom clouds.*

*Just when I'd stopped needing to fear,*
*Fiona returns to announce Armageddon is here.*
*The crack of her head snapping back still*
  *resounds in my mind.*
*The bureau is near;*
*There's so little time.*

A seabird hovers over the yard, frozen in flight above the wafting zing smoke. Erin sings the final verse:

*Isn't it cruel?*
*Isn't it grim?*
*Confessing to Jacob right now*
*All I've hidden from him.*
*But here come the clouds,*
*Those huge mushroom clouds,*
*To punish our sins.*

The party swings back into motion as the music fades. The beer flows down the funnels, a Ping-Pong ball lands wide of the cups, the clown yells *Hey!* as the boy runs off with his nose. The dancers lurch from side to side with tipsy legs and stiff torsos, their hinges rustling in time to the motorcycle revs. A female server passes with a tray of steaming nuggets; another tends to a bleary boy in a deck chair, helping him sip from a jug of Glug4Glad.

*Oh God,* Erin prays on the soundtrack, glancing between the groups. *Please let me find him. Please let me warn him. I just need a little more time.*

She presses her way up the patio stairs, struggles through chanting frat boys to the sliding doors of the mansion. Inside is an enormous living room, the vaulted ceiling two stories high, the skylights giving glimpses of a drone flying over the party, air-dropping condom packets on the guests. On the carpet stands a gigantic tube, twice as wide as the burly boy who sways inside the cylinder, his body barely visible for the zing smoke that billows from a vent in its floor. The boy takes a few deep huffs of smoke, clearing a view of his bug-eyed face, then pushes open the door and staggers out coughing.

In the kitchen, coolers of Glug4Glad surround the marble island. On each jug is a short rhyme: *Get too drunk? On your rump? Drink Glug4Glad—no stomach pump!* Behind the island is an open door, through which Erin can see the tiled length of a sunporch, its ceiling strung with glass wind chimes, its windows looking out on the mansion's foggy pier. Three figurines talk in the breakfast nook, Jacob and Olivia and Monica, the plastic girls perched on a sofa, Jacob on a wicker love seat. None of them notice Erin as she steps onto the tile.

. . . and I so *humiliated,* Monica says in a slurred, tearful voice. I such *idiot* out there. I miss whole table.

Oh, Monny, Olivia coos, rubbing her friend's back. It only beer pong. No take so serious.

Monica lifts a crumpled tissue, dabs mascara from her cheek. Tyler such *ass*hole. He *dare* me. He know I never turn down dare.

People play drunk all time, Jacob assures her. They ever miss table.

I not drunk, Monica says.

Oliva laughs. Course you not.

Erin hurries down the long porch, her passage stirring a row of chimes, the tinted glass tittering in her wake. She looks intently at Jacob—his gleaming glasses, his half-zipped hoodie, his hand on the loveseat cushion—as if this moment on the sunporch will soon be a memory, a memory she seeks to preserve with careful attention. The camera switches to a point-of-view shot, showing Jacob through her eyes, his face washed in moonlight, the mist blurring the beach in the window behind him.

Olivia turns her head, hearing the chinkling chimes. She gives Erin a bland wave of greeting, a loose bangle sliding down her arm. Jacob, she says. Your girlfriend here.

Wow wow, you make it! he cries, a little tipsy himself. No think you coming!

Erin steps into the breakfast nook, her hair pale with wood dust, her breath coming in gasps. The ankles of her jeans are soaking wet. Olivia and Monica exchange a glance on their sofa.

So glad I find you, Erin says, taking the cushion beside him. She presses a kiss to his forehead. Think maybe you not at party.

I here two hour or so. It wild, huh? Tyler fly drone outside, drop condom on everyone—so way way. I no drink much yet. You catch up easy.

You need do Zing Pillar, Oliva says to Erin. It fliiippy. Jacob no try it, though. Real party pooper.

He laughs. One hit on zing-stick, I flying. Now stand in *pillar*? I prob forget my name.

Erin rests a hand on his knee. Uncertainly she says:

Jacob, I so sorry this. But we . . . we need talk. Right now. I no have much time, prob few minute.

Few minute? But you just get here.

Sweetie, I not sure how say this. But I need tell you. Tell you quick.

Jacob hears the fear in her voice. Sure, def. What going on?

You need believe me—I want tell you truth before, truth about everything. Just scared you leave if know. Scared I lose you. We such good thing, I happiest whole life. But my past, sweetie, my old life . . . there something I hide from you. Something big big.

Olivia and Monica listen attentively. *Dra-ma,* Monica whispers under her breath. Olivia nods.

He reaches for his cane, folded on the armrest. Maybe we go outside, Erin? Talk alone for sec?

There no time. Please, I just—my sister. I never tell you, but I have sister. She disappear in college. Her name, you maybe know it: Fiona Reynolds.

Jacob grows quiet, his nylon eyebrows drawn together. You mean that dorm bomber? She your . . . family?

Holy shit, Olivia says, looking at Erin with new interest. Fiona Reynolds? She way way famous. That your sis for real?

Erin ignores this. My sister die tonight, Jacob. Her terror group kill her, because she help bureau. But before that, she tell me—

You still in contact? Jacob says, confused.

Only tonight. First time five year. She die to give me warning.

At the far end of the porch, two figurines step out from the kitchen. The first to emerge is Tyler, a look of unease on his vulpine face, the remote to the condom drone in his breast pocket. Behind him strides an agent from the Terrorism Bureau, a stern-faced woman covered in spatters of wood dust. The camera zooms in on the agent, her jacket shredded in places, her neck and chin pitted with nicks of shrapnel. Seeing Erin, she lifts her handgun and shouts:

Terrorism Bureau! Put hand in air!

Olivia and Monica shriek in unison, throwing up their arms. Erin raises her hands cautiously, shrinking into herself at the sight of the weapon.

I not armed, she calls down the porch.

Get hand up higher! No move!

The agent strides toward the breakfast nook, her wet loafers slapping the tile. In a faster voice, Erin whispers to Jacob:

Listen, there bad attack soon. Nuclear, you hear me? That what my sis tell me. You need leave country. You grandma, you need—

Leave country? Jacob says, his hands raised like hers. What mean?

It not safe here. They have nuke, six nuke. You need run.

The agent reaches the nook, levels her gun at Erin.

Get flat on ground, she orders. All four you. *Slowly.*

Leave soon as can, Erin continues. Go airport tonight. It happen any—

With a swift jerk of her hand, the agent pistol-whips Erin across the temple. The blow resonates through her skull; she flinches back in her seat, dazed but conscious.

Erin, oh God, Jacob says. You okay?

Get fuck on ground, the agent repeats. I lose four good friend tonight. Not in mood.

The young figurines obey her, pressing their hard cheeks against the tile. Tyler, in the background, takes a worried hit on his zing-stick. A few more agents step through the doorway, their suits and hair spattered with the same dust.

That her? asks a male agent, aiming his gun down the porch.

Think so. She no get immunity now. That for damn sure.

Erin barely notices these words. She struggles to slow her breathing, to resist her rising panic attack. Jacob reaches out to soothe her, but she flinches and says: *Stay still, Jacob. Stay still.*

She have anxiety condition, Jacob tells the agents. She need her medication.

The agents keep their guns leveled. They ignore him.

Closing her eyes, Erin attempts to pray herself calm. But no words will come to her now, not even words on her soundtrack, and so, zooming out from this scene, abandoning the sunporch, she disappears from her body into the darkness of her mind. There she extends an unreal finger and taps the darkness twice. This opens a video window, loaded with a brand-new episode of *Nuclear Family.*

An agent kneels beside her, pulls the handcuffs from his belt. But Erin is nowhere near him as he cuffs her trembling wrists, as the ratchet teeth click into the lock. Her hands remain unbound in the nightscape of her mind, and, as more agents surround her, as they hoist her to her feet, as Jacob says again, *Please—she need her medication,* Erin taps the play icon on the video.

The new episode starts to air.

## 18

## "THE ABSENCE"

The episode opens on a line of women in prison jumpsuits, shuffling through a maze of metal railings. The inmates queue together on a large sitcom set, designed to look like a prison holding area. They wait their turn at a window bank along the back wall, their sneakers scraping the concrete floor in a raspy rhythm, like a needle on the inner rim of a vinyl.

The camera pans across the line until it reaches Erin, who shuffles along a rail near the middle of the set. Her hair has grown out several layers into an accidental pageboy; her face looks even paler than its usual blanched sheen. She wears the same black jumpsuit as the other inmates, a number stamped on its chest in a ring of golden digits. Seven months have passed since her arrest, and it shows in her numb expression, the distance in her eyes as she nears the window bank.

There, behind the glass, sits a row of giant waffles in prison guard uniforms. The waffles smile broadly at each inmate who approaches, their rubber lips stretching their mouth squares wide. Then they set a paper cup in the drawer below their window and push a button. The squeaky runners chirr like cicadas.

*Every morning, before our workday starts, we're forced to take our dose of FocusMaxx,* Erin narrates. *The drug is strong and—I have to admit—very, very pleasant. It makes me chatty and upbeat, eager for my shift, a small miracle with the way we're treated at the call center. It lets me forget my true situation: my ten-year sentence in a bureau prison, my daily ache for Jacob, my fears of Fiona's warnings. There are no visits in a prison like this one, no phone calls or letters, no access to an attorney. Just the work, the endless waiting.*

She reaches the front and shuffles to a window. An old waffle guard with dried-out squares squints at Erin's number, his collar dotted with breadcrumbs. His grin is so wide it looks painful; his left hand squeezes a foam stress ball. He shouts above the clatter of drawers: Morning there! *Confirm 70432011?*

Confirm, Erin replies.

The waffle taps the digits into his tablet. One dose Focus-Maxx! he sings in a breezy voice. He sets down the cup and the drawer squeaks out reluctantly.

In the air above her, his propeller buzzing, a fur-cube watches Erin as she raises the cup and the capsules bulge her throat. Guk guk flazoo, he reports to the guard behind the glass. You good to go! the waffle says to Erin.

She crumples the cup, tosses it into a trash can. Then she strides along the window bank, past the other grinning waffles, until she reaches a fake hallway that leads from the set. TO CALL CENTER #9 read the words on a yellow-black arrow.

Grooba nup! Bawaa! says a fur-cube near the hall, joking with a cube who floats beside him. They hold their sides as they burst into merry laughter.

*         *         *

The next scene opens a few hours later, in the sitcom set of the call center. Erin, now bright-eyed and chipper, sits among hundreds of fellow inmates, each tucked inside a cubicle with a dated telephone console. Waffle guards stride down the aisles, stopping often to chat with each other; a flock of fur-cubes monitors the work from overhead.

Erin, on a call with an elderly man, nods as he complains about a purchase:

But I follow all instruction, the man is saying. I put Happy Flash on table, I drink water, turn out light. Then I stretch out eye—flash flash flash! But, dunno, still feel depress. I pay lot money this, young lady. Want see result.

Oh no, much sorry hear prob! Erin exclaims. The Happy Flash User Guide sits on her desk; the cover displays a square black box, an amber light bulb jutting from its center. You use eye tweezer?

Def use, the old man replies. I use both eye.

And tongue jelly?

Tongue jelly? What that?

Oh, need much much jelly, sir. You no get jelly bag in box?

Let check.

There is a sound of rummaging, a chortle of relief.

That explain! he cries. I think jelly bag just padding.

No no, sir, that special jelly. Take jelly spoon—you see inside—then spread on tongue thick layer. Then flash flash flash: you happy!

Ah, thank. I try. Bet cheer up lot now.

Bet will! Thank call Paradise Product!

The call ends. Erin, her smile undimmed, rolls back in her

chair and looks out the window, where a painted backdrop shows a prison yard heaped with snow. Around her the other women talk on their phones in gleeful voices, their words mingling together into a giddy din of chatter, a sound like a bird sanctuary at sunrise. At the next table over a woman spins her chair in rapid circles, crying out, *Wheee! Wheee!* with desperate delight.

Down the aisle from her, two waffle guards flip a coin. The loser steps behind her chair and rolls her from the room.

Erin's phone begins to ring. Lively, enthused, she answers.

Hello! Paradise Product. How help prob today?

Yeah, um . . . says an abashed male voice. I just get Dong Magnet?

Sure! How help?

Well, I use first time. And it hurt lot. Like, *lot.*

Much sorry hear! Quick question, sir: You take hour shower first?

I shower last night . . .

You read manual? Erin asks.

No . . .

Sorry tell you this, sir, but you need call ambulance. Need call now.

Ambulance?

Dong Magnet lot power. Dong go boom sometime.

Wait. Dong go *boom?*

Forty-five percent if no shower. Your penis swell any?

Um, little.

Then seventy percent. Def make call.

Dear God. Okay. I get ambulance.

Thank call Paradise Product! Have great day!

He hangs up fast. Yikes, Erin murmurs, staring down at her console. She looks as if she will never blink, then blinks several times in a row.

A woman rolls back from the cubicle beside her. She is a stocky figurine in her forties, her hair a thicket of nylon curls, her lips arched in a wide, ironic frown. The episode's laugh track, silent until now, cheers as she glides into the scene.

That Dong Magnet call? she asks.

Erin nods. Third ambulance today.

The woman shakes her head. Men! All their life, obsessed their dick—what get it hard, what lube it like, what condom feel best sex. Even buy magnet make bigger. But read *manual?* No, never. That way too tough.

The laugh track bursts into raptures.

Craze it legal anyway. Should call it "Dong Bomb," Erin says to more laughter.

Dong Bomb! Ha! They need rename!

The woman's phone starts ringing. No rest for wicked! she cries. The laugh track applauds wildly as she rolls back into her cubicle.

*That's Hannah, my cellmate,* Erin narrates. *She's the only good thing about this place. Well, her and all the drugs.*

A voice comes booming from a speaker on the wall. Lunch-time! it announces. Here come the mega yum!

The women squeal as one across the set. They raise their eager eyes toward the ceiling, as if about to receive some heavenly dispensation.

Then, above each cubicle, a panel in the ceiling screeches open. From the darkness plunges a square of wax paper, stamped with a colorful label: *Flippin' Chicken Prison Supply.* The logo shows a rooster in a prison cell, his wings raised to his mouth, playing a soulful harmonica while his cellmate drums with spoons.

·       ·       ·

After work that day, Erin sits in the set of a prison common room. Women play chess at the tables around her; one reads a book repaired with duct tape; another works on a jigsaw puzzle, an image of a Shmuglin field with several pieces missing from the goal zone. Two robot inmates are propped near the windows, engaged in a silent argument, angrily spinning their eyes and flashing their noses.

Erin sits on a wobbly folding chair, her smile gone, her pills worn off for the day. She stares with a flat expression at the television on the wall, mounted inside a wire cage. On the dusty screen plays a rerun of *Nuclear Family*.

The episode, set long after the war, opens inside a sunny hospice room. In the bed lies a gaunt figurine in his fifties, his breathing slow and pained, his body a rotted-out shape below the blanket. A tube runs under his nostrils; his jawline is coated in ash. Frail and withered, struggling for breath, the dying man is still recognizably Max.

He watches the morning news from his bed, a female anchor speaking on the small TV. Beside her floats a photo of a city street at night—rolled-down storefronts, ink-black windows—above which the sky is an absolute white, a dome of pure blankness. The headline *Sky Crisis* bars the bottom of the screen.

"We back with today top story," the anchor says in a rattled voice, her stiff hands folded on the news desk. "The sudden disappear of Earth sky. Late last night, in much tragic event, the entire Western Hemisphere see unexpected sight: night sky go from black to white strange fast. Many hope there simple explanation—solar flare, asteroid collide, satellite explode. But soon we learn true cause: the sky our planet vanish, gone like morning mist. No one know how why."

The anchor now shows a video of the occurrence, filmed in the empty parking lot of a strip mall. The night at first looks ordinary, nothing out of place, the sidewalk shadowed beneath the awnings, scraps of cloud littered above the rooftops. Then, without warning, the shade of the black sky begins to lighten. The sky pales at a steady rate, changing from charcoal to a murky ivory, then from ivory to a whiteness of a paler and paler hue, until the sky is less a color than an absence overhead, vacant as a theater screen without an image, blank to the outer reaches of the horizon.

One might expect this glaring sky to douse the strip mall with light, peel the shadows off the store signs, luster the toothsome smiles of the couple in the dental office poster. But instead it has no effect on the world below, as if not substantial enough to tint a surface beyond itself. The stores remain sunk in the soot of night; a soda machine casts a feeble flush on the sidewalk. The moon has also disappeared, though it gleams in icy patches off the windows.

Max lets out a sigh as he stares into the absence. On the windowsill beside him sit some photos of his family: Max in his thirties, wearing a newborn Erin in a chest sling; Max as a little boy, passing a Shmuglin ball with his father; Max with his mother, cheering as Blorko goes soaring off a ramp. In one photo Max receives a diploma, still boyish in his cap and gown; in another he stands with Erin at a wall-length aquarium tank, an octopus dangling its noodly arms behind them.

He turns his eyes from the TV set, looking out the barred window. A rolling lawn fringed with pine trees stretches down to the parking lot, where a carved sign reads, HALLOWED HORIZON HOSPICE. The sky is a gaping void above the treetops, no tint or depth to the dome, mere negation.

The dying man is not alone in the room. Across from the bed, on a wide stool, O sits vigil in a wrinkled T-shirt and stubby jeans. He is also in his fifties now, his squares sagging, a web of cracks around his eyes and lips. The years in prison have left their mark on the waffle: his bread scraped in places, his outer edges ragged, some patches torn from inside his cheek squares.

He holds a phone against his rim, talking in a low voice as he watches Max in bed.

"Yeah, he pretty spaced out. Lot more medication now. Last few day, he just stare at TV whole time. But it not even on."

O pauses, listening. He runs a hand down his ridged face.

"Sam, I sorry—this not good time. We talk it later, okay? I know this rough on you . . . it rough on me, too. But I need stay here in town. Not sure till when."

The waffle listens to a longer response, his forehead squares compressing. At last he says: "Erin, she so alone right now. She prob never ask me for help—that not her way. But she need me."

Sam's voice loudens on the line. O interrupts him: "I know, I know. You have garden center. Can't just pick up and move. But Sammy, I not sure . . . not sure I can leave her again. When she young, I total mess: it best I leave. But I better now. Can be there for her."

Max starts to cough in the bed, a weak and arid hacking that jerks his head up from the pillow. Clumps of his earlobe remain on the pillowcase; a chunk of his jaw breaks free.

"I got go," O says abruptly. "Max coughing again. I call back soon, promise."

The waffle jumps up from the stool, presses the call button for the nurse. Then he wobbles his bread over to the bedrail.

"Just try breathe. Just take slow," he says to Max. "I here. I right here, my love." O reaches out to stroke his cheek, then remembers not to touch his fragile face.

More ashes strew the blanket as his coughing continues; an edge of his nostril crumbles against the breathing tube. O starts to cry softly, his bread absorbing the tears, leaving little wet spots on the surface.

Finally, gasping, Max sinks back onto the pillow. On the TV, the anchor continues her broadcast about the absent sky.

"All going . . . all . . ." Max sputters, breathless. "All going . . . it . . ."

"Shhh, easy there," O says.

"Owen . . . it . . ."

"That right, it me. It Owen."

"Sky . . . sky gone . . ."

"Sky? What mean?"

"It vanish . . . it no more . . ."

"No be silly. Sky right out there. Take look."

Max glances again at the window. Outside, the sunny slope of lawn has vanished like the sky: the grass is gone, the weeds, the dirt, all earth. Only a blankness remains in their wake, a slope of smooth gloss, like coated paper. The pines that edged the property, the bushes around the building, the tulips at the entrance— these too have disappeared in the evaporation of nature. Beyond the hospice sprawls a stripped suburban landscape, the houses stranded on blank plots, the parks a pale tundra, the hills on the horizon bare of any growing thing, denuded of branches and blushing flowers, of leaves that sway in any wind, nothing growing or wilting in the sunless light of this world, an absence below that matches the absence above. A shirtless man on a riding mower rumbles across a vanished lawn, oblivious to these losses.

Max lifts his hand, then drops it on the blanket. An alarm begins to sound on his EKG machine. O hurries from the room to find the nurse.

The next scene opens in the hospice room a few hours later. Max, now alone, sleeps soundly in the bed, so still that someone might think he had already passed. He looks like his former self, the man before Brad Pitt Disease: the ash gone from his jaw, his legs bulging the blanket, his plastic smooth as if it had never rotted. Gradually his eyelids rise and he stares up at the ceiling fan, his eyelash threads stirring in the breeze.

Across the room, a patter of footfalls comes through the open doorway. Max turns his head on the pillow, but the room appears empty. He presses an arrow on the bed remote, rising to a seated position: he still sees no one. The patter ceases, replaced by a labored grunting.

"Hello?" Max asks.

"Just a second there," says a gruff, breathless voice.

Up a leg of the stool, a tiny figure shimmies into sight. He reaches the seat with a clumsy pull-up and flops down at the edge, his little dress shoes dangling above the floor. The man wears a black herringbone suit, a checkered tie below his ivory vest coat. His gelled hair is slicked straight back, a few strands of which he flattens with his pierced hand.

"Morris!" Max cries with delight, his voice now clear and resonant. "I knew I'd see you again. I knew you'd be here one last time."

Morris, still thirty-three, gives a friendly wave to the camera. The laugh track applauds ecstatically. As he turns his face to Max, a sadness fills the Savior's eyes.

"They treating you good here, kid? You doing okay?"

Max chuckles. "Well, I'm about to die. I guess I'm about as okay as I can be."

"I've been praying for you," Morris says, lowering his gaze. "That might sound dumb, coming from a jerk like me. But I've been praying."

"You're not a jerk, Morris."

"Sure I am, kid. Sure I am. All those decades together, all

those adventures, and then, one day, I up and disappear? No forwarding address, no nothing? I've always felt awful about it."

"You look good, old friend. Healthy."

Morris smirks. "What are you, enlightened now or something? You must be a little angry."

"Well . . . maybe a little. But I never blamed you much for leaving. I was such a wreck those days myself."

Morris turns to the window, looks out at the ocean of absence. "I just couldn't handle it, Max. I'm so sorry, but I couldn't. The war, the compound—I could face all that, because we always had each other, we had our family. But when *Fiona* became a terrorist, *Fiona* a killer? That was too much, even for me. I had to get out of there, had to come down from my cross. And so . . . so I'm working as a stockbroker now. I'm filthy rich, to be honest."

"Less napping, then," Max says.

"Oh no, about the same."

A mild laughter flutters from the laugh track.

"You know," Max says, "the more I lived, the more I saw I had a choice. If I wanted, I could be bitter, I could believe that life was meaningless. I could hate God, deny God because I'd lost so much. Or—or I could choose to have faith. Faith that I was put here for a reason. That it was, I don't know, my job somehow. My job to love this world of dying things."

"But you can't choose to believe in that, kid. You either have faith or you don't."

"No, I think it's a choice. Maybe the hardest choice of all."

At these words, the walls of the hospice room evaporate from view. The carpet becomes a sheen of blankness; the ceiling above them vanishes. Then the rest of the building is gone as well, the beds and chairs and IV poles, the TVs and couches and paintings, so that the patients in the other rooms—visible now through the missing walls—float on their backs in midair with no bed below their bodies, no blankets over their gowns, hovering half alive amid the nothing.

Outside, the suburb is also absent, no houses or strip malls in sight, just a sudden profusion of bodies where the buildings stood seconds earlier. The figurines seem untroubled, typing at the air in their vanished cubicles, shopping at absent clothes racks, sitting in tiers in a missing movie theater. Down the absent turnpike, seated bodies speed through empty space, shorn of their trucks and sedans, exposed in heedless motion.

"I guess that's my cue," Morris says on an exhale. He hovers in the air where the stool has disappeared, his dress shoes several feet above the ground. "Not much time left here."

Max hovers beside him, the vanished bed still propping up his back. "Thanks for visiting me, dear friend. I'll save a seat for you."

"Me, die? Hmm. Maybe when I get sick of making money." The laugh track titters. "You were the best, kid. Know that. The very best."

"You, too, Morris. You, too." There is a faint yearning in Max's tone, as if he wishes Morris would stay here, as if he knows what his leaving will mean. He says, "Hey, remember when Mom and Dad took us all to that carnival? And you flew into Anita's mouth on the Gravitron?"

Morris smiles off into the absence, as if seeing the rickety carnival ride once more. "I was so mad at her that day. It took me hours to wash off all that oil."

The laugh track roars.

"Oh, Morris."

"Goodbye, Max."

The tiny man wipes a tear from his cheek, then hops from the air to the ground. He leaves the way he entered, though now there is no door for him, no hallway or other rooms, only the bodies scattered throughout the blankness. Max remains alone in the vacant air, smiling at the space the plastic Christ departed. Floating freely, bathed in light, he shuts his tired eyes.

As the credits begin to roll, Erin stands up from her chair and leaves the set, shuffling out of sight down a false hallway. The evening news continues playing on the common room TV.

·           ·           ·

In the final scene, Erin lies awake in the set of her prison cell, stretched out in the shadows of the bottom bunk. She stares up at the springs of the bed above her, where her cellmate Hannah snores in a medicated sleep. Two capsules sit in a paper cup next to Erin's pillow, the words *NightyNightNow* on each pill.

The lights are off in her cellblock, a strip of fake moonlight on the floor. A vapor of noises wafts her way from the other cells on the block: the scrape of a chair, the drip of a faucet, a whispered conversation. Outside her narrow window is a painted backdrop of clouds, clustered above the snowy roof of a guard tower.

The camera zooms in on Erin's face, the subtle shifts of thought in her molded features. After a moment, she pulls back her blanket and rises from the bed. She strides to a corner of the set, then kneels down on the floor and clasps her hands. The silence grows around her, stretching out beyond the set, beyond the fake night, beyond the dim illusions of her world.

Erin lifts her eyes to the wall, only to see that the wall is gone, vanished like mist. Beyond the wall is a different view than before, a view of total blankness, as if someone has scrubbed the images off the backdrop of the night. Gone are the clouds in their sleepy clusters, gone the dome of winter sky, gone the guard tower and the razor wire fence. In their place is only absence, a void without color or tone, no trace of a sitcom set or any recognizable space. The void extends for miles into the distance, or perhaps for only feet, the size of the absence impossible to gauge with nothing to give it contrast.

She looks out on the void, a nothingness beyond her comprehension. It glows without a sun or moon, illumined with an uncreated light. As if in a dream, Erin stands in the cell and drifts to the edge of the floor, the juncture of the absence and the world she's known. Then she steps forward into the nothing, lets the void enfold her in its silent depths.

# 19

———

Erin stands perfectly still in the void, a body abstracted from all other beings, alone in the luminous space beyond her cell. Her body retains the darkness of the room behind her, her face and undershirt daubed with the same shadows. Hannah still snores on the upper bunk, one arm stretched beyond the bed frame, her hand dangling limply in the night.

In the void there is no camera to record Erin's movements, no soundtrack on which to narrate her passing thoughts. Both camera and soundtrack are lost in the bright expanse. She stands silent in the emptiness, her sunken eyes unglinting, absorbing the vacant vista spread before her. Then, in a quiet voice, she begins to speak out loud, no longer to a TV audience but to those of us here beside her: we who listen in the void, who return her steady gaze.

A few months from now, near the end of winter, a ceiling of storm clouds will darken the afternoon sky. The first raindrops will patter

out in the yard, and then, for five straight days, a drenching rain
will lash the prison complex. Morning after morning I'll watch the
downpour from my cell, streaking along the windowpanes, pounding
the yard to slush, dissolving the few remaining clumps of snow; I'll
hear it thrumming down the building when I lie in my bunk at night,
and again when I wake in the dimness before the dawn; I'll smell it
on the guards who've just come splashing through the parking lot,
that close, musty scent of sodden fabric. Before I lived in this prison,
the sound of rain always calmed me, even helped me fall asleep on
restless nights. But here, behind these concrete walls, it only reminds
me of Jacob. I think of the day he passed his NAT, when we shouted
with joy as we drove through the rainstorm, when it seemed like such
a different future was opening before us. We might live together while
he started college, get married after graduation, bring a child into this
tragic, dazzling world.

After five days of the downpour, it feels like a flood has arrived to
take me. Like this rain will wash me away from the earth, out into a
deeper isolation.

Then, one early morning, I wake up to a placid sunrise in the
window. The sky is cloudless behind the smog; the rain, for now, has
passed. A few hours later, in the cafeteria, I stand at the window and
watch the sky once more. It is now a glassy lavender shade above
the razor wire, striped with fluffy wisps of cirrus clouds. As if on cue,
a sleek bird comes winging through the smog haze, its back a plum
color, its breast a pure white. The two-tone bird flutters down and
perches on the railing of a guard tower.

As I watch the bird, I feel a gentle presence surround me. This
descends on me at times now, this sudden sense of peace, most
often when I pray in my cell at night. In such moments, as I kneel on
the floor, as I offer my pleas to God—begging that my loved ones
stay safe, that I won't see bombed-out cities on the evening news—

the whirring of my mind fades at last to silence. And sometimes, in that silence, in that vast absence of thought, I feel the calm of a loving presence around me. Is it God? My father? My imagination? I couldn't begin to guess. The presence lasts for a few minutes and then disappears as quickly, like a radio broadcast drifting out of range.

As I gaze at the bird, Hannah strides up beside me. I'm very fond of my cellmate—in this, I'm luckier than most—but she loves to talk, to joke and gossip, and I don't have much conversation in me these days. Hannah is here for a minor crime: not calling the bureau when a friend confided in her at work, telling her that, years ago, he'd visited a terrorist cousin with a terminal illness. It turned out her friend's smartwatch was bugged; Hannah was arrested at home, in the middle of a movie night with her husband and children. For the bureau, she got off lightly: a three-year sentence.

Sometimes I think I should tell her Fiona's warnings. But then I think: Why should I fill her life with that fear? It's not like Hannah could call her family, send them a text, write them a letter. We were cut off from everyone when they locked these doors behind us.

"Big big sky today," Hannah says at the window. She points at a larger cloud. "That one look like Ireland, no?"

"Huh. Little bit. Yeah."

She sees the bird on the tower. "Awww. Look at him. Such cutie."

"Wish knew what called," I say.

"Pigeon maybe?"

I chuckle. "That not pigeon."

"Wren? God, I bad at bird. This what happen when you web designer. Stare at screen whole life."

As if offended at our lack of knowledge, the little bird straightens its posture on the railing. Then, with a brisk movement—its claws pushing off, its wings unfurling—it takes to the air and ascends toward the Ireland-shaped cloud. Hannah blows it a kiss.

Later that day, I go back to our cell and lie down on my bunk. Dinner isn't for several hours, and, as always, I start to daydream of Jacob. Often I imagine our reunion, Jacob waiting for me outside the gates on the morning I'm released, hugging me close, pressing his avid lips to mine. I know this is self-delusion, that by now he's probably moved on, started dating at college. Why *would* he stay loyal to me, this convicted criminal, this woman who deceived him? But the Jacob in my daydreams will always adore me, will never look for other partners, will believe the best of me no matter my crimes. I won't give him up any time soon.

I roll onto my side, trying to stay inside the dream. But it's too late: I've thought of Jacob at college. Now I'm picturing the girls he'll meet there, the girls who will replace me, creative girls with quirky haircuts and poetry books in their backpacks, girls who paint and play guitar and burn incense in their dorm rooms, girls who surpass me in every possible way. I can see one in my mind, an arty film studies major, her nose stud gleaming as she sits beside him in some intro class. She is charmed by Jacob's sincerity, his self-deprecating humor; one day they exchange numbers and plan a time to meet at her dorm. After an hour or two in her room—her roommate sent away for the night—she leans over and gives him a tentative kiss, the incense fogging the air above their heads.

This, of course, is what I want for Jacob. Or, if I'm honest, what part of me wants, the part of me that puts his happiness first. The rest of me wants him to stay alone, to never fall in love again, to believe, like me, that a beautiful life could await us when I'm released. If only I could send him a letter, just one short letter—the letter I write in my head, over and over—to explain myself, to tell him Fiona's warning in more detail. That night on Tyler's porch, did he understand at all?

At times like this, my daydreams cannot help me. I am forced to stay in the present, in the bare walls of this cell. When Hannah returns a few minutes later, back from a trip to the weight room, I sit up on my bed and ask her if she wants to play some chess. "Hell yeah," she says. "Always."

We leave our cell and stride past the others on our row, then turn down the long corridor to our common room. Hannah, sensing my mood—I get like this every few days—tells me some puns she remembers from her family's huge collection: "Know why I put my bed in fireplace? I sleep like log!" "You believe I get fired from calendar factory? I just take one day off!"

I manage to laugh along with her, but I can't stop seeing Jacob in that incense-clouded dorm room, that film studies girl wrapping her hinges around him. When we step into the common room, I go straight to a chess board and start to set up the pieces.

I'd known nothing about this game in my old life, just that it came from a time before computers. My first week here, when Hannah asked me to play, I said, "Nah, not my thing." After rowing through virtual Venice, soaring among the stars, I didn't expect much fun from some stumps of wood on a board. "Same with me," Hannah said. "Back home, you think I give damn *chess?* I own Smartbody just like you. But listen, Erin, chess—you need give chance. It teach your mind be present. Teach it focus, teach it calm. Chess help me lot."

There was little to fill my free time, so I took her advice and started to learn the game. I found a strategy book in the library, memorized a few techniques, sometimes noticed myself trying out moves in my mind. Now, every few games, I can back Hannah into a corner, even get her in check if I'm clever—though I've never come close to actual checkmate. Hannah has a competitive side, wants me to become a true opponent. In our first few games, she beat me in three moves.

This afternoon I'm playing better than usual, not squandering my pawns, not taking stupid chances. I slide a bishop to e5, blocking Hannah's queen, then castle quickly before she takes my rook.

It is not until after four p.m., my knights and bishops gone—Hannah now smiling down at the board, meaning I'll soon be in checkmate—that we hear an immense sound of explosion encircle the prison. From the first baffled seconds, we can sense that our world has changed, that history has returned for its bitter harvest. The sound begins with a harsh rumbling, like a seism splitting the ground, and then rises into a rapid whirring, a column of windy clamor, a noise like all creation is being sucked back to its source, uprooted and drawn violently into the sky. Even at this distance, all these miles from the blast zone, we can imagine the explosion that has birthed such a sound—the pillar of cloud, the funnel of wind, the flood of melting flame.

The sound lasts for close to a minute. The walls shake, the windows rattle, our chess pieces skitter off their squares. All goes quiet in the common room, silenced as if by the voice of a higher authority. There is something eerily beautiful about the magnitude of the sound, as if we hear the voice of heaven, a summons from the whirlwind, calling a crowd of souls to rapture from the earth. As the news will soon tell us, over 1.2 million souls, all loosed from their melted bodies by the time the sound shuddered through our plastic.

The specifics come to us in news reports throughout the night, minute-by-minute updates from a team of keyed-up reporters, talking fast in the flashy sets of their newsroom. To me they look like addicts, like addicts strung out on their drug of choice, the heady rush of a true Historic Moment. And it is historic: six nuclear devices have gone off across the country, all in the same half hour, targeting cities, centers of government, military bases, the largest terror attack in global history. Early estimates suggest more than seven million dead from the explosions, at least eleven million wounded.

We gather around the television set late into the evening, our normal schedule canceled for the night. We stare, shoulder to shoulder, at the first satellite photo of a blast zone, a city blanketed under a river of floating ash. Through little lines in the ash we glimpse the remnants of the city: the razed buildings, the scorched parks, the fractured streets and highways, all cloudy and opaque, as if seen under ice. Are there any figurines down there, still moving, still alive, not melted to the ground where the light blazed across them? The thought makes me shiver: rising to your feet, trembling, breathless, beneath that sky of ash. Could you find the strength to flee, to care about survival, staring up at that absent sky?

From the moment I heard the explosion, I started to pray. Jacob, Owen, Katherine: their faces fill my mind as the news grows worse and worse, as, near six p.m., I learn that the target of one bomb was the power plant near our suburb, crucial to the grid of the entire region. While I sit here safe in prison, they might be plunged inside this chaos, dead or wounded or rushing from radiation. There is nothing I can do for them—just pray in helpless silence, just stare at the TV set in its wire cage.

The news now shows the "radius ring" of each explosion, six purple circles on a stark white map. One of these circles, far from the largest, encompasses every significant place in my life—my house, my school, my church, my work, the graveyard where Dad is buried; the forest where, as a lonely teen, I pretended to stroll with Patrick; the bars where, after his second death, I drank to have some other voices near me as I mourned him—and also contains, unless they had the luck to settle elsewhere, nearly every figurine I've ever known. The reporters assure us there will be survivors, that not everyone in a blast zone will die from the bombing. Starting tomorrow, a "citizen casualty list" will begin to get updates online, the dead determined in part by their cell phone location. Those not named can be held in a tenuous hope.

Hannah, beside me, sees the look on my face, my out-to-sea expression. "Come here now, Erin," she whispers and then wraps me in her arms, holds me like the mother she is, the mother I need in this massacre. Her family, I now remember, lives in a suburb far from the blast zones, but she too has friends in those circles, she too keeps weeping on and off like everyone in the common room, even the guards who stand among us to watch the TV. I breathe in the musk of Hannah's jumpsuit, her faint scent of nicotine, her strength. Then I pull away and pace at the windows, unable to bear her kindness, unable to pray more or lose myself in dreams.

I spend that night in a fog of sedatives, which the warden makes available for the crisis. The next morning she gives an announcement on the loudspeaker: today, in common room N, she will open a computer bank for the prison population. The computers will let us access a single webpage, the search page for the "citizen casualty list." I can hear the strain in her voice as she speaks; it is rumored she lost a brother and a niece in the bombings. "Check on your family," she says. "This tragic time."

There is some chaos when the computer bank opens; a few women are tased, fighting to join the first group through the door. But soon enough the crowd calms down—most of us on sedatives—and we enter a long, unnerving day of waiting. For most of the morning I stand in a line that curves down several corridors, shuffling forward every five minutes when a group completes its turn, passing guards who furtively check the list on their phones. At last I sit before a monitor for my own five minutes, start rapidly typing names into the search bar. The women around me sob softly, or let out grateful sighs, or, after seeing a certain name, simply stare at the floor for their final minutes. When our time is over, we go to the end of the line and wait our turn again.

After two rounds at the computer, I have a shred of hope: Jacob and Owen and Katherine have not been listed. But other names emerge with each new search—teachers, coworkers, high school

friends, acquaintances from CODA, Olivia and Tyler and Monica. As
I wait in line, I tell myself that my loved ones *must* be safe, that people
who have suffered so much in life cannot be suffering more, that my
months of prayer for them were not in vain. I picture them sitting in
a transport van, exhausted but unharmed; I watch the van drive off
without me, its taillights shrinking in the ashy air.

The computer bank closes for dinner, but most of us stay in
the line. It is almost seven p.m. when I sit for a third time before a
computer. For the third time I thank God when Jacob and Owen do
not appear; for the third time I type *Katherine Sillan* into the search
bar. Then I stand from my chair, too startled to think, fighting an urge
to punch the monitor, to smash it on the ground. Among the several
Katherine Sillans listed, there is one with the same age and address as
my friend. I turn and stride quickly to my cell.

There, alone, I kneel on the concrete floor. I pray for Katherine
first, that her death was free from pain, that she was napping, not even
conscious, when that blinding flash of light swept through our suburb,
that she passed into a better world if a better world exists. I pray for
the victims I knew in town, then for the million lost in my region, then
for the millions more around the nation, the cities of dead figurines
whose souls soared above the crumbling skylines. I pray for the
survivors, then for those dispatched to help them, then for all those
now in mourning—those, like me, who must go on living in the rubble
of this nation, who must wander through this fog of grief and rage.

Then my prayer goes deeper, further, encompassing more
figurines than I thought my shrunken soul could ever hold: the poor
around the planet, the oppressed and their oppressors, the sick and
homeless and hungry, the dying and the newborn, and finally, as the
circle widens, the terrorists themselves, that they'll grasp the horror
of what they've done, that their conscience will wake them up from
these dreams of destruction. I feel my anger rising, the hatred and

bitterness I've felt since the day of the aquarium shooting. *Oh God,* I pray, *don't let the rage consume me. Don't let it smother the love that I have left.*

Then I pray again for Jacob, again and again for Jacob. I plead my case to God, my forehead to the floor, offering all that I am to the mysterious presence around me. And then, lifted up somehow, as if hovering outside the Earth, I kneel here in a strange and aerial peace.

The next day Jacob is still not on the list. I rest my forehead on the screen each time his name shows no result. Perhaps he was out with friends on the afternoon of the attack, headed to some concert or party beyond the blast zone. Perhaps his college is in a distant region, far from the deadly circles. There are other reasons, of course, why his name might not be listed, reasons that make me need my sleeping pills at night. Right now he could lie in a field clinic, groaning on a narrow cot, one of the many victims succumbing to radiation exposure. Or, like many others, he might have died at once in the blast, but too far from ground zero to confirm this from his cell phone.

Sometimes I wonder: if I did see Jacob's name on the list, would I even believe it? It would only mean his phone had been destroyed. Maybe he forgot it in his dorm room that day, left it behind while he drove with his friends to safety.

There are now survivors on the news, giving their haunted accounts of the bombing, talking in weak voices from their wheelchairs and hospital beds. They describe the vicious heat of the blast, the shock wave that vaporized entire neighborhoods, that melted the figurines near ground zero to bubbling puddles infused with shreds of clothing. These survivors had wandered through the devastation, past heaps of debris that were schools or churches, past playgrounds stained with child-shaped shadows, past mangled heads half melted in their puddles. I remember my high school history classes, the "modern war" units, where our teachers played us eyewitness accounts of the last nuclear war. The shattered voices of those figurines, their downcast eyes, their trembling hands, the oddly specific details they mentioned—it is all the same on our television now.

In high school I watched with flagging interest, wishing we'd study something less depressing for a change. Today I stare at the television with my entire being, praying that news of Jacob and Owen might somehow appear on the screen. But that is too much to ask; I should keep my prayers humble. I only ask that they survived, that they live on.

This evening the president addresses the nation, his first real speech since the broadcasts from his bunker. The aging leader looks more assured behind his regular podium, not in his stark briefing room underground. With a row of soldiers behind him, a flag at half mast, he tells us that he is here tonight as a man in deep mourning. He grieves for the millions killed in the bombings, for the millions dying of aftereffects all throughout the nation, in hospitals, in outdoor clinics, in sports and concert arenas. He asks for a moment of silence, and then, lifting his eyes to the camera, he gives an official declaration of war. There will be a time for further mourning, he says, for remembering the lost—but this is a time for retribution, for reclaiming national security, for destroying the traitors who murdered our families and burned our cities to dust. He describes the new powers of the Terrorism Bureau: closing our borders to foreign travel, locking down whole regions, increasing surveillance nationwide. At this I sigh and stand to leave the common room.

Hannah starts to stand as well, but I put a hand on her shoulder. "Thank," I tell her. "I . . . I best alone right now."

In my cell I kneel on the hard floor, the only place where my fear and anger subside. I let the silence gather around me, immerse me in its peace. And I wonder: If God is in this silence, if God listens to my words, does this mean that Dad might hear me now as well? And, if he hears me, in that world beyond death, does this mean that I might join him there one day? Could there even be a world like that, a world without our chaos, a world where we never say goodbye? Where our real selves shine outside our surface, not hidden under plastic?

My heart opens as I kneel here in the shadows, to Dad and Katherine and Patrick, to Fiona, to all my dead. My love for them spreads outward to that world beyond my sight, returns to me in a deepening of presence. In this presence is a greater love, a love that knows no bounds, a love that grants me grace in every breath. It holds the depths of the universe and the creaks of my smallest hinge, shines its mercy deep inside my hollows.

Even if he hears my prayers, my father still feels far away, divided from me by the mist of death. One day, maybe soon, maybe many years from now, I'll cross that mist and meet him in the air, soar with him like seabirds high above this scorched terrain, into that absence that is fullness, that dawn of invisible light. Until then, I must find that light in a world of care and carnage, reflected off our cracked and chipping plastic.

I doubt I am the only one who stares into this mist, who longs for a world beyond my sight. Maybe all of us are searching for a path that has no end, that makes death just a turn of trail, a brief, benign confusion, before we soar up into vaster spheres of light.

n the depths of the void is an absent apartment building, eighteen floors of bodies floating against a departed sky. No trace of the building itself remains, no roof or walls, no floors or ceilings, no furniture or appliances. Instead there are only figurines suspended in the air, unaware of the void that surrounds them: some dressed and some naked, some jogging on absent treadmills, some boiling water on absent stovetops or making love on absent beds or rinsing off shampoo in absent showers, a woman with an open blouse nursing a fussy infant, two little boys running through vacant space for a ball that they seem to see, a family of four eating absent chicken around an absent table, many sleeping on their backs or sides, or staring at vanished screens—and together, in stillness or motion, swathed in darkness or light, the eighteen stories of bodies resemble a single towering hive, a collective being that functions for a single, specified aim, though this goal remains obscure from a glimpse of the hive itself.

Midway up the building, Erin sits in a varnished kitchen,

tying on a worn pair of sneakers. She is now in her midthirties, no longer thin and short-haired, dressed in linen pants and a canvas jacket. The light of an absent ceiling lamp gleams off her fuller face. In the next room, behind a vanished wall, Owen lies fast asleep in midair, his eyelids fluttering as he dreams on a missing pillow. He too is over a decade older, his hair receded to a faint rim, the crackles wider in his forehead as he floats in the luminous void.

Erin stands inside her lost kitchen, zips her jacket halfway to the collar. Then she leaves the apartment and strides through the air down an invisible hallway. At the end, she stops and presses an absent elevator button. Soon she is falling from floor to floor, plummeting past her neighbors, her lightweight clothes unstirred despite her speed.

Her sneakers come to a halt on the blank ground. She steps into the vacuity of the lobby, where a stubble-faced security guard reclines in empty space, laughing to himself as he scrolls an unseen phone. Erin strolls past him and the light slips off her body, her face and clothing shadowed as she enters the invisible night.

In the blankness of the parking lot she strides an absent aisle, her plastic brushed with the shimmer of missing streetlamps. She thumbs a fob she does not hold, climbs inside a vanished car, curls her fingers as if around a wheel. Then she pushes down her sneaker and glides forward through the void, bouncing briefly as she crosses the ghost of a speed bump. Her hovering neighbors recede behind her, shrinking smaller and smaller as they sleep, bathe, argue, jog in place—until, as Erin picks up speed, as their bodies blur to outlines, they no longer look like figurines but slivers of soot smudged in the air, wisps of fog that soon will thin to light.

She glides forward at a moderate speed, the voidscape without feature. Here and there the absence swarms with other busy hives of plastic people. In a vanished supermarket, which now passes on her right, customers stroll with their arms out, pushing unseen shopping carts; they pause and reach to either side and grasp invisible products; they wait together in checkout lines while figurines in uniforms make motions of scanning the items—the entire process calm, sincere, like a crowd of mimes in normal dress performing without an audience, a coordinated illusion for its own sake. She passes an absent strip mall, a long and varied illusion: a hair salon, a restaurant, a tax preparer, a gym, each hive composed of figurines who mime their tasks in fluid rhythms, a dance of marionettes with hidden strings. Then, gliding faster, Erin turns her hands in a crescent arc, steering her airborne body to the left. She ascends above the ground in a swift diagonal line, climbing up the slope of an unseen on-ramp.

Here a vaster emptiness envelops her. No figurines swarm in the distance, not even a sliver of life, so that she seems not to change position at all, arrested in the bright enormity. Time passes in this isolation, her fingers curled, her speed unclear, until, on the far horizon, a ghostly sight rises from the void: a thousand or more dark slivers arranged in curving rows, a spare and orderly pattern on the blank earth. As she nears the pattern, it coalesces into a lucid location, a burial ground that stretches for miles across the barren land. In this stark, lustrous vista, emptied of other visions, the limits of the graveyard seem to mark the boundaries of physical space itself.

Erin glides to a stop near an outer row, steps out on the pale terrain. Then she strides off toward the headstones, the obelisks, the crosses, the figures of saints and angels and Christs and hooded Virgin Marys, all jutting up from the earth like the tallest points of a flooded city, the last symbols shored against the ruins. Her face glows brighter outside the car, lit like the gravestones around her in a soft palette of moonlight. To her left she passes a statue of Gabriel, his horn held at the ready; to her right a statue of Saint Bernard, a gracious gladness in his eyes, his stone hands clasped in supplication.

A wind comes chasing across the graveyard, ruffling the threads of Erin's longer hair. At this another layer of her world dissolves from view: the blank ground below her feet turns all at once transparent, its surface clear like a floor of polished glass. Below this glass the rows and rows of corpses can be seen, suspended on their backs in rigid rest inside the void, no earth or coffin to hold them, no moon or sun to light them, cast in silhouette as if against a depth of cloud. The bodies have not shrunk in death, their lonely plastic unrotting, static shapes awaiting the trumpet's cry.

Erin steps up to a granite headstone, one of the taller markers in its row. Pine shadows swim across the name of the departed: *Jacob Sillan.* She stares down at his vanished plot, her eyes alert but distant in the craters of her sockets, as if gazing into another world, which only she can see.

The wind grows louder in the graveyard, the lost pine trees soughing in the gale. Now, for miles, the rows and rows of headstones fade from sight, absorbed into the blankness like the sky and clouds and earth, like the animals and plant life, like all the passing worlds that we have known. Only Jacob's headstone remains, in a space that could be infinite or the size of the spare rock, so little is it defined. The wind rises moaning and we hear the branches swaying and we hear among the branches water falling through the leaves, a light and then a stronger rain across the unseen earth. The rain runs down her smooth dark hair, disappears the instant it flows off the nylon.

Erin steps onto the base of the marker, and then, lifting a sneaker, hoists herself to the top of Jacob's headstone. There she assumes a diving stance, her chin sunk to her chest, her knees bent at their hinges, her hands outstretched before her palm to palm. She holds this stance for a long moment, lacquered in light like the figure on one of her trophies. Then, tilting forward, rising on her toes, she pushes off and hurtles herself toward the nothing.

It seems her fingertips will strike the ground, perhaps fracture from the force. Instead they slide through the clear surface at a smooth diagonal angle, followed by her wrists and arms, her head and chest and legs, swallowed as if by water but for the lack of splash or ripple. Passing through the barrier, the plastic woman is changed: her face transformed to flesh, her crackles into wrinkles, her body to blood and bone. Her hair, no longer nylon, streams behind her as she plunges into the depths.

Under the ground Erin swims from us with a steady, fluid breaststroke. Her arms push outward and inward in the stroke's circular pattern; her sneakers pump behind her like the flippers of a seal. She slips past the rows of buried bodies, the only moving form among the stillness. Soon the graveyard is behind her, its static husks of grief, and she swims out farther and farther toward the void of the horizon, shrinking from a sliver to a dot to a pinpoint until she is no more, like a lost memory, a lost vision, beyond our senses, beyond our language, fading onward, gone.

Alone now in the nothing, we hear the rhythms of rainfall. Then, raising our eyes to heaven, we strain to see the ghost of any star.

# ACKNOWLEDGMENTS

This novel would not have been possible without the incredible support of my writing community, who read multiple drafts of the book, gave me incisive guidance and feedback, and offered much-needed encouragement whenever the way grew murky. Writing a novel is often a very solitary activity, and I'm so grateful for the brilliant and delightful people who cheered me on through every step of the process. I owe you more than words can say.

My partner, the wonderful Rachel Cochran, could have earned a degree in *Plastic* studies for the time she put into reading, editing, and discussing this book with me. Not only this novel, but the entire time in my life that led to *Plastic* is thanks to her. My dear friend Mark Hitz has been with this book since our first graduate workshop and has given masterful feedback on every draft of the novel. My agent, Bill Clegg, a writer and reader of profound insight, worked with me on several drafts to evolve the story, characters, and world of *Plastic*—an unforgettable education in craft. My editor, Anna Kaufman, brought a wealth of brilliance and dedication to our drafts together, inspiring new directions for the book, providing creative space to embrace my queerness, and teaching me so much through her expert grasp of form and structure. An enormous thanks is also due to editor Tim O'Connell, who acquired the book for Pantheon and provided an incredible first round of feedback, transforming my sense of what this novel and my writing in general might achieve. Thanks as well to editor Zack Knoll, who encountered *Plastic* in its infancy and gave important advice and encouragement at a crucial time.

I will be forever grateful to my writing mentors at the University of Texas and the University of Nebraska: Elizabeth McCracken, who read the very first excerpts of *Plastic* and breathed life into the whole project; Deb Olin Unferth, who transformed my aesthetic outlook and opened a new door into the power of sentences; and Timothy Schaffert, who restored my confidence in my writing and deepened my sense of literature and the writing life. I'm very thankful to Stephen Harrigan, James Magnuson, and Jonis Agee for their fantastic workshops and the insights I gained in their classrooms. Thanks also to Matt Cohen, James Hynes, Wendy Katz, and Guy Reynolds for their astute feedback on the book.

A huge thanks to my friends who have read and discussed this novel with me through the years: Elena Makarion, Parini Shroff, Ilana Masad, Ryler Dustin, Talitha Greaver, Meg Freitag, Lucas Schaefer, Greg Marshall, Cassandra Powers, David Henson, Abbey Chung, Vincent Scarpa, and Matt Cutts. I have so much gratitude to everyone at Pantheon Books for their commitment to *Plastic* and their powerful work in the literary space—it is such a privilege to be working with you—and to the team doing unbelievable work bringing *Plastic* into the world: Julianne

Clancy, Demetri Papadimitropoulos, Kayla Overbey, Jo Anne Metsch, Helen Maggie Carr, and Tyler Comrie. To everyone at the wonderful Clegg Agency: You have been such brilliant readers and supporters of my work in every way, and I can't begin to express what your insights and enthusiasm have meant to me through the years. Marion Duvert, Simon Toop, David Kambhu, Nik Slackman, Nik Wesson, MC Conners—you are amazing. An enormous thanks also to my musical collaborators, the extraordinary artists bringing the album of *Plastic* to life: Anna Hoone, Jonny Rodgers, Levi Cecil, Peter Katis, and Alan Douches.

I doubt I'd be a writer at all if not for the amazing teachers I encountered in my teens and twenties, who opened my eyes to writing and reading as a lifelong creative journey. First and foremost I must thank Marc Pfister, who took my work seriously when I was a bewildered high school sophomore, introducing me to the beauty of craft and to writing as a daily practice. Along with my wife, this book is dedicated to you. Jeffrey Roets, Tom O'Connor, Mary Beth Jordan, David Athey, Lylas Rommel, Jaysinh Birjepatil—some of you are no longer with us, but I thank you all for being an inspiration. Last but certainly not least, a tremendous thank-you to my family, who have always encouraged me on the path of writing: my mother and father; my stepmother, Bonnie; my brother, Stefan; my grandmother; my aunts, Joan and Jackie; my uncle, Tom; and my cousins Megan, Cristin, Chris, Muriel, Ron, and Leeza. Lots of love also to David, Angie, Viridian, Jessica, Mark, Axolotl, Steve, and Patty.

## A NOTE ABOUT THE AUTHOR

Scott Guild received his MFA from the New Writers Project at the University of Texas at Austin, and his PhD in English from the University of Nebraska–Lincoln, where he was a Michener Fellow. He served as assistant director of Pen City Writers, a prison writing initiative for incarcerated students. He is currently an assistant professor at Marian University in Indianapolis, where he teaches literature and creative writing. Before his degrees, Scott was the songwriter and lead guitarist for the new-wave band New Collisions, which toured with the B-52s and opened for Blondie.

A musical companion to this novel, *Plastic: The Album,* is available now on all major streaming services. The album tells Erin's story through a cycle of dynamic pop songs, featuring lyrics from her songs in the novel and original music from an eclectic array of musicians. Find the album on your favorite streaming service or at scottguild.com.

Or simply use the QR code:

A NOTE ON THE TYPE

This book was set in Caledonia, a typeface designed in 1939 by W. A. Dwiggins (1880–1956) for the Merganthaler Linotype Company. Its name is the ancient Roman term for Scotland, because the face was intended to have a Scottish-Roman flavor. Caledonia is considered to be a well-proportioned, businesslike face with little contrast between its thick and thin lines.

*Typeset by*
*Scribe, Philadelphia, Pennsylvania*

*Printed and bound by*
*Berryville Graphics, Berryville, Virginia*

*Designed by Jo Anne Metsch*